Gal

# Owl's Silent Strike

A Gabriel Hawke Novel
Book 9

Paty Jager

Windtree Press
Hillsboro, OR

OWL'S SILENT STRIKE

Contact Information: info@windtreepress.com

Windtree Press
Hillsboro, Oregon
http://windtreepress.com

Cover Art by Christina Keerins
Print cover by Covered by Karen

PUBLISHING HISTORY
Published in the United States of America

ISBN  978-1-957638-19-5

## Author Comments

While this book and coming books in the series are set in Wallowa County, Oregon, I have changed the town names to old forgotten towns that were in the county at one time. I also took the liberty of changing the towns up and populating the county with my own characters, none of which are in any way a representation of anyone who is or has ever lived in Wallowa County. Other than the towns, I have tried to use the real names of all the geographical locations.

## Special Thank You to:

Louis Brewer, Angie & Dan Conner, Lloyd Meeker, and my awesome team of beta readers.

# Chapter One

The wind wailed, shaking the tall pine and lodgepole trees and blowing snowflakes the size of Gabriel Hawke's favorite corn flakes into a white frenzy. He had taken a week's vacation from his job as an Oregon State Trooper with the Fish and Wildlife Division to bring his friend, Dani Singer, owner of Charlie's Lodge, up into the Wallowa Mountains. They came by horseback, one of the only ways, besides hiking or flying in, to get to the lodge. Dani had flown her airplane out two weeks earlier after the horses and staff had headed down the mountain for winter. Now they were up here so she could fly out her helicopter. She had repairs she wanted to do to the aircraft over the winter.

When they'd swung up onto his horses' backs and headed up the trail the day before, the storm that was now piling up snow and causing visibility of only ten feet had been heralded to arrive Thursday. Four days from now.

The day he had planned to be back down snug in Dani's apartment spending the rest of his week with her.

"How are we going to find the lodge in this storm?" Dani yelled above the wind as her horse bumped into Hawke when he'd stopped to try and figure out where they were.

"We're going to have to sit it out until we can see where we're going." Hawke had noticed an outcropping of rock when the wind had let up five minutes before. He was headed in that direction. Dot, his young gelding, was doing his best to continue in the face of the blustering wind and snow flurry.

"Jack wants to take the lead," Dani said, her leg brushing by Hawke's as the older gelding did indeed press on by.

"Maybe he knows the rocks I'm looking for," Hawke yelled, sticking Dot's nose right on Jack's tail to not lose them in the white world. Horse, his mule, who had more horse attitude days than mule attitude, was lagging behind, holding Dot back.

"Dani! Stop!" Hawke yelled to keep her in earshot and sight while he dealt with the stubborn mule.

She turned and came back to them. "What's wrong?"

"Horse is being stubborn, and Dot doesn't have the stamina to keep pulling on him and get through the snowdrifts. We need to trade horses. Jack will make Horse more comfortable." Hawke stood in his saddle to dismount.

"Just hand me Horse's rope." He saw Dani's gloved hand reach out.

"If he continues to be a mule, you could end up pulled off Jack. Let's just switch horses." Hawke again readied himself to dismount.

"Just hand me the rope. It can't be that much farther to the rock outcropping if you saw it. And if Horse is more comfortable with Jack, then he should be fine." She grabbed the rope, turned Jack, and made kissy sounds to Horse.

Hawke held Dot back as the mule walked on by. He'd bet if he could see clearly in the snow, Horse would have a smirk on his lips and a twinkle in his eyes. The mule hadn't liked being led by Dot from the start of the trip. But Hawke hadn't felt comfortable having Dani ride the younger horse or leading the mule with Jack.

He urged Dot, or Polka Dot, as his friend Kitree, a twelve-year-old, had named the gelding due to his Appaloosa heritage and white coat with black and brown spots, to stay close to Horse. They traveled for fifteen minutes when the horse and mule ahead of him stopped.

"I think Jack found what you were looking for," Dani called.

Hawke dismounted and led Dot forward. The outcropping would barely keep all of them out of the snow, but it was a dry place to wait out the storm.

Dani dismounted and they led the animals under the covering of basalt.

Dog walked out of the snow and shook, spattering water droplets and clumps of snow on the ground.

"Leave them saddled, but loosen the cinches," Hawke said. "If we take off the saddles and blankets, they'll be sweaty underneath and it will make them colder." They settled the animals to one side of the area and Hawke dug in Horse's pack for a Sterno stove and pan. Once the small one burner stove was going, he scooped up snow and put the pan on the burner.

"We'll get something warm in us and then I'll feed the horses." He glanced at Dani. She'd pulled out the tarp they'd used for a tent the night before and spread it on the ground at the back of the rock recess.

"I shouldn't have relied on the weather station," Hawke said, walking over to Horse and the pack on his back. Hawke pulled out two cups and the instant coffee crystals. "When I called Mom and told her we were making this trip, she told me it wasn't a good idea. Her bones told her the weather was changing sooner."

The water began boiling. He shook crystals into the tin mugs, poured a little bit of water in, and swirled the two cups until the crystals had dissolved. Adding more water to the tin mugs, he handed one to Dani.

"Will this snow cause problems with getting the helicopter out of here?" He sipped his coffee while adding more snow to the water.

"It will depend on how much protection the trees are giving my bird." She held the tin mug in her gloved hands as if warming them.

Hawke set his cup down. "I'll put feed bags on these three. They can use all the energy they can get to haul us to the lodge."

He pulled the feedbags out of the pack on Horse, scooped grain into the canvas pouches, and pet each animal as he took off their bridles and attached the bags to their halters. At Horse, he grudgingly attached the bag. "You know you didn't have to work Dot so hard."

The mule's eye looked at him and then closed as crunching sounds came from inside the canvas pouch.

Hawke turned back to Dani and found her and Dog snuggled together. "Do you want me to pull out the sleeping bags? You could wrap up in those to stay warm."

"If you think we'll be here a while, I wouldn't mind trying to get warmer." Her teeth chattered.

"Why didn't you tell me you were this cold?" Hawke dropped to his knees beside her and rubbed his gloved hands up and down her coat sleeves.

"I thought we'd get to the lodge soon and didn't want to stop our progress the way the snow was coming down." She peered into his eyes. "I wanted us tucked safely in the lodge."

Hawke rose and walked over to Horse. He pulled Dani's sleeping bag out of the pack and unzipped it as he walked toward her. "You have to stay warm. Getting cold out here can be deadly." He wrapped the bag around both her and Dog. The animal's heat would help warm her up.

"Aren't you cold?" she asked.

He shook his head. "I'm used to being out here and dress for it. I have feet warmers in my boots and long johns on." He pulled the sleeping bag up around her neck. "You and Dog sit tight. I'm just going to step out to the front and see if I can figure out where we are."

"Be careful."

"I'm not going far." He straightened and walked to the front of the outcropping. Large flakes landed on his chest and fluttered by his face. The wind seemed to be easing up. He could see a little farther than when they'd entered the shelter. Stepping out into the now two feet of snow, he peered around and had a pretty good idea of where they were at. He recognized a tree that had the top blown out by lightning several years earlier. They were off the trail to the lodge by about seventy-five yards.

He walked back into the recess, stomping the snow

from his feet.

"Did you learn anything?" Dani asked, taking a sip of her coffee.

"We'll get something to eat and wait out the storm. We're not off the trail by much and we're only about an hour from the lodge. The wind is letting up. After we eat, if it's died down enough for us to see, we'll head out of here. I'm looking forward to the fireplace and a soft bed tonight."

"Me too." Dani held her cup out to him. "Can you heat up some soup to put in here?"

"I'll melt some snow for Dog to get a drink and then I'll get that soup." Hawke grabbed the dish he carried for Dog to eat from and filled it with snow before drizzling the hot water over it. When the snow had melted, he placed the dish on the ground. "Dog, get a drink."

The dog's furry head appeared from under Dani's sleeping bag. He spotted the dish and crawled out, stretching.

Hawke retrieved the soup from the pack and stopped when he caught Dog staring at him. "Aren't you thirsty?"

The animal dropped his gaze to the cans of soup.

"As soon as I get these warming up, I'll get you something to eat." Hawke chuckled as he crouched by the Sterno burner and poured the soup into the pot. Using the water Dog hadn't drank, Hawke swished water in the cans, pouring the soup-flavored water into Dog's dish. The rinsed cans were flattened and returned to the pack. While his hands were in the pack, he found the container of dog food.

He walked over and poured some food on the ground next to the water in the dish.

Dog smiled at him and began crunching the kibble.

"I think he was hungry," Dani said, a chuckle in her voice.

"He's always hungry. If I let him eat everything he wanted, his legs wouldn't be able to hold him up." They both laughed at his comment and fell into a companionable silence. That was one of the things Hawke liked about Dani. She didn't have to be talking all the time. He liked the quiet. You could learn as much about a person when they were quiet as when they told you things.

The soup steamed. Hawke poured some into Dani's cup, drank the rest of his now cold coffee, and filled his cup.

<><><><><><><>

An hour later the visibility was better and they left the outcropping. Hawke was back to leading Horse with Dot. Dani had taken the lead when Jack gave a snort and pushed by Hawke, knowing he was getting closer to the lodge and rest.

Hawke kept an eye on the horse and rider to make sure Jack did go in the right direction. The lead rope tugged Hawke's arm as Horse stopped and Dot continued. Pulling back on the reins, he stopped the young horse and glanced back at Horse. "Come on, Horse. We're almost there. The more you balk the longer it will take."

He yanked on the rope, stretching out the mule's neck but not getting him to move his feet.

"What's wrong?" Dani called back.

"Horse is being a mule, again!" Hawke replied. Shifting his gaze to the woman and horse, he caught sight of them as Jack slid and fell to his side, taking Dani down into the snow under him.

# Chapter Two

Hawke bailed off Dot, dropping the reins and shoving through the path made by Jack to get to the horse and woman. The longer Jack remained on his side there was no telling what could happen to Dani. Dog raced ahead of him to his friend. The horse and dog had been friends since Hawke brought Dog home.

His heart thudded from exertion and fear. He cursed the weathermen for being wrong and himself for thinking they could make a leisurely trip up here to get her helicopter. If they hadn't stopped and camped last night, they would have already been at the lodge when the storm hit.

At the horse, he scanned the snow for Dani. Her leg was pinned under the large animal. Her eyes were closed. Hawke dropped to his knees beside her. "Dani? Dani, I need you to tell me if your foot is still in the stirrup."

He touched her face and her eyelids popped open.

"Shit! My leg hurts. You'd think snow would make

a good cushion." Her face was pale, and her breathing came in fast bursts.

"Any chance you know if your boot is still in the stirrup? I don't want to jerk you around if it is." He kept his face neutral from all his police encounters with injured people, but his head was going through all that could be wrong if her leg hurt that bad. He knew she was a woman who could endure pain. For her to complain, it wasn't good.

"I can't tell. I was trying to get it out when I felt Jack slipping."

The horse moved and she sucked in. "Shiiiit!"

"Want something to bite on while I get the horse up?" he joked.

She glared at him. "Just get the beast off me. I'll deal with the pain."

Hawke stood and grabbed Jack's lead rope, figuring out the best way to get the animal up in the snow. Jack's head was downhill. Dog lay beside his friend's head, comforting the horse. He needed to get the animal's legs pointed downhill, but that would put more weight on Dani.

Hawke went back to Dani and started digging at the snow around where her leg disappeared under the horse. "I have to get you out. To try and get Jack up will hurt you worse."

"But it's not good for him to lie here too long either," Dani said.

"I know, but I can't get him up without spinning him." Hawke continued to dig to the side and under her leg. His hand hit something hard. Damn. She'd landed on a rock. That was why her leg hurt so bad.

"I'm going to dig out the snow in front of your lower

15

leg and then I'm going to have to pull it to the side. It's resting on a rock." He pulled out his hands and there was blood on his glove. "I think you have a compound fracture."

Dani dropped back into the snow. "Do what you need to do."

He shoved the fact this was the woman he loved out of his brain and automatically went to work to save her.

Another fifteen minutes and he had all the snow dug out. Jack had started to breathe out of rhythm. Hawke patted his neck. "I'll get you up soon." Jack was the best horse he'd ever owned. He wasn't about to lose him and the woman he planned to spend the rest of his life with at the same time. He'd never set foot in these mountains again if that happened.

"I'm going to pull your leg forward." He studied Dani.

She had her eyes shut tight. "Do it."

He lay down and worked her leg forward as quickly but carefully as he could. She moaned twice and then he didn't hear anything. The leg was in the spot where he'd removed the snow. He stood and reached under Dani's arms to pull her out from under the horse. That's when he realized, she'd passed out. At least she wouldn't feel the pain of her leg dragging.

When he had her out of the way of getting Jack up, Hawke checked out the damage to her leg. He tore the bottom of his shirt off and used it to apply pressure to the wound to stop the bleeding. Packing snow over the wound, he hoped to slow down the flow of blood. "Dog, lay down. Keep her warm," he said, pointing to Dani before heading down to the mule and Dot.

He led the two animals up closer to Dani and pulled

a rope out of the pack. He tied the rope to Jack's back hocks and pulled, sliding the animal's backend to be level with his head and his feet facing downhill. Untying the rope, he felt Jack trying to get his feet under him. "Just a couple more minutes, boy."

Coiling up the rope, Hawke draped it over Dot's saddle horn and then grabbed Jack's lead rope. "Come on, Jack, up on your feet." He gave a steady tug on the rope, helping the horse raise his head, and then his shoulder. Jack tucked his feet under him, sat for a minute, and shoved to his feet. The animal wobbled like a newborn. Horses didn't lay on their sides for very long. Their weight pooled blood and put nerves to sleep.

"Good boy," Hawke patted the animal checking him for injuries. He didn't see anything other than a scrape on his hocks from the rope and blood on his side from Dani. He left the animal standing and went to see what he could do for Dani. The cold weather and snow had helped to stop the bleeding.

Now he needed to find some limbs to use as splints to stabilize the leg until they reached the lodge. There he could assess and doctor the injury better.

Dani woke up sounding like a tire losing air. The hiss revealed the pain she felt. "Son-of-a-bitch," she said through clenched teeth. "Is it as bad as it feels?"

"I won't know until we get to the lodge. I'm going to stabilize it the best I can to get you there." Hawke grabbed a small multipurpose tool from his pack and hacked two limbs two inches in diameter off a pine tree.

After delimbing and splitting the sticks and making a flat side on four pieces, he dug in his pack and found the roll of emergency bandaging wrap. He knelt beside Dani's leg, placing a stick on four sides of the leg. "Can you hold each stick in place while I do the first wrap?" he asked, peering into her pain-dulled eyes.

"Yeah." She rose slightly, holding each stick as he quickly wrapped the sticky elastic wrap around the sticks and her leg, leaving the shirt and snow underneath. He held out a hand when he'd finished. "I'll help you stand and get on Dot."

Her neck popped as she peered at Jack, still standing where he'd gotten up. "Is Jack hurt?"

"I don't think it's anything permanent. But I'll tie him on behind Horse and lead you on Dot."

"That's going to be hard work for you to break trail." Dani put a hand up and grimaced as Hawke pulled her to her feet.

"If I get tired, I'll ride Horse, but that will make the going slower because he doesn't like to lead." Hawke led Dot over to Dani. The young horse snorted. Possibly from the scent of blood.

"It's okay, Dot. Dani needs your help." Hawke stopped with Dani at Dot's head. The gelding sniffed her hand, up her arm, and touched her cheek with his nose.

"He wants to help," Hawke said, drawing the horse a couple of steps closer to place Dani next to the saddle. He knew Dot would come through when needed. "You'll have to keep that leg straight." He grasped her around the waist and using all the strength he had, he lifted her up so she could throw her uninjured leg over the horse's back and saddle.

"Does it hurt for the leg to dangle?" Hawke asked.

"A little."

"I can make a rope sling that might help." He dug in the pack and found the climbing rope. He made a sling around the toe and heel of her boot and tied it to the saddle. "Ready?"

"I have to be."

"If you feel faint or need to stop for any reason, just say so." Hawke led Dot and Horse over to Jack. He tied Jack to Horse. Dog leaped through the snow in the direction Hawke planned to go, so he followed.

After half an hour, Dog sat down, his tongue hanging out. Hawke felt the same but wasn't going to let Dani know his legs felt as soft and limp as a rubber band. They only had another mile to go. "Dog, do you need some fuel?" Hawke stopped, dug in the pack, handed Dog a couple of biscuits, and himself and Dani a candy bar.

"It isn't much further, is it?" she asked.

"No. About a mile. Twenty to thirty minutes." He pulled out a bottle of water, handed it to Dani who drank half before she handed it back to him. Hawke finished it, put the bottle back in the pack, and started walking.

They had planned to arrive at the lodge around noon today, so Dani could get the helicopter ready to fly and they would both head back in the morning. Thanks to the storm arriving early, the dark shape of the lodge loomed ahead in the dusky light of early evening. The helicopter sat in a large drift of snow to the left of the barn and corral. Even if they had made it here as planned, it would have taken them several hours to dig the helicopter out.

Hawke led Dot up to the lodge porch. He helped Dani down, up the three steps, and into the log building. "Want to sit by the fireplace while I get it started?"

She nodded. Her face was pale, and her teeth chattered. He settled her in the chair closest to the fireplace and lit the wood in the hearth. It soon crackled and took off, the pitchy kindling popping and snapping.

A swirl of smoke stung his nostrils, but it meant Dani would soon feel warmth.

"I'll grab some blankets." He stood.

"My room's locked, you'll have to grab some from one of the guest rooms," Dani said, not opening her eyes.

Hawke walked across the room to the closest guest room and grabbed the quilt off the bed. He wrapped it around Dani. "I'll tend to the horses and be right back to check out your leg."

"I'm not going anywhere," she said. Her head was tipped back, and her eyes were closed.

Hawke placed a piece of split wood under her foot to elevate the broken leg. He placed a kiss on her forehead and left the lodge.

Dani clenched her teeth, trying to ignore the pain radiating from her shin up her leg. It was stupid to have asked Hawke to bring her back up here in December. But she had enough maintenance to do on the helicopter to keep her busy all winter if it were down in the valley. They'd both checked the weather reports and had been foolhardy enough to think they could get in and out of the mountains before the storm hit.

She snorted. Hawke gave off so much confidence when he was in the mountains that she hadn't worried. Even if the storm arrived early, he'd get them in and out. She grimaced as she moved her toes and caused a new spasm of pain.

Jack had been walking along and then his foot had hit something and they went down. No one's fault. Even though she'd been in unbearable pain, she'd noted how Hawke had kept his cool and taken care of her without letting his emotions take over. She wondered why he hadn't stayed in the army. He would have moved up the ranks quickly, just as she had.

She shivered and pulled the quilt tighter around her. With a broken leg, there was no way she could fly the helicopter out. This trip had been for nothing. Well… not nothing. She was getting to spend a lot of time with Hawke.

Grasping Dot's lead rope, Hawke led his tired crew over to the barn. They'd appreciate a warm dry place to spend the night.

Opening the door, Hawke grabbed for the large flashlight inside on the righthand wall. He switched it on and headed to the stalls on the right. Dog woofed and ran by him into the shadowy corner of the building. They must have disturbed a critter who was using the barn for a home while the summer occupants were away.

He unsaddled the horses and took the packsaddle off Horse. Using a burlap bag, he rubbed all three down before putting them in the stalls. He gave them grain and went in search of hay. That's when he found Dog sitting next to a body lying in a pool of blood.

"What have you found?" Hawke ran the beam of the flashlight the length of the man, taking in everything he could. The body was on its back. Blood pooled under his head, from a large gash from the ear to the forehead. The blood hadn't dried, it shined in the light. There wasn't a need to check for a pulse. The lips were pale, the skin waxy. But the body had barely begun rigor mortis. Only the muscles in the face seemed to be tightening. That meant it had been less than four hours since this person had been killed. Possibly more given the cold temperatures.

He did a quick scan of the interior. No one else lurked in the shadows. There wasn't anything he could do tonight.

"Come on. We'll check it all out tomorrow," he said to Dog. Packing hay over to the horses, he decided to get as many photos as he could while the scene was untouched. Dr. Vance, the medical examiner, would appreciate that.

Hawke walked back over to the body and took photos with his phone, which was only good for pictures up here anyway. Then he dug in the victim's pockets. They were empty other than lint and change. What would someone be doing up here in early December? Without any identification, it couldn't be good. And since he didn't hit himself in the head, there had to be someone else on the mountain. As much as his curiosity wanted to be sated by checking the body out and determining how the victim had died, Dani was in the lodge needing medical care.

# Chapter Three

"You found a body in my barn?" Dani opened her eyes as he went on to tell her that he thought the man had been killed only a few hours before they'd arrived.

"You need to get on the radio and have Search and Rescue come up and get the man." Her gaze traveled around the great room. "Do you think he stayed in here? I leave the door unlocked so anyone who is up here during the winter and needs to warm up can use the fireplace and kitchen."

Hawke knelt by her leg with the first aid kit he'd retrieved from the kitchen and the vet supplies he'd brought in from the barn. "I'll do a look around after I get your leg doctored better." He set out the supplies he figured he'd need, including more of the adhesive wrap he'd taken out of the packsaddle.

Dog sighed as he lowered onto the rug in front of the fireplace.

Hawke unwrapped Dani's leg, saving the used wrap to put on the outside of the new he'd use after doctoring the wound. He'd also brought a chair from the dining room. He replaced the piece of wood her foot rested on with the chair. Taking all the wrap loose and removing the sticks and snow, which was melting, along with the bottom of his shirt, he studied the wound that had stopped bleeding.

"I'm going to move a bed out here to put you on. Then I'll need to make a pulley system to pull your leg and set the bones back together." He studied the woman with whom he'd started planning a future. "It's going to hurt like hell, but if you want to start the healing process, the bones have to be fit back together."

"I want to be able to use this leg. Without it, I can't fly." She stared into his eyes. He saw the pain deep in the brown depths wasn't physical, it was mental. Flying had given her the ability to go beyond her own expectations, both in the Air Force and in life.

"I'll do my best." He went into the closest guest room and dragged out the twin-size mattress and then the bed. Once he had it all back together, he helped Dani move from the chair to the mattress. He took her boots off and then her snow pants. Tucking the quilt around all of her but her injured leg, he cut the shredded legging off that leg, revealing the end of a bone poking out of the skin on her shin.

Hawke had gathered several towels as he'd brought together the supplies he'd need. This bed had a metal head and footboard. He could use the footboard to tighten and pull the leg, while Dani held onto the headboard.

"I'm going to clean this wound now. I don't want to

24

get any dirt or cloth in the wound when we set it."

Dani nodded and closed her eyes.

Hawke washed his hands with soap and water he'd boiled. Then using a betadine solution he'd found in the barn, he flushed out the wound. Dani didn't need to get an infection. He used a sheet from another bed to tie to the footboard and then around Dani's foot. While twisting the sheet, he slipped a stick of kindling through the twisted fabric to use as a tightening device.

"Grip the headboard and don't let your body move when I tighten this. It's going to hurt like hell, but we need to get the bone pulled back to set it in place." He ran a hand over her forehead, pushing back her shoulder-length, curly brown hair. When he'd first met her, she'd kept her hair only an inch long, he liked the length it was now. He peered into her brown eyes. "Do you want something to bite on?"

"Are you afraid I'm going to call you names?" Dani said, her spunk coming through even in her pain.

He smiled. "You can call me anything you want as long as it helps you get through the next few minutes." Hawke placed everything he would need on the bed within easy reach. He glanced at Dani, holding onto the headboard, watching him. "I'm going to start twisting this tighter to pull the bone down. When I can see or feel it in place, I'll try to quickly put ointment on the wound, place a pad over the hole, and wrap this towel around your leg with the clean wrap. Then I'll put the splints back on and wrap them with the wrap we had on before. I can't let your leg loose until the splints are on. I'll work as fast as I can."

Dani nodded.

He tightened the sheet. Dani made a sound. He had

to shut out who she was and do the job that needed to be done. Turning the kindling until the bone disappeared under the skin, he tipped the betadine bottle, running the brown liquid over his fingers and felt the shin, measuring if the bone had settled into place. Satisfied the bone was back in place, he hurried to get the leg wrapped back up, being mindful of doing everything correctly. By the time he finished the last wrap and reached to release her leg, it had taken him fifteen minutes.

Hawke studied Dani as he pulled her down in the bed, to use the footboard as a means to elevate her splinted leg. Her knuckles were white where she'd gripped the headboard. Her diamond-shaped face was sallow and her eyes dull with pain.

"You did better than I would have," he said, kissing her forehead and placing her hands underneath the quilt. "I don't think I could have endured that pain."

"That's because you're a man," she said, the corners of her lips barely tipping into a smile.

"Do you want whiskey or painkillers?" he asked, wanting to get her comfortable before he did some reconnaissance and called the body in on the radio.

"Will you give me both?" she asked, peering up at him.

Hawke shook his head. "Not a good idea. How about painkillers? They'll help you sleep better."

She held out her hand. He dropped three strong Ibuprofen pills into her hand. "I'll get you a glass of water." He stood.

"I don't need water." She popped them in her mouth and swallowed.

"How about some coffee then? You should get more liquid in your body after losing blood." He stood.

"Water sounds better than coffee. But can you make it warm water? I'm still cold." She pulled the quilt around her shoulders more.

"Hot it is." Hawke put the quilt over her wrapped leg and grabbed a blanket off the shelf in the bedroom where he'd snatched the bed. He settled the blanket over her and went to the kitchen to start a kettle of water.

Water to the hand pump in the kitchen came from a spring. This time of year, the water in the pipes would be frozen. He grabbed a large pot and walked back through the dining room and down the short hall to the back door and Dani's room and office.

The door to her bedroom had been kicked in. Hawke set the pot down, pulled his knife out of his boot sheath, and advanced to the gaping door with caution. Holding his breath, he listened. Not a sound from the room. He mentally went through any spots in the room where a person could hide and stepped through the doorway.

The hiding spots were all empty. His gaze landed on the radio. Whoever had killed the man in the barn had made damn sure no one else would contact the outside world. The radio was smashed to bits. Which had Hawke wondering how the person had known there was a radio locked in here?

After checking everything else in the room and noting it was only the radio which had been destroyed and nothing taken, he went out to the great room to tell Dani.

Her head was to the side. By the soft snoring, he had a feeling she wouldn't be awake any time soon. He'd go check around outside. If he didn't know for certain the person had fled, he wouldn't be able to sleep.

"Come," he said softly to Dog. The animal pushed

to his feet, stretched, and walked over to him. "Let's go see if we can determine if the killer is still around or if he took off."

Dog trotted to the front door.

Hawke followed, but not before picking up the shotgun he'd brought into the lodge with him. He wanted to be prepared if they ran into the person responsible for the body in the barn.

Using a large beam flashlight from his pack, Hawke searched the inside of the barn for any sign of the killer. No one hid in the corners or behind boxes or bales. He did discover drops of blood too far from the body to belong to the dead man. Using those as a starting point, he swung the beam of light in a half-circle across the floor. More drops darkened the dirt in a line toward the only opening in the barn, the door that faced the bunkhouse.

Outside, Hawke followed the drops around the side of the barn and to the shower house. From the square of packed snow and drops of blood on the wood step outside the door of the building under a large black water tank, the suspect had either stood listening to see if someone was inside or fumbled with the latch. Hawke opened the door and swung the beam of his light around the eight-by-eight building. A towel with smeared blood lay on the floor. The person had found a way to staunch the blood he was losing. Hawke hoped he could pick up the trail in the morning. For now, he'd check the three cabins and bunkhouse to see if the person had holed up there.

But first, he walked into the bathhouse and picked up the bloody towel. "Dog." He held the towel out for the animal to sniff.

Dog sniffed the side without blood and the bloody side.

"Keep a sniff out for him," Hawke said, tossing the towel into a corner and leaving the shower house.

He continued behind the barn and corrals, past the snow drifted helicopter, and over to the first cabin. When Dani's Uncle Charlie owned the lodge, the lodge and cabins were barely livable for anyone except a diehard hunter who just wanted a roof and a bed. Dani had not only made the lodge inviting, sanitary, and safe, but she'd also upgraded the cabins, making them habitable for anyone who wished to experience the Wallowa Mountains. She'd taken her inheritance and made the lodge into a recognized vacation resort. While it was remote, with electricity from a generator that was used only when needed, water from a spring, and outhouses, she had turned a profit the last two years and was proud of her accomplishment.

Heck, he was proud of what she'd done.

Hawke walked along the side of the first cabin, listening. At the door, he opened it and searched the twelve-by-twelve interior with his flashlight. Nothing seemed out of place. Dani or Sage, her cook and housekeeper, would know better than him, but as far as he could tell, no one had entered the building.

He moved on to the next one. Same result. And the third cabin was empty. It appeared the person hadn't stayed in the small cabins. He wondered if the dead man and the person he was looking for were friends who'd had a fight or if one had been looking for the other? The only way to find out was to find the man who was still alive.

Dog trotted ahead of him toward the bunkhouse. At

the door, the dog sniffed the weathered wood and particularly the handle.

"Is he here?" Hawke whispered. He hadn't seen any indentions in the snow to indicate someone had walked to the bunkhouse from the barn during or after the blizzard stopped.

Cautiously, he turned the doorknob and eased the door open. He didn't hear a sound other than some creature scratching on the wall of the structure. Dog shoved through the open door, his nose to the wooden floor.

"He was in here, wasn't he," Hawke said quietly, watching Dog follow the scent to Kitree's small walled-off room that had a blanket for a door. The hair on the back of Hawke's neck tingled thinking the person responsible for the body in the barn had slept in the child's bed. He'd saved Kitree from the people who killed her parents. He'd been happy when Sage and Tuck, Dani's cook and wrangler, wanted to adopt the girl. After spending all the time he had with the child here in the mountains, hiding from the people looking for Kitree, he and the girl had bonded. Now he saw her whenever he came to the lodge to see Dani, and he spent time with Kitree, Sage, and Tuck when they were in the valley for the winter.

Dog whimpered. He also knew the room was Kitree's.

Hawke stepped behind the blanket and ran the beam of light over the bed. It was rumpled. The possible killer had slept in the child's bed. Nothing seemed to have been bothered.

He stepped back into the main room and checked the larger bed that Tuck and Sage shared. Those covers had been rumpled as well. Did that mean both people had slept here before one was killed?

The cupboard that usually held canned goods and snacks for Kitree was open. Hawke knew that they cleared out all products that would encourage rodents when they left for the winter. The canned goods were knocked over as if they had been looking for something else.

He exited the bunkhouse and headed straight across to the lodge. At this time, he believed the injured person, who had presumably killed the man in the barn, had taken off on foot. Hawke would go after him tomorrow if Dani felt well enough to stay by herself.

# Chapter Four

"What do you mean the radio is smashed?" Dani asked when she woke up at three a.m. moaning from pain.

Hawke held out two more Ibuprofen tablets and a glass of water. "The door was busted in and the radio smashed." He leaned back in the chair he'd been sleeping in. "I'm wondering how they knew there was a radio in there or just because the door was locked, the person decided there must have been something worth stealing and smashed the radio when they saw it. But why? Did the person who is injured think the other person wasn't dead? Maybe he wanted to make sure that person couldn't call anyone?"

"Have you been awake all night spinning all these scenarios?" Dani asked, handing him the glass.

"I spun them before I fell asleep." He grinned. "How are you feeling, other than the leg?" He reached for the glass with one hand and felt her forehead with the other.

There was always the chance infection could set in.

"Uncomfortable from laying on my back and my leg hurts, otherwise not too bad." She put a hand on his thigh next to the bed. "You?"

"Sore muscles from trudging through the snow. Nothing I haven't dealt with before." He set the empty glass on the table he'd pulled up beside the chair he'd positioned by the bed. "Let's get a few more hours of sleep. If you think you can handle being alone, I'd like to see if I can catch up to the suspect." He searched her eyes. He didn't want to miss any signal she didn't want him to go.

"We'll talk in the morning." She closed her eyes. Her mouth slackened as the pills pulled her into slumber.

Hawke picked her hand up, holding it in his. If they had a way to contact officials, he'd stay here and not worry about catching the suspect. Someone else could do it, but they didn't have a way to get someone else out looking.

He was positive there had only been the two people here. But who knew they would be up here? Could there be someone else on their way?

Worry about leaving Dani alone tugged at his mind, keeping him from falling asleep until the fire had started to die.

Hawke woke as his body shivered and someone tugged on his hand. Opening his eyes, he stared at Dani.

"I need to pee," she said.

He wiped a hand over his face, feeling as if he'd been rolled over by a boulder. "Yeah. Got any ideas? You can't make it to the outhouse."

"There's a bucket with a toilet seat on it in my closet.

I use it nights I don't feel like hiking to the outhouse. You could set it next to the bed." She gave him an apologetic crooked smile.

He shoved out of the chair and went in search of the bucket. She'd never used it the nights he'd stayed in her room. But he was glad she had the contraption. It would make leaving her here alone easier.

Back in the great room, he shoved the chair he'd been sitting in away from the bed and placed the bucket in its place.

"You're going to want to lift and not drag your leg across the bed," he instructed.

"How do you know that? Have you had a broken leg?" she asked, focusing on him.

Hawke pulled the blankets back, giving her room to navigate to the edge of the mattress. "No. I had a friend in high school who broke his leg. When I'd visit, he'd want to sit in a chair. Watching him move to the edge of the bed, I realized dragging his leg across put pressure on it. He had a cast, all you have are splints. The main thing is to not do anything that could tweak your leg and pull the bone apart."

She nodded, sliding her good leg across to the side of the bed and using her arms to lift and move the splinted leg beside her left leg. "I just realized you splinted this so I can't bend my knee." She studied him.

"That's to keep the lower leg more stable. Bending can pull the bones apart." He put a hand on her cheek. "It's going to be a bit more difficult, but without real medical care, I'm not taking any chances on that leg not healing correctly."

She nodded and stood on her right leg, shimmying her leggings and underpants down her thighs before sitting on the bucket with her broken leg out in front of her. Beads of sweat popped out on her forehead. He was glad she'd kept on exercising after her retirement from the Air Force. She was in good enough shape to move around a little at a time. But crutches would help.

"When I go outside, I'll see if I can find a couple of sticks that will work for crutches." He handed her the roll of toilet paper he'd grabbed when retrieving the bucket.

Dog whined.

Hawke walked over to the door and let the dog run out and take care of his business. Which gave Hawke the notion he needed to do the same. But first, he had to make sure Dani made it back into bed.

He faced the great room and found her sitting on the side of the bed, the splinted leg sticking out in front of her. She spun her butt, moving the injured leg onto the bed with her hands. Then scooting her body over, she raised her right leg up onto the mattress. Dani remained sitting and grabbed the covers, pulling them up to her waist.

"Can you get this fire going again?" she asked.

"As soon as I make a trip out back." While he went to the outhouse to take care of his business, he thought about how he could make it easy for Dani to keep the fire going.

Hawke finished stacking the wood on the hearth in a pyramid. As long as a spark didn't pop out and catch the pile on fire, Dani could use the pitchfork he'd brought in from the barn to push a log into the fireplace. He'd also fashioned a pair of crutches from old rake and pitchfork handles. He'd cut short pieces for arm braces and wrapped them with a towel and duct tape, after screwing them onto the ends of the handles. Then he'd brought them in and had Dani stand up with the crutches to see if they needed to be shortened. They did. She was five feet eight inches tall. Four inches shorter than his six feet. He took the makeshift supports back out to the barn and sawed them to the correct length.

Returning with the crutches, he worried that the suspect had another half a day's travel on him. But in the daylight, he'd discovered the direction the man had headed. With a pair of snowshoes and Dog, Hawke had no doubt he'd catch up to the man by tomorrow night. The snowshoes would make his walking faster than the man trying to plow through the two-and-a-half-feet deep snow and even deeper drifts.

Dani was looking better after he'd heated up soup and she'd eaten a whole can by herself.

"I think I have everything here that I can think you might need." He'd brought in the Sterno burner and half a dozen cans of spaghetti, soup, and chili. Melted a bucket of water. Filled all the canteens he could find and hung them from the back of the chair by the bed. He'd even scrounged up some magazines from Dani's room and had dressed her in a pair of her pajamas, placing a set of clothes in the seat of the chair.

"Go. Bring the man back so we can both learn why there's a body in the barn," Dani said, waving her hand toward the door.

Hawke stared down at the strong woman. "I'd leave Dog with you for company, but he has the man's scent."

"What about the horses?" she asked.

"I put them out in the corral. They can eat the snow for water, and I forked a good portion of the hay out there. They should have enough to not starve by the time

I return. I'm hoping to catch up to him by tomorrow night. I should be back Wednesday night or Thursday by noon, depending on how far this guy has gone and if he's traveling straight or trying to hide his trail."

He leaned down and kissed her on the lips, lingering to let her know he would be back as soon as he could. Straightening, he peered into her eyes. "Don't go beyond this room. The leg will heal quicker if you don't use it."

She saluted him. "You be careful."

He kissed her again. "I will. And keep this beside you." He handed her the Beretta M9 she'd slipped into her saddlebags before they'd headed up the mountain.

"I might need more bullets than are in the magazine," she said, smiling.

Hawke joked, "You need more than 15 rounds to take down one person?" and handed her the box he'd found in her room. "Just don't shoot me when I return."

"I'll try not to." She raised a hand and he grasped it, giving it a squeeze.

"I'll be back. In the meantime, think up where you want to go on a real vacation."

She nodded and slipped her hand from his.

Hawke hated leaving her alone, but he needed to get the suspect captured, to make sure they were all safe.

# Chapter Five

Hawke set down the pack and took a drink of water as he scanned the trees ahead of him. He'd been following the vague indentions in the snow all afternoon. He only had another half hour to forty-five minutes before the sun would be gone. He'd have to rely on his flashlight and keep going until his legs gave out.

He'd told Dani he'd be back by Thursday noon at the latest. He didn't want her left alone longer than that or she'd come looking for him, broken leg or not. That was the problem with being in a relationship with a tough, determined woman. They didn't always do what was best for them.

Dog trotted over to a tree, sniffed, and sat down.

"What did you find?" Hawke put the lid back on his canteen and shouldered his pack. He walked over, studying the ground and the bark on the tree. Twelve to eighteen inches of bare ground could be seen around the base of the two feet in diameter pine tree. The snow tapered down in depth the closer he walked to the tree. Something had bedded down here the night before. A dark spot on the ground drew Hawke's attention.

He knelt on one knee and pressed a finger of his leather glove on the spot. Studying the residue on his glove, he determined it was blood. That must have been what Dog had smelled that drew him to the tree. The man's wound was bleeding enough to leave a visual trail and to slow the man down as he weakened from the blood loss.

"Let's see if we can find his trail." Hawke rose to his feet but walked stooped over, shining his flashlight on the snow, looking for…there it was, a small pink dot. The snow had diluted the drop. "Looks like he left this way."

Dog sniffed the pink quarter-sized spot and walked out in front of Hawke.

Using the beam of the flashlight, sweeping across the snow, he caught sight of the next drop as Dog stopped to sniff. Dog's nose was following the drops better than Hawke and the flashlight.

The thought he could catch up to the suspect kept him going long after he'd planned to stop. Finally, Hawke called Dog back to him, and found a spot under a tree to rest his legs, fill his stomach, and catch a few hours of sleep. He hoped Dani was behaving herself.

Dani shoved a piece of wood into the fireplace with the pitchfork and leaned back, biting her bottom lip from the pain in her leg. Every time she leaned or reached it made the leg hurt. But they would be stuck on this mountain if she couldn't prove to Hawke she was ready to travel when he came back.

That determination had her taking two more painkillers and moving to the edge of the bed. She grabbed the crutches Hawke made for her to use when she needed to go to the bathroom and instead, walked across the room and back, before collapsing on the bed. She was going to make it to the kitchen and back by the time he returned.

A sound outside had her reaching for the Beretta she'd slipped into her coat pocket when Hawke left. If there was someone still hanging around, she'd make sure he was here for Hawke to question. She stared at the door until her eyes blurred and she fell asleep with her hand on the weapon.

A golden glow lit the tops of the trees as Hawke continued following the footprints and blood drops. He noticed the man appeared to be stumbling. There were spots where he'd fallen and struggled to get up.

They came across another spot where their suspect had spent last night. The ground was still slightly warm.

"We're close," Hawke whispered to Dog, motioning for the animal to heel rather than lead. Dog was a unique mix of breeds and more than once a hunter in the wilderness had thought he was a wolf. They just saw size and color not the wiry hair on his face and body.

Thirty minutes later, Hawke had a visual. The suspect stumbled and fell in the snow, face first.

Hawke hurried over as fast as his snowshoes would allow. He knelt on one knee and rolled the man over. A gun barrel pointed at him.

"Hey, I'm a good guy." He pulled his State Police badge out of his coat pocket. "I'm State Trooper Hawke.

I've been following your trail to help you."

The hand holding the gun shook. The man dropped his arm holding the weapon.

Hawke grabbed the handgun, shoving it into his pack. "Can you walk back to the Lodge?"

"I'm not going back there. He tried to kill me." The man's eyes widened, and he struggled to get to his feet.

"The dead man in the barn?" Hawke asked, studying the man who appeared to be in his thirties. His face was pale compared to his tanned neck. The man wasn't dressed to be hiking around in the mountains. He had a regular coat, jeans, and hiking boots, not insulated or waterproof. And no gloves. His hands were turning blue.

"H-he's dead? How?" The man's body shook.

"Get up. You aren't dressed to be laying around in the snow. Or even hiking around on a mountain." Hawke grabbed the man by the front of his jacket and stood him on his feet. The man's feet sunk in the snow while Hawke remained on top. He could fix that. He had a smaller pair of snowshoes in his pack.

"Follow me. We'll get to a spot under a tree where you can put a pair of snowshoes on." Hawke took several steps and glanced back. The man hadn't moved. "We're going back to the lodge if I have to drag you the whole way." He wasn't going to leave Dani alone any longer than necessary.

Dog caught the menacing tone and growled at the man.

The man's eyes widened as he took a step backward.

"Dog, no. He won't hurt you." Hawke walked back and grabbed the man's arm.

"Ouch!"

Hawke stared down at the blood trickling out the

sleeve of the man's coat. "Who shot you?"

"The man in the barn."

"What's your name?" Hawke had released the man's arm, but walked behind him, prodding him along to the nearest downed log.

"Kieran."

At the log, Hawke put a hand on Kieran's shoulder, making him sit. Then he pulled an extra set of heated socks out of his pack along with the smaller set of snowshoes.

"Take off your boots and socks."

The man stared at him.

"I have heated socks to put on your feet instead of those wet cold ones." Hawke held out the pair he'd pulled from his pack.

Kieran tried to untie his boots, but his hands were too stiff and cold. Hawke handed him a pair of gloves and took the man's shoes and socks off, revealing feet that were in the first stage of frostbite.

"You're lucky I found you when I did. You would have lost your toes and probably died of hypothermia if I hadn't come along. You aren't dressed for walking around in the mountains in the snow."

When Kieran had both shoes back on, Hawke attached the snowshoes to the man's feet. "This should help you walk with less effort." He stared into the man's dull eyes. "We're going to get back to the lodge tonight. I have a friend there who has a broken leg. I'm not leaving her alone any longer."

Kieran's eyes widened. "You left an injured woman alone at the lodge?"

"She has a gun and knows how to use it. Why? Are you expecting more people to show up?" Now Hawke's radar was lighting up. This man was part of something that had caused him to kill a man and run into the wilderness ill-prepared.

"I'm sure someone came looking for the man. That's probably who killed him."

"Why would they kill him?" Hawke finished strapping the snowshoes on the man's feet.

"Because he didn't have me." Kieran wearily stood.

"How did you get away?" Hawke decided he'd wait until later to ask the man why he was in the wilderness in this kind of weather. He walked away from the downed log and glanced back to see if the man followed. He didn't. He sat on the log, shivering and looking as if he didn't have any energy left.

Hawke handed him an energy bar from his pack and a bottle of water. "Fill up on this and we need to get going. We aren't that far from the lodge. You've been zigzagging so much you only traveled about three miles in a straight line."

The man ate, drank, and studied Hawke. When he'd finished, he asked, "What are you doing up here?"

"I brought my friend up to fly her helicopter out before the storm hit. Only the snow came earlier than we'd calculated. Her horse slipped, falling on her, and she broke her leg." Hawke motioned for the man to get up. "She owns the lodge. She'll be wanting you to pay for the radio you smashed and the door you broke to get to the radio."

The man stared at Hawke. "Why would I smash the radio?"

"That's what I'm asking. Why would you?" Hawke grabbed Kieran by the coat sleeve on his uninjured arm and pulled him to his feet. "Move out."

Hawke was impatient to get back to Dani. If Kieran hadn't smashed the radio, either the other person did before he was killed or someone else was on the mountain looking for the dead man and the one Hawke was practically dragging back to the lodge.

After the third time they had to stop because Kieran collapsed, Hawke pulled out his utility tool and hacked down two ten-foot trees, delimbing them. He lashed braces across on both ends and tied a tarp he had in his pack to the sides and ends, making a travois to drag the man back to the lodge. He attached the snowshoes from Kieran's feet to the poles that would be dragging, hoping it would keep the travois from digging too deep into the snow as it was towed.

Once he had Kieran wrapped in the emergency blanket Hawke carried in his pack, he used a piece of the climbing rope, that would soon be too short to use for climbing, to tie the man on the travois.

Hawke grasped each tree handle and started off through the trees and rocks in as straight a line as he could manage toward the lodge. Dog trotted ahead of him, coming back each time Hawke needed to give his arms a break or pull the backend of the travois out of a hole it dropped into when he'd walked too close to a bush or tree.

He was using up his energy, but it had been evident Kieran wasn't able to walk another step. Hawke had no way of knowing how much blood the man had lost. The drops had been minimal but the inside of Kieran's coat could be soaking it up.

He smelled the smoke of the fireplace before he saw a small light that disappeared when he'd turn this way and that around the trees. The knowledge he was almost there, gave Hawke's legs renewed energy. Not only could he rest but he would see that Dani had been fine.

The darkness increased as the grays of evening deepened into black. The moon wasn't high enough to shed light. And even if it was, the waxing moon wouldn't have lighted their path under the trees.

Finally, the back of the lodge appeared. That's when he noticed the light he'd seen was from the kitchen. Dani wasn't supposed to get up. Had she disregarded his orders or had the people Kieran was afraid of arrived? He gave a soft whistle to Dog, calling the animal back to him. "Let's go easy," he said, motioning for Dog to heel.

Wanting to not take the man into a situation that could get them all killed, Hawke dragged the travois into the shower house. "Stay here until I scope things out," he told Kieran, leaving the man tied to the travois so he couldn't try to run. Hawke wasn't in the mood to drag him back to the lodge again tonight.

Once the shower house door was closed, Hawke snuck up to the kitchen window and listened. He couldn't see in as the window was too high in the air. The lodge had been built on stilts to keep the building from flooding when the snow had a fast melt in the meadow and ran down the sides of the mountain the lodge sat upon.

Rather than quietly entering the back door, in case someone was watching it from the inside, he walked the length of the back of the building, and along the end where the fireplace sat to the front corner of the lodge. He studied the area between the bunkhouse and the lodge and the cabins. He didn't see anything that looked out of place. He slipped onto the porch and eased close to a window to see into the great room. Dani sat in the chair, her leg propped up on the bed, reading a magazine. She didn't seem the least bit worried.

He did an extra scan of the interior he could see and determined that she was the sole occupant of the lodge.

Hawke retraced his steps and untied Kieran from the travois. There wasn't any sense in worrying Dani until the need arose about his suspicions there might be others on the mountain looking for Kieran.

# Chapter Six

Hawke put Kieran's arm over his shoulder and around his neck and helped him up the steps to the back door. He shoved it open and walked Kieran down the hall and into the great room.

Dani's head spun and her gaze latched onto them. She grabbed the crutches Hawke had made and stood. "What does he need?"

"Heat and medical aid." Hawke dropped Kieran on the bed that was near the fireplace.

Dani moved to the man's feet and began unlacing his boots.

"I told you to stay off that leg," Hawke said, pulling his hands out of his gloves and placing a palm on her warm face.

"I'm not on it. See." She swung her leg slow and gentle back and forth. "You didn't expect me to stay lying in the bed for days, did you?" The frown on her face told him what he'd already known about the woman. She wasn't one to be kept down for anything.

Kieran moaned as she pulled the boots and socks off his feet.

"Oh!" Dani exclaimed.

One glance at the man's bright red feet, and Hawke headed to the next room. "I thought the socks I gave him would help. Looks like it wasn't enough heat. We need to warm them up." He hurried into the room where he'd taken the bed from and grabbed four towels. He knew the man's hands would be worse. "Warm the towels by the fire, then wrap one around each foot." Hawke unzipped Kieran's coat and eased it off him. The man had been shot in the upper arm. It appeared he'd tried to tie a bandana around his arm to stop the bleeding. But because the man had kept moving, other than lying down at night, he'd not allowed the wound time to coagulate but kept the blood pumping out by moving.

There was an entrance and exit wound, which gave the blood an extra hole to seep from.

"Now what?" Dani asked.

"Wrap his hands in the warm towels and give him Ibuprofen. I'm going to get some water and clean up this gunshot wound." Hawke strode out of the room through the dining room and into the lit-up kitchen. It was evident Dani had been in here making something to eat earlier and left the oil lamp lit. He poured the water from the kettle on the lit wood stove, which had to have been lit and stoked by Dani. Hawke shook his head. The woman didn't know how to take care of herself.

He carried the bowl of water and a clean kitchen towel out to the great room.

Kieran's eyes were open. His face pinched in pain.

Hawke knew from experience that having frostbitten extremities warm up hurt like a son-of-a-bitch.

"I'm going to clean up your bullet wound and bandage it," he said to Kieran. Glancing over at Dani who was sitting in the chair, he asked, "Did you make introductions?"

She shook her head.

"Kieran, this is Dani. She owns the lodge and is who you'll pay for damages to the radio." Hawke wrung out the wet cloth and began cleaning out the bullet wound.

"Ow! I said I didn't smash the radio," Kieran said through gritted teeth.

"You said the dead man did. When? How?" Hawke kept his gaze on the wound but listened for any hesitancy that Kieran was thinking something up.

"He must have done it while I was hiding in the barn. That's where he found me. He shot, hit my arm, and I ran out of there as fast as I could." The man sucked in air as Hawke raised his arm to clean up the other wound.

"Why didn't you fire back since you had a gun?" Hawke asked, keeping his attention on the wound.

"Gun? Oh, right, the one you found me with." He stopped. It was clear he was trying to piece out what to say.

Dani rose. "Are you two hungry? I can heat up some soup."

Hawke put a hand on her crutch. "I can do that when I finish here."

"Nonsense. I can have the soup ready for when you finish." She swung her way across the great room.

He let out a small hiss of air.

"When did you say she broke her leg?" Kieran asked.

"Two days ago." Hawke finished cleaning the wound and shoved some of the antibiotic ointment in the wound.

"She must be on some hardcore pain meds to be getting around like that. Or she's one tough woman." Kieran winced as Hawke placed gauze over both the holes and wrapped the arm with cotton gauze and then a couple of wraps of the adhesive binding.

"She's tough. Too tough to realize she could be jeopardizing her future of flying."

"I heard that. I'm not doing more than I can bear," Dani said, swinging back into the room. "The soup is heating, but you'll have to carry the bowls in." She lowered onto the chair.

"I've finished dressing the wound." Hawke walked into the bedroom and grabbed two more towels. He hung them close to the fireplace and then picked up the bowl of bloody water and towel. "I'll go get the soup."

When he returned, Kieran was asleep. Dani sat in the chair studying the sleeping man.

Hawke placed the tray with the soup bowls and utensils on a table. He motioned for Dani to stand and he moved her chair over closer to the fireplace at the foot of the bed. When she was settled back in the chair with her foot propped on the end of the bed, he pulled another chair over close to hers. Then he handed her a bowl of soup and settled in the chair beside her with his own bowl.

They had eaten about half of the soup in their bowls when she asked quietly, "Did you learn anything from him? Why he ran? What he had to do with the body?"

"Not much. Other than he believes there will be friends of the dead man coming here to look for them."

He studied Dani. "Right now, I don't know whether he's telling the truth or just didn't want to come back here because of his connection to the body."

"I heard how he dodged the question about the gun. I think it's strange he didn't shoot back if he had a weapon when he was shot." Dani scooped up a spoonful of soup and sipped, staring at the man.

"Yeah. I'm going to ask him where he was when he was shot. Then I'll go see if I can find a slug. But I think—" Kieran stirred, and Hawke stopped talking. He had decided since he hadn't found a weapon on the body, that after being shot, Kieran had overtaken the man, perhaps knocking him in the head with a board, and grabbed up the gun before he left the barn.

The man on the bed moaned and his eyes opened. He stared straight up at the beams of the log structure for several minutes before turning his head toward the fire. His gaze landed on Dani and Hawke sitting in the chairs.

"How long was I asleep?" he asked, starting to push up on his hands and moaning.

"Now that you're awake, you can drink some soup while I change the warm towels on your feet and hands." Hawke placed his empty bowl on the tray and stood. He unwrapped Kieran's hands and handed him a mug of soup. Hawke had figured it would be hard for the man to hold a spoon with his hands stiff, cold, and hurting. The warm mug would help his hands.

While Kieran drank the soup, Hawke replaced the towels on his feet with the newly warmed ones by the fire. He'd set the ones that had been on the man's hands by the fire to warm up while he drank his soup.

"How did you get here, to the lodge?" Dani asked.

Kieran glanced at her. "The dead man brought me."

"Why?" She set her empty bowl down on the tray.

The man shrugged. "I don't know."

"How did you know the man in the barn?" Hawke asked, easing back down into the chair. His muscles were tired and sore from breaking trail the last few miles to the lodge the other day and then dragging this man through the snow to get here tonight.

"He showed up at my home three days ago, grabbed me, shoved a gun in my side, and said we were going on a trip." Kieran closed his eyes. "I was his hostage."

Hawke glanced over at Dani to see what she thought of that. Her eyebrows rose but she didn't seem convinced. Neither was he.

"Why would he take you hostage?" Hawke studied the man who lay on the bed, motionless, his eyes closed. When the man didn't answer he asked, "How did you get up on the mountain?"

Nothing.

Hawke turned his attention to Dani. "Why don't you sleep in your room tonight. I'll heat up a hot water bottle to put in bed with you."

She peered at him. "What about you?"

He nodded to the sleeping man. They knew nothing about him, only his first name. Hawke had to assume he killed the man in the barn. And he didn't buy the line he was a hostage. It could have been the other way around. The body in the barn could have been the hostage and when he tried to get away Kieran killed him.

He wished he knew Kieran's last name. Maybe it would help him decipher what had transpired and how he should treat Kieran, victim or suspect.

Dani smiled as Hawke studied the radio pieces on

the table in her room. He'd used hot water bottles to warm the bed before he'd helped her into it. That was one of the things she liked about him. While he appeared aloof and brusque, he had a soft kind heart and always went out of his way to make people comfortable.

She hoped he didn't notice she had been trying to put the radio together enough to make a call. So far, no luck. There wasn't any way to use the helicopter radio to contact anyone. Its range was too short. If they knew there was a search and rescue party on their way up the mountain there was a possibility she could contact them when they were close enough. But she knew with the weather as it was, they wouldn't attempt coming up here until the storm had completely passed. And no one would start looking for them until after today.

"What do you think of the man in the great room?" she asked Hawke when he continued to linger.

He walked over and sat on the edge of her bed. His deep brown eyes held concern. "I'm not sure. I'll go out tomorrow and really take a good look at the barn and see if I can figure out what happened." He picked up her hand and held it in his broad palm. "He knows the dead man but for some reason won't tell us. I'm going to see what I can find in his pockets during the night."

"Be careful, if he wakes up and doesn't like you snooping..." She knew his job was dangerous and that he couldn't leave a puzzle unfinished. Dani put her free hand at the back of his neck to keep him close. She like how soft his hair was when it was "grown out' as he called it. While doing his job during the fall months when he spent most of his days in the mountains checking on hunters, he was allowed to let his hair grow to look less like a Fish and Wildlife officer and more like a hunter. Less chance of him getting a bullet in his back. The inch and half of black, sprinkled with gray hair made him even more handsome to her.

"I'm not injured. And I have Dog." He smiled. "You rest and get stronger. It isn't going to be an easy trip off this mountain for you. We'll stay here until the storm has passed and then we'll go back. If I know my landlords, they'll have Search and Rescue out looking for us by Friday."

She laughed and said, "That is one thing I am envious of, you have someone to keep tabs on you and know when things aren't right." In the Air Force, she'd always had another pilot or officer who had her back. Since becoming a civilian, she'd missed having a partner to bounce ideas off. Yes, she had Sage and Tuck, but it wasn't the same. While the lodge was their livelihood, it was her heritage. Her uncle had left it to her to keep in the family. Her cousin Tyson was interested in taking it over, but he'd been going to school to be a lawman after meeting Hawke.

"You have me to keep tabs on you from now on." He smiled and patted her uninjured leg. Then he leaned forward and kissed her. He rose off the bed. "Go to sleep. I'll make sure our guest stays put and no one storms the lodge."

# Chapter Seven

A sound woke Hawke. It was a low growl. He dropped his hand down beside the chair to pet Dog. The animal wasn't there.

Opening his eyes to the dark room with barely a glow from the fireplace, Hawke peered at the bed. Kieran wasn't in it. He shot to his feet. Dog's growl grew in volume and fierceness. Hawke followed the sound with his eyes as he found the flashlight with his hands. He clicked the button on the light and caught Kieran in the beam.

"Where are you going?" Hawke asked, striding across the room toward the man, standing with his back against the wall by the front door.

"I need to pee." Kieran didn't take his eyes off Dog.

"Step out on the porch, but you better be back in here in a reasonable time or I'll send Dog after you." Hawke kept his tone hushed to not wake Dani. "Dog quiet," he added.

Dog plopped his butt on the floor, stopped growling, and watched the man walk to the door.

When Kieran stepped out the door, Hawke patted Dog on the head. "Good boy. I was so tired I didn't hear him get up."

The door opened and Kieran hurried through. That's when Hawke noticed the man was still wearing the towels wrapped around his feet. "Get back on the bed and I'll check your feet and hands."

Kieran walked over to the bed as if his feet hurt and sat on the edge of it. "Are you some kind of EMT or something?"

"Oregon State Trooper with the Fish and Wildlife Division. I've spent a lot of time in these mountains and come across lots of people who needed first aid and didn't think to bring a kit with them." He unwrapped the first foot. It had the color back and while the skin wept a bit, Kieran was lucky it only seemed to be the first stages of frostbite. Which was fortunate for him considering how long he'd been hiking around in the snow without proper footwear.

"I'll put salve on these and wrap them in gauze. Then you can put your socks on over the top." Hawke walked over to his pack and pulled out the salve his mom made from beeswax and other ingredients she harvested from her yard and the Blue Mountains that were part of the Umatilla Reservation.

Kieran didn't say anything as Hawke worked on his feet and handed him the tin of salve. "Put some of that on your hands."

The man took the tin and sniffed. "What's in it?"

Hawke shrugged. "I don't know. My mom makes it

and I've used it for years."

Kieran studied him. "Your mom makes it?"

"Yeah. You have a problem with homemade remedies?"

"No. But I have a problem with Indian remedies." Kieran shoved the tin back at Hawke without putting any on his hands.

Hawke shrugged again. "I guess when you realize your feet are healing and your hands aren't you'll take wisdom over bigotry." He scratched around in the fireplace, bringing up embers, and tossed two more pieces of wood on the fire. It was three in the morning. Another three to four hours until daylight. He might as well try to get more sleep before he did another thorough check of the barn and the body to see if he could reveal anything that might get Kieran to talk to him. Hawke had a feeling the connection between the dead man and Kieran was more than a hostage situation. Otherwise, Kieran would be spilling his guts about being kidnapped.

"Go back to sleep. It's going to be dark for several more hours."

Dog walked over beside the chair Hawke sat in and stared at Kieran.

The man swung his legs up on the bed and laid down.

Hawke patted the dog's head and closed his eyes.

The smell of coffee brought Hawke out of a dream where an owl with piercing yellow eyes and tufted ears was peering down at him. He shook off the dream and glanced at the bed. Kieran was sleeping.

Hawke softly walked across the room, stopping at the doorway to the dining room. "Dog, stay and watch him." He made the hand signal for stay and then pointed to the man in the bed.

Dog lay down in the doorway, watching the man.

Entering the kitchen, Hawke found Dani leaning on her left crutch and mixing something in a bowl. "What are you making?" he asked.

She jumped, splattering whatever she mixed out of the bowl. "Shit, Hawke, you shouldn't sneak up on me like that." She glared but a smile curved her lips.

"Sorry. I didn't realize you were so deep in thought." He walked up beside her and peered into the bowl. "What is that?"

"Pancakes. Sage leaves a few dry ingredients in tins in case someone shows up needing food. They can make simple foods. Enough to fill their bellies and give them the energy to go on their way. But not enough for them to squat all winter." She winked. "Are we going to be up here all winter?"

"No. We'll head out as soon as I think you're ready and I have a plan." After the fall Jack and Dani took, Hawke wasn't excited to have the animals carrying the two injured people. But Dani couldn't walk out of here with a broken leg.

He took the bowl of batter from her. "You go in and rest that leg. I'll make the pancakes and bring them to the great room."

She glared at him. "I'm fine. I can sit when you go out and check on your horses after we eat."

Dog growled.

"Kieran must be moving around. Make the pancakes but come get me to carry the food out when you're done." He kissed her on the temple. "I don't want you taking chances of that leg not healing correctly."

58

"I'll be careful. I can't lose the use of it, I need to be able to fly clients in and out. I can't afford to pay a pilot." She waved her hand as Dog's growling grew louder. "Take care of our guest."

Hawke grinned and hurried out of the kitchen. Dog stood in front of the main door, not letting Kieran through.

The man had put his boots and coat on.

"Where are you going?" Hawke asked.

"I need to pee."

"Do the same as you did during the night. No farther." Hawke slapped his leg. "Dog, come."

Dog moved away from the door, but his gaze remained on Kieran.

"What kind of mutt is that?" Kieran asked.

"The best kind," Hawke replied.

The man stared at him for thirty seconds before opening the door and stepping out.

Hawke moved to the window and watched the man's back as he relieved himself, stared in the direction of the bunkhouse, and returned to the lodge.

"Dani's making pancakes. Might as well take off your coat and get ready to eat." Hawke waved to the bed. He'd gone through the man's pockets during the night and found it interesting that he also didn't have any identification. Hawke had found granola bar wrappers, lip balm, a pocketknife, and used tissues, but no wallet or ID.

Kieran sat on the bed and let the coat slide down his arms. He pulled his good arm out of the sleeve and then used that hand to work the sleeve off his injured arm.

"You fell asleep last night before you told me why the dead man kidnapped you and why you were both on

59

the mountain without proper clothing for the weather." Hawke sat in the chair and studied the man on the bed.

"I was a hostage. He had me at gunpoint."

Dani entered the room. "You can bring in breakfast. It's all on a tray." She sat down in a chair and propped her splinted leg on the corner of the bed.

"Think about what I just asked you and when I get back you better tell me the truth." Hawk strode across the room and into the kitchen. He found the tray ready for him to carry into the great room. His first impression of Dani, and subsequent encounters before she finally dropped her guard around him, had Hawke thinking she had more male qualities than female. After watching her with Kitree, he saw the soft side of the woman. The caring and giving side. That's when he started to see that her straightforward abruptness had been a skill she'd learned in the Air Force. It was a way to not be seen as inferior to her male counterparts.

Staring at the coffee in three mugs on the tray and the neatly folded paper towels for napkins, Hawke smiled. Now that she was out of the military, she was starting to soften and let herself indulge in being a woman.

He walked into the great room and discovered Kieran sitting in a chair he must have pulled up to the other side of the fireplace. "Looks like this bed can go back in the room I pulled it out of." Hawke placed the tray with breakfast in the middle of the bed so everyone could reach the coffee, pancakes, and sugar.

Hawke picked up a plate, silverware, and cup of coffee, placing the plate in Dani's lap and the mug on the arm of her chair. Picking up the sugar canister, he held it out for her to sprinkle on her pancakes.

When he turned around to set the sugar down and gather his meal, Kieran had nearly eaten all of his pancakes.

Sitting in the chair next to Dani, Hawke peered across at the man who ate as if he hadn't had a meal in weeks. "Care to tell us how you came to be on the mountain?"

Kieran slowly raised his face, his gaze meeting Hawke's. "I told you. I was taken hostage by Patrick."

The man had slipped up. This was the first time he'd given a name to the body in the barn. "I find it odd that you know the first name of your kidnapper. And even odder that he didn't have any identification on him."

The man's eyes widened as if he'd just realized his mistake.

Ahh. Hawke had a feeling Kieran knew where the identification was. Why would he hide that information? If indeed, the man had kidnapped him. "How did you get on the mountain? You don't have clothing to indicate you had planned to be here. And neither did the dead man, you called Patrick."

"We were snowshoeing and became lost." Kieran shoved half a pancake in his mouth.

Hawke shook his head. "You were an amateur on the snowshoes I put on you yesterday. And you aren't dressed to be out snowshoeing or anywhere near a trailhead to have become lost. I know these mountains."

Hawke ate his meal, watching Kieran and answering the soft questions Dani asked him.

When he'd finished, Hawke gathered up the empty dishes, packed them into the kitchen, and gathered up a length of small white clothesline rope he found in the room off the kitchen. He returned to the great room.

"Dani, I want you to rest while I check on the horses." He faced Kieran. "Since I don't trust you and I don't want Dani bothered…" Hawke held up the clothesline. "You are going to be tied to that chair until I come back in."

Kieran jumped up and started to run but Dog was on him before the man could reach the bedroom. Hawke grabbed Kieran, yanking his good arm behind his back and propelling him to the chair. "I'm going to find answers out in the barn and when I do, I'll be back in here expecting to hear the truth from you."

Once in the chair, Hawke tied the man's hands, wrapping the rope around Kieran's torso and the chair, then down, tying his feet to the chair legs.

"You are no better than the man who kidnapped me!" Kieran shouted.

Hawke stared down at the man. "If you'd tell me the truth and not act like you killed the man in the barn, then I would treat you fairly. But until I know the truth, I'm not trusting you." He faced Dani. "Shove something in his mouth if he gets rowdy."

She saluted and smiled.

Hawke grinned and called Dog. Pulling on his coat and gloves and picking up his shotgun on his way out, Hawke headed to the barn. He wanted to check every inch inside the barn in the daylight with all the time he needed to ponder what had happened that one man ended up dead.

# Chapter Eight

Hawke brought the horses and mule into the barn to give them a reprieve from the snow and wind. They all stood in their stalls, crunching on grain as he began his inspection of the body and the barn. Hawke opened the hidden door to Dani's room full of expensive aircraft parts. He'd placed the body in here before they'd left. He hadn't wanted an animal to find the body and nibble. He also didn't want anyone to stumble across the body and leave evidence that would incriminate them. Since it would be a while before anyone official would get a chance to look at the body, Hawke wanted to learn all he could.

As he'd remembered. The man had on a coat, long-sleeved shirt, slacks, and dress socks and shoes. He wasn't dressed to be wandering around on a mountain. Kieran was dressed more for hiking, only he was dressed for a summer hike, not a winter one. Hawke leaned close to check out marks on the body's head and neck and caught a whiff of airplane fuel underneath the iron scent of blood. Due to hair being oily, odors adhere to the strands. He leaned closer to the side of the man's head opposite his wound. There was a definite underlying odor of airplane fuel. If the body had been in warmer weather, the gases of decay would have covered it up.

Airplane fuel. He knew Dani didn't have any fuel in here. All she kept in this room were parts for the helicopter and airplane, and the jumpsuits she wore while doing mechanical work. He stood and walked over to them. One had a faint smell of airplane fuel like the man's hair. It wasn't strong enough for the hair to have picked up the odor since he'd deposited the body in this room.

Hawke stood staring at the jumpsuit, his mind whirling. For two people to end up on a mountain without proper clothing meant they were either dropped off by helicopter or a plane crashed. There was a good possibility if a small aircraft was flying close to the mountains in the snowstorm it could have crashed. The only aircraft that had a reason to be in the air over the mountains were Dani or Fish and Wildlife. They all knew better than to fly through the mountains during a storm. Someone trying to avoid radar could have been flying low in the mountain.

He pivoted and knelt beside the body. Hawke turned all the pockets inside out and checked the whole body for any other injuries. He found some bruising in a strip from his left shoulder to his right side and on the left arm. While checking the right hand, he noticed the scent of gunpowder. This man, as he'd suspected, had fired the bullet that caused Kieran's injury. Hawke was pretty sure the weapon he'd taken from Kieran was the same gun.

When he couldn't find anything else useful on the body, Hawke picked up the board with blood and hair and studied it. He was 99% sure the board was the murder weapon. But whether it was murder or self-defense, that was what he hoped to discover. He returned to the barn area, closing the hidden door to make sure if anyone arrived looking for the two, they wouldn't find the dead man.

Hawke walked over to the spot where Dog had found the body. He studied the area. There wasn't a lot of room for a fight to take place. The length of the board would have required more room to swing it hard enough to land a killing blow. He walked over to where he'd first discovered the drops of blood from Kieran. There wasn't a clear view from the area where the body was to have shot at Kieran.

Hawke thought about that for a moment. He hadn't paid attention when he'd dressed the wound if the bullet had entered from the front of the arm and out the back or the other way around. Had Kieran been facing his shooter or running away from him? If he'd been running away, then how did he manage to hit the man with the board?

Dog ran into the barn through the door and headed for the stall where Jack munched his grain. Hawke smiled as Dog jumped up into the trough and licked Jack's ear. The two had been buddies for a long time.

"When you get done saying hello, I could use your help," Hawke said to Dog.

When Dog joined him, Hawke pointed to the dark spot on the floor where he'd found the body. "Sniff."

Dog sniffed the dark spot thoroughly.

"Search," Hawke said and watched the animal walk

around the inside of the barn with his nose to the ground. Dog stopped in the middle of the barn and sat.

Hawke walked over and studied the dirt. There was a pattern of dark droplets that made him think this was where the dead man had been hit in the head with the board. "Stay."

While Dog made a visual reference to the spot, Hawke stood where he'd found the blood spots from Kieran. Pivoting to look behind him, Hawke walked up to the barn wall and scanned the wood. A hole the right size for a slug pierced a wall brace. He pulled out his knife and dug into the pole. Within minutes he had the slug in his hand.

His best guess was a 9mm. It had an odd pattern on the end of the slug. There was one way to find out if the gun he took away from Kieran was the same as the one that shot him. Hawke slipped the slug into his coat pocket and headed to the lodge. If the storm hadn't covered the tracks of the dead man and Kieran arriving at the lodge, he could have found out where they'd landed or crashed. But there was too much snow covering their tracks for that to be an easy job.

When he entered the lodge, Dani sat in a chair reading a book and Kieran sat staring into the fire. Hawke walked over to his pack and pulled out the gun. He checked the magazine to see if it still held cartridges. It did.

Back out at the barn, he stood where he believed the dead man had stood and shot into the same board. Of course, the bullet wouldn't be slowed down by the arm the first bullet had gone through, but he hoped they looked similar enough to prove it was the same weapon.

The other thing he could do was comb the area for

the spent cartridge. He dug the slug out of the pole and pulled the first one he'd found out of his pocket. The funny mark near the end matched on both slugs.

Now to get Kieran to tell him what had happened.

Hawke returned to the lodge. Dani was just sitting back down in her chair with what smelled like a cup of coffee. He detoured into the kitchen to get himself and Kieran a cup. Back in the great room, he set the cups down and untied the angry man. As a peace offering, he held out the cup of coffee.

Kieran stared at him a second and took the cup, sipping the steaming brew.

"From what I can determine, you and the dead man must have been in a plane crash."

The man's eyes widened. Yep, he'd discovered the way they'd ended up on the mountain.

"Why do you say that?" Kieran held the cup of coffee in front of his mouth. Hiding half of his face and peering into the cup.

Hawke went on to reveal the smell of aircraft fuel, the lack of winter clothing, and the bruising on the dead man's body. "I also believe you swung that board and hit him out of self-defense." Hawke studied the man across from him and Dani.

Kieran's gaze searched Hawke's face.

"Why didn't you say you hit him in self-defense?"

"Why do you say I did?" The man now seemed genuinely interested.

"Because I believe the weapon you had when I found you is the same weapon that shot you in the arm. You didn't do that yourself. I dug the slug out of a brace in the barn. It matches the weapon. I think, you struck the man with the board to get away. As you were running, he shot at you, the bullet went through your arm, and you hid, waiting for him to come after you. When he didn't, you returned to find him dead. You dragged him into the area that was hidden from view when a person entered the barn. You tossed the board next to him, took the gun and his identification, and left." Hawke cocked his head to one side. "Because you didn't stay where it was warm and out of the weather, knowing the man was dead. I believe he used the radio to call whoever he is working for to let them know his location and then smashed the radio in case you found a way to use it."

Kieran stared straight at him.

"And that is why you took off through the snow unprepared for the cold. You were less scared of the weather than whoever would be coming to retrieve the two of you."

Dani shifted in her chair. "You believe there are men who want Kieran dead on their way here?"

Hawke nodded. "That's why he's been trying to get away from here. I'm sure the storm has slowed them up, but we need to head back tomorrow morning. I'll make a better travois to put you on. We aren't going to ride the horses. It's too dangerous. Kieran and I will walk in snowshoes and Horse will pull you."

"Horse? Is that safe?" Dani asked.

"I need to lead him ahead so he can break trail for the other two. He's taller and stronger than the horses. His path and the travois will make it easier for Jack and Dot." Hawke nodded toward Kieran. "Do you think Tuck left any winter gear in the bunkhouse?"

"I'm sure you'll be able to find something better than what Kieran is wearing," she answered.

Hawke studied the man. "Now that I know where you came from and that you killed the man in self-defense, are you willing to help us get you out of here alive?"

Kieran glanced down at the cup in his hand, over at Dani, and finally locked his gaze with Hawke's. "Yes."

"Then come with me over to the bunkhouse and see if we can find some warmer clothes for you to wear."

# Chapter Nine

Hawke and Kieran found clothing in the bunkhouse and then returned to the lodge to put the furniture back where it belonged. Dani had heated up canned spaghetti.

"After I eat, I'll gather up enough food for six days and put it in Horse's pack."

"It's going to take us six days to get off this mountain?" Kieran asked.

"I'm hoping four, no more than five. But it's nearly seventeen miles to Little Bear Creek Trailhead and with the two feet plus of snow, it will be slow going. Horse and I will have to break trail the whole way because you don't know which way to go." Hawke spooned a bite of the food into his mouth and chewed.

"Don't you think the people looking for me and the man in the barn will come up the trail to here?" Kieran asked.

Hawke glanced at Dani. "That's why we aren't

going down the Moss Springs or the Minam trail. I'm taking you out to Bear Creek. We'll come out near Eagle, closer to help."

Dani's eyebrows rose but she didn't say anything.

"What do you mean by that?" Kieran asked.

"We won't come out in the areas that would be logical. Once we cross the Minam River, we'll take the North Minam trail over to Bear Creek and follow it down. When we get within cell service, I'll call a friend to pick us up." Hawke knew by the time he called Herb, his landlord, and Darlene, his wife, would be worried. Hawke had told them he'd be back Thursday. That was today. If he didn't turn up by dark tomorrow, they would surely contact his superior Sergeant Spruel who would contact Search and Rescue. There wasn't much they could do other than fly a helicopter over and see what they could see before they sent Search and Rescue in after them.

But that gave him an idea. "Do you still have that old wooden bear your uncle had sitting on the corner of the porch?" he asked Dani.

"I think it's out in the barn. Why?"

"I know how to leave a message for Search and Rescue whether they come by helicopter or snowmobile." He set the food down, walked to the door, and pulled on his coat. He went out to the barn and discovered the carved bear in a corner. The carving looked like Kitree had been playing with it. The animal wore a red and black checked scarf.

Hawke looped a rope around the statue's neck and dragged it out into the snow and over to the lodge. There was a hole all the way through the middle of the bear's body. He had another idea to make sure whoever was looking for them saw the bear from the air and the ground.

Stomping his feet on the porch to rid his boots of snow, he entered the lodge. "Do you still have your uncle's box of flags?" he asked.

Dani nodded. "They're in a box at the back of my closet."

He strode down the hall and entered Dani's room. Moving aside the summer clothing she left in the closet year-round, he found several boxes stacked in the corner of the small closet. In Dani fashion, they were all labeled making it easy to find the box of flags. He found the flag he was looking for. It was a Nez Perce flag Charlie had at one time hung on the wall in the great room. He carried the folded and faded flag out to Dani.

"I'll hang this on a pole so anyone from Search and Rescue who comes by will see the rest of the message. But whoever is after Kieran won't know the significance."

"How will Search and Rescue know?" Kieran asked.

"Everyone in the Search and Rescue knows me. They'll know the Native American reference is from me and will see the significance of the rest of the message." Hawke walked out of the lodge, across to the barn, and using a staple gun attached the flag to a wooden pole he took off a push broom.

Back at the lodge, he climbed up onto the porch roof with the flag, wooden handle, and rope in one hand. Once up on top, he lay down the pole with the flag attached and began pulling the bear up to the roof. When the wooden statue was on the roof, Hawke shoved it up to the top of the porch roof. He was happy to see a large metal hook. Using the rope, he attached the bear to the hook and then covered the rope with snow. Then he placed the pole with the flag down through the hole in the bear. To make sure the pole wouldn't fly out with a gust of wind, he cut off the end of the rope, unraveled it, and shoved the smaller rope pieces down into the hole with the pole. He pushed and shoved until the pole was wedged tight.

Back down on the porch, he stomped the snow from his boots and clothes, and entered, taking off his hat and coat to sit down and eat his cold dinner.

"How is that going to tell anyone anything?" Kieran asked, looking skeptical.

"The flag will alert my friends that it is me leaving the message and the direction the bear is pointed along with the significance of the bear will tell them where we are headed." Hawke sat back down and finished his spaghetti.

Kieran stared at Hawke the whole time he finished eating.

Hawke didn't care if the man thought he was crazy. He had faith in the people he'd worked searches with to figure out it was a clue to where they'd gone. The people coming after Kieran wouldn't know he was with two Nez Perce and would most likely ignore the flag and bear as something decorative.

The following morning, Hawke rose before dawn, saddled the horses and put the packs on the mule, and refurbished the travois he'd made to bring Kieran to the lodge. He'd tightened the cross braces and added a metal skid plate across the ends of the travois to make it easier to pull without it, hopefully, plowing up snow. He'd found an old tarp in the corner of the barn. After shaking it out, he folded it into thirds and put it on the travois, adding Dani's sleeping bag on top to help keep her warm. She would get colder than he and Kieran because she wouldn't be working her muscles to stay warm.

Once the animals were ready, he led them out past the barn and into the woods a quarter of a mile then back again. He attached the travois to Horse and walked over to the front of the lodge. Now that the sun was up, he didn't like the gloominess that hung over the mountains. It appeared as if they were in for another snowstorm. He hoped it wasn't the magnitude of the last one. The nearly three feet of snow they would be plowing through was more than enough for the animals and themselves.

Hawke glanced up at the bear with the flag. It was hard to miss. If one of the other Fish and Wildlife troopers came with Search and Rescue, they would immediately know that wasn't normally on the roof. And those members of SAR would realize no one would leave a flag out during the winter, knowing that no one lived here from December to May. He entered the lodge and found Dani trying to get her splinted leg into her snow pants. She needed the clothing to help her stay warm.

"It looks like I'll have to slice the inside seam, then I'll use some string and tie it together around your leg. You need that insulation to stay warm." He studied her, wishing he could do more than cut up her clothing.

"Do what we need to do. You didn't cause the storm, and I insisted we come up to get my helicopter."

"I was wondering why we don't use that to get out of here?" Kieran asked, standing by the door in the winter gear they'd borrowed from Tuck's trunk in the bunkhouse. He looked like a cowboy getting ready to go out and round up cattle. Except he wasn't wearing a cowboy hat.

"Because Dani can't fly the helicopter with a broken leg." Hawke pulled his knife out of his boot sheath and began slicing up the inseam of the insulated pants.

"You fly the helicopter?" Kieran asked in surprise.

Hawke glanced at the man. He was staring at Dani as if he'd heard something ridiculous.

"What's the matter? Never heard of a woman pilot before?" Dani smiled at the man. "I've transported the president and vice president and I've also flown top military leaders in and out of war zones. If I didn't have a broken leg, we would have been out of here by now, believe me."

Hawke had finished cutting the pant leg. He helped her pull it up her other leg and then rather than use string which could be uncomfortable to lay on, he used more adhesive wrap to hold the pant around her leg. Then he helped her put on her coat, hat, gloves, and boots. He'd given her his last pair of heated socks. He didn't want her getting frostbite because she wasn't moving enough to circulate blood to her feet.

"Grab that sleeping bag by the door," he told Kieran, picking Dani up and carrying her to the travois. It didn't hurt to have extra sleeping bags when dealing with winter weather. He'd found it in Dani's room while getting the flag the night before.

He placed Dani on top of her sleeping bag and then took the sleeping bag from Kieran. He opened the sleeping bag and tucked it around her. Then he pulled out the emergency blanket, unfurling it over Dani and tucking it all around her.

"Ready?" he asked.

"Yes," replied Dani.

Kieran shrugged.

Hawke handed the man, he still considered a suspect, Jack's lead rope. Dot's lead was tied to Jack's saddle. "Follow in the tracks we make." He pointed back toward the barn. "I walked these guys out and back about a quarter of a mile, hoping someone not used to tracking will think a herd of elk came through."

Kieran nodded his head.

"Let's go." Hawke walked ahead of Horse. They would follow the Minam River a short distance, then cross over it and go east on the North Minam Trail to North Minam Meadows. From there they'd go up Wilson Basin and over to Bear Creek Trail.

By noon, they'd crossed the Minam, not an easy feat. Hawke had untied the travois from Horse, led the animals across, and then he and Kieran carried Dani on the travois across the knee-high cold river. Hawke was thankful they had found waterproof clothing in the bunkhouse for the younger man to wear. Otherwise, he would have frozen to death from the exposure. As it was without his heated socks, Hawke's toes were feeling cold.

Once the travois was tied back on Horse, they continued, crossing several small streams. One had appeared iced over but Horse had broken through the ice and cut his leg. The animal was ornery on a good day, but breaking trail and getting injured, leading him was like tugging on a square wheeled wagon.

Hawke's arms and legs were throbbing. He and Horse needed a break. They stopped before another trickle of water that ran twice this size mid-summer. Hawke handed Dani her crutches but the only way she could use them was to stand. There was no walking around in the deep snow.

Hawke pulled out his Sterno burner and melted snow for instant coffee to drink with the energy bars that would only last one more day. He'd brought enough to tide him over for two days of his return trip. That wasn't enough for three people for five days. It was normally a one-day ride out to Moss Springs and a two-day ride out the Minam Trail. With the threat of several people out to get Kieran, Hawke had opted to take a longer route. And the weather conditions weren't helping. The animals couldn't cover as many miles as on a summer day.

He handed Dani and Kieran a cup of coffee to help wash the energy bars down.

"How long is this going to take?" Kieran asked.

"I figure at the least four days. We can't go any faster." Hawke had turned to doctor Horse's leg.

Dog growled. He'd been following in their tracks. Now he sat beside Jack, looking back the way they'd come.

Hawke finished wrapping Horse's leg, grabbed his shotgun out of the scabbard on Dot's saddle, and scanned their back trail.

"Hawke, be careful," Dani said.

He nodded, tapped Dog on the head, and pointed. Dog bounded back down the trail with Hawke as close behind as he could move on snowshoes. They went a hundred yards and Dog leaped into the tall snow to the side of the trail. That's when Hawke caught sight of a tawny flash through the trees.

"Dog! No!" He didn't want his friend to become a meal for a cougar. "Come!"

Dog turned around and bounded back to the trail.

"Don't go chasing that size of cat. They'll have you for dinner." Hawke walked slower back to the horses. They were going to have to call it a day as soon as the sun went down. He and Horse were already tired. At this rate, it would take them longer than he'd figured.

"What was it?" Dani asked, holding his now cold cup of coffee and energy bar out to him. Hawke slid the shotgun back in the scabbard and sipped the coffee before saying, "Cougar. Probably was looking for a meal. We're going to have to take turns guarding the animals at night. If a cougar or wolf shows up, shoot the shotgun in the air. That should scare them away." He bit into the energy bar.

"What if it doesn't scare them?" Kieran asked.

"The second shot should be at the predator. I won't have my horses or mule killed by a wolf or cougar when I'm right there with them." Hawke glared at the man making it known his animals meant a lot to him. "I'll throw you out there for bait if I have to."

Kieran's face paled.

"He won't have to do that if you stay awake and shoot in the air if a predator comes around," Dani said, taking Kieran's energy bar wrapper from him. She turned to Hawke. "I need to pee."

"Kieran, see those bushes over there? Walk over, smash the snow down behind them and then walk the same path back." Hawke noted Kieran didn't look happy about having to break a trail but he'd been walking all morning in the packed snow Hawke and Horse had made.

When Kieran came back, Hawke carried Dani over behind the bushes and held her while she did what she needed to do. Then he carried her back and placed her on the travois, once again making sure she was tucked in from the cold.

He grabbed Horse's lead rope. "Let's see how far we can get by dark."

Traveling along the ice-edged stream of the North Minam River, Hawke did his best to try and keep them on the trail. However, with so much snow, there wasn't a trail to follow, only the path of snow with fewer trees and bushes and maneuvering around downed trees and boulders.

Hawke's legs felt as if he couldn't take another step when Horse balked for the third time in half an hour. They had come to an opening that Hawke realized was North Minam Meadows. With all the snow, it appeared larger than when the ground was covered with grass and wildflowers. It was an hour before dark and snowflakes had started falling from the gray sky.

"Let's find somewhere to set up for the night."

# Chapter Ten

By dark Hawke and Kieran had dug out a space in the snow for the tent Hawke had brought. The first night he and Dani were on the mountain, they'd spent a cozy night with their sleeping bags zipped together. Tonight, they'd be sharing the space with a stranger.

They'd piled the snow they'd dug out along the sides of the tent to help insulate it from the wind and cold. He hoped the shelter would hold up to however much snow accumulated overnight. The space was large enough for the three of them to sit and two to lay down. One person would be on guard outside with a flashlight watching for predators. Dog would lie in front of the opening.

Dani offered to take the first shift of guarding the animals since she had been riding all day and wasn't as worn out as the two men.

Hawke studied her. "You'll just sit on the downed tree by the animals wrapped in the emergency blanket?"

"I won't wander off. How can I in all this snow? You'll have to help me get there and get me back." She finished off the instant coffee and soup Hawke had warmed up on the Sterno burner.

Then he crawled out of the tent opening and reached in grabbing Dani under the arms to pull her out. With her leg splinted, she couldn't crawl on her hands and knees to enter and leave the shelter.

Dani had the shotgun in her hands. Hawke carried her over to the downed log under the trees where he'd tied the two horses and mule. They still had their feed bags on but were standing slack-hipped with their eyes closed. Hawke patted each one on the neck and whispered he was proud of them in their ears as he took off the feedbags. They'd all deserve a long rest and plenty to eat when they got home.

"I'll get you in two hours. If you start feeling cold, move as many body parts as you can to keep the blood moving." Hawke kissed her on the forehead.

"You should have Kieran break trail tomorrow," Dani said.

Hawke just grunted and walked away. The snow was coming down harder. He doubted a cougar or wolf was out hunting in this weather, but he didn't want to lose any of his animals to a predator.

Kieran was asleep in the tent, wrapped up in the sleeping bag from the lodge. Hawke pulled off his boots and shoved his body down in his sleeping bag. If it wouldn't have made Dani's bag wet, he would have had her wrap up in it while sitting out there. At least he and Kieran could walk around while guarding the horses. His exhaustion overtook him.

Dani sat on the downed log as long as she could before she started feeling cold. She'd unloaded the shotgun as soon as she'd sat, knowing she'd need to use it as a cane. Now, she used the shotgun, barrel up and butt down, to push to her feet. The movement pulsed blood through her body and unfortunately to her leg that now throbbed. She groaned and eased back down on the log. She waved her arms around and patted both thighs with her hands.

One of the horses snorted and pulled back on the rope tying it to a tree.

"It's okay, I just need to get warm," she said quietly. Something bumped her arm and she jumped. Looking over she stared into Dog's eyes. "Hello. Did you come to see what I was waving my arms at?" He licked her cheek and sat down. She put an arm around the animal and leaned her head on his. His warmth was welcome.

Dani sensed a branch not far from her bounce as something cold stung her neck. She opened her eyes. Her brain was foggy. When did she fall asleep? The flapping of wings caused her to look to her left. She stared at a large owl. The bird had penetrating yellow eyes and tufted feathers on its head that gave the impression of ears. She'd never been this close to an owl before. Its unwavering gaze held hers. What did it want?

As if in answer a voice said, "Be watchful."

She blinked and shook her head, and the bird was gone without a sound. The branch barely fluttered against the snow-white backdrop.

<><><><><>

"Hawke! Wake up, I'm freezing." Dani's voice shot Hawke out of deep sleep. He looked down and saw her head and shoulders in the opening.

"What are you doing?" He quickly grabbed her arms and pulled her in on top of him.

"What's going on?" Kieran asked, wiping a hand across his face.

Dani's lips were white, and her body shook.

"What time is it?" Hawke asked, lifting his arm to look at his watch. "Shit! Kieran, get your ass out there and watch the horses. Dani's been out there four hours." Hawke took his anger at himself out on the other man.

Kieran slid out of his sleeping bag, shoved his feet in his boots, and laced them up. He shoved his arms in his coat and crawled out the opening. He stuck his head back in. "Where's the shotgun?"

"Leaning against the tent. I unloaded the shotgun to use it as a cane to move around." Dani's teeth chattered.

Hawke slid her boots off her feet and unzipped his sleeping bag, pulling Dani into it with him and shifting her body to the side away from the zipper. "I'm sorry. I don't usually sleep that sound up here." He rubbed his hands up and down her arms and back, trying to warm her up.

"The first two hours weren't bad. I talked to Jack and Dog came over and visited a couple of times. But the last hour, I started feeling colder and colder. I figured you both needed the sleep. I can sleep on the travois." She shivered.

He pulled her close, warming her with his body heat. When her teeth stopped chattering, he slid out of the sleeping bag and fired up the Sterno. "I'll make you some hot water to warm your insides."

She nodded.

"Did you see or hear anything?" he asked, getting down on his hands and knees to crawl out and fill the pan with snow.

"There's six more inches of snow. I heard a bird fly by and a soft 'who-whoo' called out up the mountain."

Hawke didn't like the idea of more snow. Outside, he stood and studied the white world. The wind wasn't blowing causing a whiteout but more snow would make traveling even more difficult. If he trusted Kieran, he'd leave him and Dani here with the horses and hike to Bear Creek and call the Search and Rescue to bring snowmobiles. They could get Kieran and Dani out and he would bring the horses out. But he didn't trust the man would take care of Dani and the animals. And he didn't trust sending Kieran for help. He'd just find a ride to wherever and never say a word to anyone that they were up here.

He scooped and pressed the snow down adding more until the pot was packed. Setting the pot in the opening, he stood staring at the dark shadows of the trees through the falling white snow and peed.

The snow would cover up their tracks from anyone who didn't know tracking. And would make it harder for a search party to find them.

He zipped up his pants and crawled back through the opening, pushing the pot of snow ahead of him. Dani was still shivering. Her eyes were closed.

"Are you asleep?" he asked quietly in case she was.

"No." She opened her eyes and stared at him in the light of the battery-operated lantern he'd turned on when he got out of the sleeping bag. "Have you ever experienced…" Her voice died away and she lowered her eyelids.

"Experienced what?" he asked, sitting beside her.

"It's nothing. I must have drifted off and didn't

know it. It was probably a dream."

Now he was even more curious. Dani was half Nez Perce but raised off the reservation in a White world. She had told him she'd only been to one powwow and hadn't been taught any of her people's ceremonies or stories. For her to have seen something and now say it must have been a dream, Hawke's curiosity had been lit.

"What was the dream about?" He glanced at the melting snow in the pot. If she needed to say this without him watching her, he could watch the melting snow.

"That owl I said I heard...I'm sure it sat on a limb not far from me and told me to be watchful."

He glanced over at her as she opened her eyes.

"I heard the sound of a branch creak and looked over. An owl stood on a branch of the tree I sat under. I stared into his yellow eyes and admired his tufted feathers that looked like ears. That's when I'm sure he told me to be watchful." She swallowed. "I blinked wondering if I was having a dream and then he was gone. All I heard was his call from up on the mountain." She wiped a hand across her eyes. "Is the cold making me crazy?"

Hawke shook his head. "I think an ancestor is trying to warn you about either the weather or the man who is traveling with us." He poured the steaming water into a cup and handed it to Dani after she sat up and pulled the sleeping bag around her shoulders.

"You don't believe all that stuff about our people once being able to speak to animals, do you?" she asked.

He smiled. "That's the first time you called the Nez Perce our people."

She scowled. "Don't change the subject. Am I hallucinating from the cold?"

"I think you and I have been warned. Something is coming." Hawke waited for a reply.

Dani only sipped the hot water, staring into the cup.

Hawke glanced at his watch. It was twelve-thirty. He had an hour and a half before he needed to take over for Kieran. This time he set the alarm on his watch. He left the lantern on and slipped into the sleeping bag with Dani. She remained sitting up until she'd finished the water, then slid down beside him.

Hawke drifted off until his watch woke him. He slipped his boots on, grabbed his coat, and shooed Dog out of the tent ahead of him. The snow had added ten more inches to the already two and a half feet and large flakes were still falling.

Hawke followed the almost indiscernible path to the horses under the trees. He found Kieran asleep, leaning his back against a tree. The shotgun was across his lap. He stepped behind the tree and hoped the man didn't shoot a horse when he tapped him on the shoulder.

"Huh? What?" Kieran's head snapped back, hitting the tree. "Ouch!"

"I'm here to relieve you," Hawke said, grabbing the shotgun off the other man's lap.

"I haven't seen or heard anything other than the horses snorting and breathing." Kieran stood, stretched, and walked toward the tent.

"Make sure you don't trip over Dani's leg," Hawke said.

Kieran raised a hand in acknowledgment.

Hawke sat on the downed tree and stared out at the snow falling as if it didn't plan to stop until spring. Dog put his head on Hawke's knee. "I know. It's up to me to get Dani home safe and get Kieran over to the authorities. If this keeps up, we're going to have to worry about avalanches." Hawke wasn't usually a worrier. He'd never seen a point in it. But right now, he worried about Dani and his animals. If he didn't make it out of these mountains with all of them, he wasn't sure he'd be able to patrol the Eagle Cap Wilderness anymore.

<><><><><><>

To Hawke's surprise, Kieran came back out in two hours and Hawke was able to get a couple more hours of sleep before he woke, made instant coffee, and helped Dani go outside to pee.

After Dani was settled back in the tent with a cup of coffee and an energy bar, Hawke told Kieran to go in and warm up and get breakfast. Hawke remained with the animals, slipping the feedbags on, and staring out at the deep white blanket coating everything. The snow had finally stopped. They now had over three feet of snow, and a foot of two more where the wind had caused drifts, to travel through. The terrain this morning was uphill to get up to the top of the ridge between them and Bear Creek. A slight incline in this much snow was going to be hard for the animals. The extra ten inches of new snow would drag on the snowshoes straining muscles and draining energy. Especially when they were only being fueled by energy bars and canned goods.

The sun was already making the newly fallen snow glitter. Branches cracked and creaked under the weight of the overnight snowfall. Hawke led the horses and mule out from under the trees to make sure they didn't get clobbered by a branch or pile of snow.

Kieran crawled out of the tent. He turned around and the emergency blanket rolled out like a rug. Then a sleeping bag was shoved out. Kieran picked it up and handed it to Hawke.

He placed the bag on the travois. They duplicated the steps until everything was out of the tent except Dani. She held her arms out and Hawke grasped her hand, pulling her out on her back. He pulled her up to her feet, holding onto her arm on the side of her splinted leg.

"It feels good to stand. If there wasn't all this snow, I could at least walk a little bit. Laying down and sitting all the time is more tiring than working for fifteen hours." She breathed deep and let it out slowly. "How far do you think we'll get today?"

"Today will be the shortest, miles wise. We have to go over this ridge." He pointed at the ridge between them and Bear Creek. "And this extra snow won't help."

He let Dani stand by Jack while Kieran helped him take the tent down and stow it in the packsaddle.

Hawke scooped Dani up in his arms and carried her over to the travois. He placed her on the conveyance, tucked the sleeping bag around her, and then the emergency blanket.

He glanced at Kieran. "Ready?"

"Not really but we don't have much choice, do we?" The man seemed less antsy. It appeared this escape was wearing on him.

"Not if we want to stay alive. We have enough food for four more days and the animals will be running out of grain in three."

Dog made a noise.

"And Dog says he won't share his kibble."

That made Dani and Kieran laugh.

Hawke ran a hand up and down Horse's face. "I know you're tired. We all are, but we have to get out of these mountains to rest." He grabbed the lead rope and headed toward what looked like the easiest route to get over to Wilson Basin and then on over to Bear Creek.

# Chapter Eleven

Hawke sensed something was different before he heard the helicopter. They couldn't cover up their tracks and there were few trees to hide under this high up on the side of Wilson Basin. He'd remembered seeing what looked like an outcropping with snow curling down over it. He veered in that direction. "Hurry, we need to try and get out of sight before that helicopter gets here!" he shouted to Kieran.

Dani raised a hand. "Let me listen."

Hawke didn't stop pulling the stubborn mule until he and the mule and travois were out of sight of anyone from the air.

The thump of the blades grew closer as Kieran managed to get Jack and Dot under the rock and snow cover.

Dog started to howl. Hawke hushed him.

Dani raised up and pulled the stocking cap away

from her ear. She listened intently as the aircraft grew closer. "That doesn't sound like the Fish and Wildlife helicopter."

Hawke had a visual out the side of the curl of snow. "It isn't. It's too fancy. Too shiny."

They must have seen the tracks because the helicopter dipped lower following the tracks up the side of the basin.

"Press in closer to the rock," Hawke ordered, pulling Horse farther under the snowy overhang.

"Dog, come," Dani said, wrapping an arm around the animal when he stood by her.

Kieran maneuvered Jack and Dot further into their hideout. He turned and looked out at the helicopter flying by twenty feet off the ground. The man groaned.

"You know them?" Hawke asked.

"They're the people who had me kidnapped." Kieran glanced around as if he were looking for a way to flee.

"How many were in the airplane with you?" Hawke asked.

"Just the man in the barn, and me." Kieran glanced out at the now empty sky. "Shouldn't we get going?"

"I'm thinking." Hawke ran all the scenarios he could think of through his mind. "If they believe we are you, they will lower someone down to check it out."

"If that's the case, they can do that anywhere they feel safe to hover," Dani said. "Too bad there isn't a good wind blowing. That would hinder where they can let a person off."

"Stay put. I'm going to step out and have a look around. See if I can figure out if they kept on going or if they are dropping someone off." Hawke pulled his binoculars out of the pack, grabbed his shotgun, and stepped out from under the snowy outcrop.

The bright sunshine on the white snow blinded him for several minutes. When his vision returned, he did a full circle, listening for the sound of the helicopter and using his binoculars to catch a glimpse of the aircraft.

The pilot must not be as skilled as Dani. He was dropping two people off in the basin. They would have to climb up the side of the basin to get to them. Hawke lay in the snow, watching, deciding what to do. He couldn't take too long. The two men would make faster progress in their snowshoes without horses. He had to take the chance if they saw him, they would follow him and not the tracks into the overhang.

Hawke hurried up to the overhang. "You two stay here. Dog, Jack, Dot, and I are going to lure the two men who dropped out of the helicopter around the top edge of the basin."

"What happens when they catch up to you?" Dani asked, her gaze leveled on him as if he were an insubordinate private.

"I'll find out who they are and pretend I know nothing about Kieran. Once we are all out of sight, I want you two to continue up over the top of the basin and down toward Bear Creek." He studied Dani. "Just keep heading downhill and you'll come to the creek. Follow it to the bottom. I'll catch up to you as soon as I can." He scooped two feed bags with grain and shoved them in Jack's saddlebags. "I need to go to draw them away from here."

He peered at Kieran. "If anything happens to Dani or Horse, I'll come looking for you."

The man swallowed.

Hawke handed Dani her Beretta. "Keep this with you, but out of sight."

She nodded, holding his hand for several seconds. "Be careful."

He grinned and winked. "Dog, come."

Hawke led the horses out of the overhang and headed along the side of the basin, slowly working his way up the side. He glanced down once and noticed the men had split up. He hoped Dani managed to find out information before she shot the man headed in their direction.

It was obvious his ploy hadn't worked quite as planned. As long as the man headed toward Dani and Kieran didn't shoot first, they had a chance. Hawke also had more of a chance with only one man after him. In this snow, leading the horses, he couldn't lose the man, but he could outsmart him once he topped the rim and set up traps in the trees.

Dani sat up on the travois watching Hawke, the two horses, and Dog work their way along the edge of the basin. "Can you see if the men are following him?"

Kieran stepped close to the snow overhang and peered out. He pulled his head back in. "One of the men is coming this way. The other is headed after Hawke."

Dani cursed and stared out at the dark spot that was Hawke. "Keep track and as soon as you see him getting close, you hide behind Horse. I'll see if I can persuade the man you are Hawke, and he found me hurt and planned to get me back to the valley until the two men showed up. He'll either leave me or I'll get a chance to shoot him." Her heart raced, making her leg hurt. She evened her breathing and stilled her heart. She knew how to squelch her nerves; she'd had to do just that while on several missions.

She'd never told Hawke about the men she'd killed in the line of duty. But she had an idea he knew. He'd wakened her a couple of times when she'd been dreaming about the events.

Kieran looked out again. "He's getting closer," he whispered.

"Get behind Horse, but stand still and don't fidget or the mule might bite you." She didn't know if the animal would bite or not, but it might keep Kieran still enough the stranger wouldn't realize he was nearby.

She adjusted her Beretta, making it not so obvious when she'd pick it up if need be. Lying on her back on the travois, knowing she was at the mercy of a man who had been stupid enough to try and run away in inadequate clothing, didn't help her nerves.

The crunch of snowshoes grew closer.

Her heart picked up speed. She slowly breathed in and out.

The muzzle of an assault rifle appeared. She closed her eyes, feigning sleep.

The travois shook as if he'd kicked it.

Horse took a step forward.

Dani opened her eyes and stared up at a man in a full-face cold mask and stocking cap. She sucked in air to appear startled as she watched his every move. "Where did you come from?" she asked.

"I'll ask the questions," the man said. His gaze left her and moved up the travois tied to Horse and then the animal. "How did you get here?"

"A man came along after I fell and broke my leg." She rubbed a hand on her splinted leg. "I own Charlie's

Lodge. He helped me and said he'd use my animals to get me off the mountain." She frowned staring in the direction Hawke had gone. "But as soon as he heard the helicopter, he cursed and stuck me in here. I wanted him to stop and get help. He just said, 'good luck' and took off." She hated to act like a helpless woman. It wasn't in her. But for the sake of getting off the mountain alive, she said, "Will you help me get off the mountain?"

The curving of his lips could be seen through the hole for his mouth. "Lady, you're on your own." He pulled out a radio and spoke into it. "There's a woman with a broken leg. Says the man you're following helped her to this point but left as soon as he saw the helicopter. Over."

"He just went over the top. I'm going after him. Over."

"Want me to trail behind? Over."

"What about me?" Dani said, as simpering as she could stomach.

"I'm sure that mule will pull you somewhere, eventually. Or this might end up being your gravesite." The man turned his back, looking out into the bright sunshine.

The voice on the radio said, "Yeah. But come up over the top sooner. We can get him in between us. Over."

The man glanced back at Dani and grinned. "Headed your way. Over." He stepped out of the overhang.

Just to make it sound authentic, Dani yelled, "Don't leave me here! Please!"

A laugh echoed in the cold air.

Dani relaxed and whispered, "Kieran, I think you can come out now."

She didn't hear him moving. She leaned up on one arm. Fear circled in her gut for several seconds as she waited for the man to appear. If he had left her here, she'd untie the travois from Horse and find a way to get up on the animal and ride down to Bear Creek Trail.

The crunch of snow from the opposite side of her hiding place had her reaching for her Beretta.

Kieran eased down into the hole. "He's heading as fast as he can to the rim. He should be over it in about ten more minutes, and we can go out this way." He pointed over his shoulder.

She nodded. "When did you sneak out?" Dani wondered at the man's stealth now that he was no longer around Hawke.

"When I moved to hide behind the mule. I figured if he did look it would be better for you if he didn't find me."

"Did you hear he has a radio to talk to the other guy?" Dani didn't like they were setting up a trap for Hawke. Would they see that he wasn't Kieran, or would they just shoot figuring from what she'd said he was?

"I heard what was said." He walked over to the larger opening and looked out. "He's out of sight. Let's go." Kieran walked up to Horse and grabbed the lead rope. He walked but the animal stood still.

Dani groaned. This wasn't going to be easy getting the stubborn mule to be led by a person he didn't know and no buddies around to make him feel comfortable. "Grab a handful of grain out of the pack and see if you can make friends with him. Horse is a grumpy mule."

While getting the grain, Kieran asked, "Why is he called Horse when he is a mule?"

"Hawke thinks it makes him act more like a horse

than a mule." She'd never understood his reasoning but if it made Hawke and the animal think that, then it was working.

Kieran laughed and walked up to the mule's head.

"Don't curl your fingers up around the grain, he'll bite them. Just put a little on your palm and let him use his lips to pick it up." Dani couldn't see everything the man was doing, but the animal walked, and she lay down. She'd never been a praying person, but she asked the Creator to keep Hawke safe and bring him back to them soon.

# Chapter Twelve

Hawke knew he and the two horses traveled at half the speed the man on the snowshoes could. As soon as he topped the basin and found a good grove of trees, he tied the horses to a tree and he and Dog made three trails away from Jack and Dot before circling around to come up behind the man when he found the horses.

The man arrived ten minutes later. He crouched down when he caught sight of the animals. Hawke caught a glimpse of the assault rifle the man held out in front of him. He had to hope Dani had outfoxed the other man if he had an assault rifle too. He hadn't heard any shots. Which led him to believe she'd convinced the man she'd been left.

Not wanting the man in front of him to accidentally shoot the horses when Hawke grabbed him from behind, he sent Dog to the right to catch the man's attention.

When the man swung the rifle to the right, Hawke

crept up behind him and lunged, taking him down. The snow effectively trapped the man. The only problem— Hawke's hands were under both of them.

Hawke lay on top of the squirming man, working one hand out from underneath, and snapping a handcuff on his wrist. Tugging on the second arm, Hawke noticed the man no longer fought. Not sure if it was a ploy or the man had run out of oxygen with his face pressed into the snow, Hawke managed to get the man cuffed behind his back and pulled him up and out of the hole in the snow. Using Dot, Hawke tied a rope to the man's waist and dragged him over to a tree. Sitting the man with his back to the tree, Hawke tied him to the pine and went back to the hole to get the rifle. That's when he saw the radio.

Hawke shoved the assault rifle into the empty scabbard on Jack's saddle and dialed the radio to the Search and Rescue frequency. "This is Hawke. Can anyone hear me?" He didn't know how far the radio would work, but it was worth a try to contact someone.

He walked over to the man and studied him. His stalker wore a full-face stocking cap. The clothing was all brand name outdoor gear and top of the line. He had a feeling this man was a mercenary for hire. *Great*. Not what he wanted to be dodging as they made their way off the mountain. He didn't know what happened to the one that had gone in Dani's direction. Standing around here wondering about both men wouldn't get him back to Dani and Horse any quicker. Especially if the man's partner was headed this way.

Hawke didn't like leaving the man out here tied to a tree, but he didn't need the extra weight of a resistant body on one of the horses. It could kill them all if the man became unruly while they were traveling a rough patch on the mountain. He'd take down the horse he was on and the horse it was tied to and possibly Hawke.

He'd let Search and Rescue know to pick this guy up when he managed to get in contact with them. That made him think about the radio. He put it back on the frequency it had been on. If the other person after Kieran tried to contact this man, Hawke would know what was happening.

Learning more about Kieran would have been nice, however, he didn't want to wait around for the man to be able to speak. He had a feeling the bound man wouldn't tell him anything. Not if he was, indeed, a mercenary as Hawke suspected. But why had Kieran been kidnapped? And why had these men dropped out of a helicopter to get him?

Hawke grabbed Jack's lead and whistled for Dog. They headed out in a northwest direction to try and catch up with Dani and Kieran.

"Listen close. We may have someone or even both the men coming up behind us," Hawke told Dog when they had traveled over an hour.

Dog's ears perked up and he stared back down their very visible trail.

Jack was breathing hard. Hawke had been making him slog through the snow faster than he liked. But being the faithful horse he was, Jack had been doing his best to keep going.

"I'm sorry, my old friend." Hawke stopped and let the animals eat some snow. He also pulled out four alfalfa cubes and fed them each two. "We have to catch up to Dani and Horse. That city slicker with them doesn't know the wilderness and I'm sure Horse isn't listening to him." Which had Hawke wondering if maybe he should cut up higher. They may not have made it down this far yet.

One look at Jack and he knew the animal wasn't going to be able to go uphill. All he needed was to get Jack down to the Bear Creek Trail and he could let the horses loose. Jack would lead Dot down to the bottom at their own pace.

Hawke decided to keep on going down with the horses until he hit the trail. Then he'd let them go and head back up to find Dani and Horse. Another hour and Dog started growling. Only he wasn't looking back, he was looking to the left.

Stopping, Hawke stared into the trees to their left. There was something moving. He couldn't tell what, but it wasn't as tall as a man. The hair along Dog's spine stood up. Whatever it was, Dog didn't like it.

That's when Hawke saw another movement. There was more than one. Gray flashed between the pine trees. Wolves. He didn't want to fire a rifle. It could possibly pinpoint him to the men after him. And it might make Dani try to take action if she thought the men were shooting at him.

He decided rather than let the animals think he and the horses were huddling up scared, he'd keep them moving. As if the wolves didn't bother them.

"Dog, keep an eye on them. We aren't going to engage." Hawke pet the horses on their foreheads and whispered in their ears. "Be brave and keep moving." They continued, and soon, Dog's hair lay back down, and the horses seemed to be calmer. But now he wondered if the wolves had found easier pickings. Like Dani, Horse, and Kieran.

Kieran didn't keep up the same pace as Hawke had with the mule. But Dani couldn't fault the man, he was doing the best he could with the stubborn animal. Horse had balked and stopped so many times, she'd become frustrated and tried to get off the travois and walk.

"Stay there. I'll not have Hawke hunting for me because you and this damn mule didn't arrive wherever the hell we're supposed to be going." Kieran put his hands on her shoulders.

Dani settled down. She didn't want the man beat up by Hawke because of her rash behavior. "I'm sorry. I'm as frustrated with Horse as you are." She motioned. "Can you get him over under those trees? The snow isn't as deep and I need to go pee."

Twenty minutes later, Kieran dragged Horse under a small grove of pine trees that were so thick the snow hadn't been able to penetrate the limbs that sagged under its weight piled on the boughs. Dani hung her uninjured leg over the side of the travois and then her splinted leg. By then Kieran arrived at her side with her crutches.

He handed them to her and stood back as she rose to her feet. "Ummm, how are you going to, you know? Hawke helped you before."

Dani shrugged. "I'll figure it out. Just stay here with Horse. Maybe give him a small amount of grain. That might appease him until we find a place to stay for the night."

She paid attention to where she planted her crutches, missing small limbs and pinecones that could make her sprawl face-first on the ground. It seemed like half an hour had passed by the time she stood behind a large tree. Standing on her right foot, she surveyed the situation. There was a log back a little bit. She could drop her pants and sit with her butt hanging over the back of the log. It was worth a try. Better than having Kieran try to hold her up. She wasn't impressed with his muscles or stamina so far.

At the downed tree, she undid her snow pants and shoved everything down to the top of her splint. On her right foot and using the crutch on her left side, she lowered onto the log. The exertion had started her injured leg throbbing. She bit back the curse trembling her lips and peed.

Now to get back up. After struggling twice and only making her left leg hurt worse, she called Kieran.

He hurried back but stopped when he saw her pants down and her butt hanging over a log.

"Grab this arm and pull me up," she ordered.

Kieran sprang forward, grabbing the arm she'd extended to him and pulled. They got her up.

"Turn around," she ordered again, in her best Lieutenant tone.

He spun around, and she pulled her pants up, zipped and buttoned, then swung by him on her way back to the travois. She needed a pain pill but didn't want to take one and go to sleep. She didn't trust Kieran to keep going downhill.

"Why don't we just spend the night here?" Kieran asked when she asked him to put the sleeping bag and emergency blanket back over her.

"We need to put as much distance between us and the men who want you. Stopping too soon could put us in harm." She studied him. "Why are they after you? I'd think since I put my life on the line for you, I should get an answer."

Kieran walked over to Horse, opened the pack, and

handed her a water bottle and an energy bar. He took a bar out and opened it. "I decided I didn't want to launder money anymore. The man in your barn was taking me to see the head of the organization. He was going to explain to me why I couldn't stop helping him."

She chewed on a bite, swallowed, and took a drink before asking, "Do you think the men following us no longer care if you work for the organization? That maybe they are just here to silence you, so you don't get their boss in trouble with the law?"

He nodded. "I figure by now they just want to shut me up. They don't care if I won't help them, they don't want me informing on them." Kieran stared at the energy bar in his hand. "Right now, with them after me, I'm ready to tell them I'll keep helping."

Dani thought about that. "You'd continue to work for people who would kill you if you wanted out? What kind of life would that be?"

"I'd be alive." He grabbed Horse's lead and started walking.

"Go to your right. Remember, stay downhill." Dani laid down and winced as the travois bounced over a stick. Where was Hawke? How soon would he meet up with them?

Hawke kept a steady pace downhill and soon came to the Bear Creek Trail. He breathed a sigh of relief. His horses would soon be safe and could travel at their own pace. He wanted to wait until morning to set them free so they wouldn't be afraid or worried, but he wanted to go back up and look for Dani.

He gave the horses the rest of the grain he'd brought along. While they and Dog ate, he drank water and ate the last protein bar in his saddlebag. He'd not thought to grab food for himself, and he'd used up his emergency bars on this trip. When he shoved the wrapper into the saddlebag, Hawke pulled out a small notepad and wrote a note for anyone who found his horses. He mentioned whom they belonged to, to call Herb Trembley to pick them up, and contact the Search and Rescue to find Hawke up Bear Creek Trail. He wrote four of the same note, putting one in Jack's saddlebags, one in Dot's saddlebags, and tucking a note in each of their scabbards after he took the shotgun and assault rifle out.

"Jack, take Dot home," Hawke said, tying their lead ropes to the saddles. He led Jack forward on the trail. The snow was now only two feet deep as the trail slowly went down in elevation.

He pulled the horse by him and slapped him on the rump. "Go! Go home!" Jack flinched, walked a few steps, and looked back. "Go!" Hawke grabbed Dot's halter and led him down to Jack. He slapped them both on the rumps. "Go!" He waved his arms and the two started walking. He watched until Jack stopped looking back, and then he picked up a small pack with extra shotgun shells, a first aid kit, and dog food he'd pulled out of the saddlebag. Slipping his arms through the straps on the pack, he grabbed the AR and slung it over his shoulder and gripped the shotgun.

"Come on, Dog. We need to find Dani and Horse."

# Chapter Thirteen

Hawke walked uphill following the Bear Creek Trail, hoping to run into Dani and Horse. The moon was in the early cycle barely illuminating his way. However, the white snow on the bare mountainside glowed.

Dog had sniffed out a rabbit earlier when they'd been in the trees. Hawke had clubbed the creature and tied it to his pack. It would make a fine meal when he had the time to build a fire and cook it. Right now, finding the others pulsed in his head.

And something else bothered him. There was no way the two men who dropped out of the helicopter knew that only Kieran was alive. If they'd been to the crash site, they'd know that both men had made it away from the downed plane. And if the dead man had radioed them, they would expect him to be alive. Which made him wonder if the person who had gone toward Dani was holding her and Kieran, waiting for the man who Hawke had tied up to bring back the person he'd followed?

This thinking had him moving as fast as he could in snowshoes traveling uphill. Which was faster than him leading horses through the deep snow.

*Whumpf.* He heard the sound and within seconds it registered. The large snowfall and warming conditions had caused the snow on the bare mountainside to slide.

"Dog, Go!" Hawke shouted and pointed to the side, hoping he was sending his friend in the right direction to get out of the way of the river of snow that would be coming their way. Dog shot off as if chasing after something.

Hawke headed to the side as well, hoping he wasn't running into the river of snow.

Swooshing sounds grew in volume and his feet were taken out from under him by the snow sliding under his feet. Hawke kept clawing and crawling on his hands and knees trying to get to the edge of the wave of snow in hopes he wouldn't be covered.

When everything went silent, he found himself buried from the chest down. His arms and head were above the snow. Dog came back, whining and licking him.

Hawke pointed upwards, hoping if Dani and Kieran had found Bear Creek Trail they were up above and hadn't ended up in the avalanche. "Go find Dani," he said to Dog. "Go. Find Dani." He waved his arm. Dog peered at him for several seconds before turning and racing up the mountain.

When the animal was out of sight, Hawke started using his hands to dig himself out.

Dani leaned on her side, her heart hammering. They

had caused an avalanche. She'd not let Kieran stop for the night. She'd feared the man coming back and wanted to meet up with Hawke as soon as possible. Now she wished she'd allowed Kieran to rest. He'd fallen and caused the snow to break off and rush down the mountain. It was clear he'd never been on a mountain in the winter and didn't realize how easy it was to start an avalanche when so much snow had fallen in such a short time.

"My god! We could have ended up buried in the snow!" Kieran shrieked, staring at the snow floating in the air from the mass of snow that had slid downhill.

"Shhh. Keep your voice down. It carries a long way up here. Especially on the cold still air." She said it sterner than she'd meant. After all, they had just avoided death.

"Move to the side. But be careful. If we get into the trees there is less chance of causing an avalanche. And we can stop for a few hours." The moon was heading downward. The sun would be coming up in four or five hours. They'd continue on then.

Horse slowly moved, pulling the travois up a bit and then across to the trees they'd avoided after seeing shining yellow eyes, and Horse had become nervous. Dani decided she'd kill whatever creature came after Horse. It was better to remain in the trees than out in the open during the day anyway.

Just as they moved into the trees, Horse snorted.

Dani sat up, her Berretta in her hand.

She saw a flash and then heard a bark. Cougars and wolves didn't bark.

"Dog?" she called.

The animal sped over to her. He whined and started

to trot away.

"What is it?" she put her hand out. He walked over to her, whined again, and walked away.

"Something's happened to Hawke. I'm sorry. We can't stop now. Follow Dog." Dani ordered and waved her hand.

Dog spun in a circle and headed downhill.

"How do you know he's just not happy to see us?" Kieran asked, his voice weak and tired.

"Because he wants us to follow, and Dog and Hawke are rarely separated. Hawke is in trouble." She sat up, her heart pounding with dread. "Go!"

Hawke had the snow removed to his waist, but his arms were too weak to help pull his body out. His feet were still attached to the snowshoes, and they were like roots holding him tight. The snow pressed against his body like a hand squeezing slowly. He leaned back and closed his eyes to take a breather. It seemed as if he and Dani had headed up the mountain months ago, not a week ago. He was so tired.

A breeze blew across his face. He opened his eyes and peered into the yellow eyes of an owl. Hawke lowered his eyelids and opened them again. The bird still sat not ten feet from him on the snow. The creature looked like the owl Dani had said talked to her.

"Hello, my friend. Are you here to tell me this is the end?" Hawke studied the regal-looking creature. "If this is to be my resting place, I will be in good company with my ancestors. But should this be where I spend the rest of my day, please make sure my animals and Dani come to no harm."

The owl blinked. He took that as meaning the owl

would care for those he loved. Hawke closed his eyes and felt the breeze again. The owl was gone on silent wings.

While his visit with the owl had settled his mind, he wasn't about to give up yet. Scooping the snow from around his hips, he continued to dig himself out.

His hips were uncovered when Dog raced up to him. "Dog, it's good to see you. Did you find help?"

He heard the crunch of snow and stared into the darkness. He made out the shape of a man, a mule, and a travois. "I'm over here. I'm stuck," he said, only loud enough his voice would carry to Dani and Kieran.

He grasped Dog's head and scratched his ears. "Thank you, my friend."

"Is it safe to come over there?" Kieran's voice quivered.

Hawke couldn't tell if it was from fear or tiredness. "If you can tie a rope to Horse and throw me the other end, I'll tie it around my waist, and he can pull me out."

"I can get the rope to you, but I can't guarantee that Horse will move," Kieran said.

"Dani? Are you okay?" Hawke asked since he hadn't heard a word from her.

"Yes. Kieran and Horse are very tired. I've kept them moving."

Now Hawke understood the man and mule's tiredness. "Once I'm out we'll go in the trees and all rest."

"Where are Jack and Dot?" Dani asked.

"I'll explain." He caught the rope that landed next to him and tied it around his waist. "Pull."

The rope pressed into his back and side. He held on with his hands to ease some of the pressure. Hawke wiggled his legs, hoping to help break loose of the snow packed around him. He felt his right leg release. Using all the energy he had, he wiggled the left leg and soon he was being pulled across the snow. One snowshoe was in the snow, the other scraped across the snow. He could use one of Dani's snowshoes to get off the mountain.

"Whoa!" he called, and Horse stopped immediately at the sound of his voice.

Hawke rolled to his back, untied the rope, and by that time, Kieran was kneeling beside him.

"Are you hurt?" the man asked.

"Not that I can tell. Everything is cold, stiff, and I'm hungry." Hawke held out a hand. "Help me up."

The two of them walked over to the travois. Dani reached up from where she lay on the travois and grasped his hand in both of hers. "We started the avalanche. I'm so sorry." The sorrow in her words warmed his heart.

"It could have been anything that caused it. I should have been paying more attention. I know after a snowfall like we had the last few days there would be weak spots." He walked up to Horse.

The animal rubbed his big head on Hawke. "Hi, boy. We need to get into the trees, and you can rest. Come on." He pulled one of Dani's snowshoes from the pack, attaching it to his boot. Then he grasped the lead rope and led the mule and woman, he'd been hell-bent on reuniting with, over into the trees. He continued in about fifty yards before stopping in a bit of an opening.

"I'm too tired to worry about a tent. We'll just spread it on the ground and sleep on top of it." Hawke moved along Horse and opened the pack, pulling out the tent and handing it to Kieran.

Dani stood beside him as he reached in to get

Horse's feedbag. "What happened to Jack and Dot?" She placed a hand on his arm.

"I'm hoping that by morning, or at least noon, they are spotted at the Bear Creek Trailhead or even walking down the road headed home if there isn't anyone at the trailhead. I put notes on them. Saying to call Herb to get them and call Search and Rescue." Hawke placed the feedbag on Horse. He patted the animal's neck. "You'll have to keep the pack on again. I hope you aren't getting any sores."

"Did that other person catch up to you?" Dani asked.

"Yes. He's tied to a tree." Hawke turned and cupped her face. "What about the man that went toward you?"

Dani glanced toward Kieran who was already curled up in his sleeping bag on the spread-out tent. "I had Kieran hide behind Horse. The man asked how I got there. I told him you, as the man who was leaving me, had found me at the lodge with my leg broken and was helping me get off the mountain until he saw the two men get out of the helicopter."

Hawke peered at her. "Did he believe you?"

"I couldn't tell. He had on a full-face stocking cap and was wearing sunglasses." She reached in the pack and pulled out the Sterno burner, pan, and two cans of soup, depositing them in his hands. "I'll make you something to eat and then we'll rest."

"Where did he go when he left you?" Hawke asked, carrying the items she'd given him, following her to a spot by a downed log.

"He headed after the two of you. But he didn't go all the way around like you did."

A muffled voice caused them both to stop moving and listen. Hawke realized he still had the small pack with the rabbit dangling. He slid the straps off his shoulders and down his arms and opened the pack. Someone was on the radio.

Hawke held it up to his ear, keeping the volume down so Kieran couldn't hear it.

"Arlo, can you hear me? Why aren't you talking to me? I can't find you. I'm going back to see if that woman was lying and helping get away with the suitcases. Over."

Hawke stared at Dani.

"Who was that? What did he say?" Dani asked in a whisper as she placed the pot of soup on the burner.

"I took this from the man I left tied to a tree. That was the man who had talked to you. He can't find his friend and is going back to see if you are helping Kieran get away with the suitcases." He studied her.

Dani's brow furrowed. "Suitcases? Kieran told me that he had been laundering money for someone and when he wanted to stop, that's when the other man kidnapped him. He was taking Kieran to see the boss."

Hawke's gaze drifted over to the sleeping man. Had he killed the other man to steal whatever was in the suitcases? But he would have had to have hidden it somewhere. Since there hadn't been ID on the dead man and he'd found none on Kieran when he'd searched his pockets while the man slept, they had only the man's word he was Kieran and not possibly the other man.

This was getting more complicated than he liked. Now he wanted to go back to the lodge and see if he could find the hidden suitcases, but his first priority was getting Dani off the mountain and to a doctor. Then he'd come back up and take a look around.

"Don't let him," Hawke dipped his head toward

Kieran, "know that we have the radio."

Dani nodded and poured the warm soup into a cup, handing it to Hawke. "Do you think he is Patrick?"

Hawke sipped his soup, blew on it to cool it down, and then said, "We'll know when we get him off the mountain and check out his fingerprints."

# Chapter Fourteen

The sun was flickering through the trees when Hawke opened his eyes. His body hurt all over and his limbs were stiff. He rolled his head toward Dani. She lay with her eyes wide open, staring up at the sky. He grasped her hand. They'd zipped their sleeping bags together before bedding down so they could share their body heat.

Her head moved and she gazed into his eyes, smiling.

Hawke rolled his head in the other direction. Kieran wasn't in his sleeping bag. Hawke sat up, ignoring his screaming muscles and caught a glimpse of the man over behind a tree.

"Time to get moving," he said, dragging his body out of the sleeping bag.

Kieran returned. "I have snow melting to make coffee."

"Thank you." Hawke went over behind a tree, relieved himself, and then came back and helped Dani do the same.

By then Kieran was pouring hot water into cups.

Dani sat on the log, and he handed her a cup. "Thanks."

Hawke reached down and took the cup the man offered. He'd tried to think things through last night after he and Dani slid into the sleeping bags, but he'd fallen asleep before he even thought about places the man might have hidden the money.

"How much farther to the trailhead?" Kieran raised his cup to his lips.

"It depends on how much cooperation we get out of Horse today. I'd say we'll be at the trailhead tomorrow mid-day. As we travel down the mountain, the snow will get less and less which will be easier for Horse to walk through."

Kieran nodded.

"Dani told me that you have been forced to launder money for someone and that was who kidnapped you." Hawke sipped his coffee, watching the man over the rim of his cup.

Kieran ran a hand over his face. "I got into some money trouble, and Patrick, the man who is dead, came to me and said he could help me with my money problems. I thought it was a one-time thing, but he kept coming back over and over again. I finally told him I'd had enough and wanted out. He said that wasn't going to happen. I told him I wasn't doing it anymore. He said, I'd have to take it up with the boss and that's when he took me to the airport, and we got on the plane that crashed."

Hawke took time to think through everything this man had said. "Then if Patrick is the only person you talked to, how come you knew those men in the helicopter?"

Kieran gazed into his cup of coffee for a long time. He didn't glance up when he said, "One of the men came with Patrick once."

Hawke met Dani's gaze. The man was lying. Now Hawke wondered if the situation hadn't been the other way around. Or Kieran and Patrick had come up with a plan to get away with laundered money and both men became greedy. One killing the other for the money.

Either way, he would no longer give this man the benefit of doubt. While Hawke wouldn't let Kieran know he no longer considered him having killed Patrick in self-defense, he'd definitely keep a closer eye on him.

"We're out of energy bars. You'll have to eat chili for breakfast," Dani said. Breaking the awkward silence.

"I'll get it heating." Hawke walked over to the pack, pulled out three cans, and carried them back to Kieran. "Open those and put them in the pan. I'm going to feed Horse."

The man did as he was asked.

Hawke pondered what they knew as he took care of Horse and checked the supplies left in the pack.

"The chili is ready," Dani said as Hawke shoved the tent into a pack. He'd already shoved in his and Kieran's sleeping bags, leaving Dani's out to cover her with.

They ate in silence. Knowing the trailhead was only a little over a day away, they were all anxious to get moving.

Kieran cleaned up the dishes with snow while Hawke settled Dani on the travois and tucked her in.

"I missed this," she said quietly.

"Missed what?" Hawke peered down at her, his hands still resting alongside her body.

"Your kind touch."

He grinned. "I don't plan on leaving you alone with him again." He kissed her cheek and walked by Kieran who was storing the pot and cups.

"Do you want to lead?" Hawke asked him.

"No. That mule doesn't like me. I'm surprised we made it as far as we did." Kieran walked behind the travois.

Hawke grunted. Yeah, the man just wanted easy walking. He could have used a day to let his body recuperate but it wasn't happening until they were tucked in at Dani's place outside of Eagle.

"Come on Horse, let's get home." The mule's long ears stood up and his eyes brightened. He knew the word home.

The morning went smoothly. By the time they stopped at noon, Hawke's muscles had warmed, and the aches were just in localized spots and not all over. It also helped the snow was only two feet deep now, and he'd found Jack and Dot's trail. They were heading in the right direction. Jack had been in these mountains enough times over the thirteen years Hawke had owned him to know which way was home. He felt confident someone would find them and contact both Herb and the Search and Rescue.

"What are we eating for lunch?" Kieran asked after Hawke had helped Dani hobble behind a tree.

Hawke reached into the packsaddle. "It looks like we're down to eating MREs." Hawke handed a packet to Kieran, then opened the one in his hands. "These are only in the bottom of the packsaddle for emergencies. I'm not guaranteeing they will taste good, but they'll put food in our bellies until I cook that rabbit tonight." He pointed to the rabbit dangling from a rawhide string on the packsaddle. He'd cleaned and filled the carcass with snow to keep it cool and ready to eat.

Kieran turned the package over in his hands.

Hawke handed one to Dani. "I'm sure you know what to do with this."

She nodded, dropping the inside packet into the melted snow in the pan over the burner. Hawke dropped his in. Kieran stared at the pot and finally opened his MRE and started to drop the heater portion in the pot.

"Hey! Not that one. See what it says on the side?" Hawke put his hand out to stop the man from dropping the warming container into the pot of water.

Kieran's face reddened. "Heater. What does that mean?"

"If we didn't have this water already warming, you could put water in that package and then put the packet of food in there and it would be warm in five to ten minutes depending on the food," Dani said.

He dropped the heater envelope back in the main container and pulled out the food packet. He dropped that in the now steaming water.

Hawke used a stick to fish out Dani's MRE. He placed it in her gloved hands. She ripped it open and used the dual-duty utensil Hawke had handed her to eat the spaghetti.

He pulled out his packet, dropped it on the ground, and used his knife to cut the package open. He ate, giving the last packet in the pot a few more minutes before he pulled it out and put it on the log beside Kieran.

After finishing his meal, Hawke took the empty container over and filled it with dog kibble, before pouring it all out on the ground for Dog.

As he walked over to put the trash in the packsaddle, Hawke heard a muffled voice. He turned the volume down on the radio and slid it into his coat. Walking deeper into the trees until he was out of sight, he pulled the radio out and listened with it next to his ear.

"Dammit, Arlo, where are you? That woman and mule are gone. I'm following the trail. Over."

Hawke grinned. The two men hadn't met up. But the one was on their tail. He dialed the Search and Rescue frequency. "Hello, this is Hawke. Anyone on the mountain?"

There was some static and a voice he knew came through loud and clear.

"Hawke, where the hell are you? Over." His counterpart in the Fish and Wildlife Division, Trooper Tad Ulman.

"Tad, we're heading down Bear Creek Trail. Dani's with me. She has a broken leg. And we have a suspect in a murder. We could use some assistance ASAP. There is someone after us. Over."

"We're headed up that way with snowmobiles. Your horses were found this morning and we were called out. Over."

"We'll keep heading your way. Over." Hawke's worry lifted. They would soon have medical care for Dani and Kieran would be interviewed and they'd discover exactly who he was.

He shoved the radio in his coat pocket and found the other two ready and waiting for him when he returned. Hawke leaned down to tuck the sleeping bag around

Dani. "Help is on the way. Should see them before dark," he whispered.

She smiled. "Good. I'm tired of riding on this."

He grinned, knowing she'd be put in something similar when the snowmobiles arrived.

Hawke took the feedbag off Horse, stowed it in the pack, and they headed down the trail with Kieran bringing up the rear.

Hawke heard the snowmobiles before he saw them. He glanced back at Kieran. The man stopped. His head whipped around as he peered in all directions. Before he started to run, Hawke called back to him, "It's Search and Rescue."

"How do you know?" the man asked skeptically.

"Because I talked to them." Hawke continued on the trail and within minutes four snowmobiles appeared.

The sound died as the machines were turned off and Tad, Deputy Alden, and two local people Hawke had worked with before walked over to them. One of the locals happened to be a nurse. He hurried over to the travois and started asking Dani questions.

Hawke walked over to Tad. "You need to get Dani down to a doctor. I did the best I could, but she has a compound fracture. And the guy with us needs to be interviewed. You'll need to figure out who he is. Neither he, nor the body we found when we arrived at the lodge, had identification on them."

Tad wrote all of that down in his logbook. "Okay, what about you. You look like you're ready to collapse."

Hawke shook his head. "I'll lead Horse on down to the trailhead. Just have someone there to pick us up." He glanced back up the mountain. "Are there any other

Search and Rescue members up in the mountains looking for us?"

Tad shook his head. "Today was the first day that we were cleared to go looking. If it hadn't been for the horses with the notes coming out at Bear Creek, we would have all gone up Moss Springs where you left your truck and trailer."

"I tied a man up to a tree on the north side of Wilson Basin. He had an assault rifle that I lost when I was caught in a small-scale avalanche. But his partner is following our tracks." Hawke held up the radio. "I got this from the man I tied up. They are after the man that is with us."

"Why?" Tad asked, looking up from the book he'd been writing in.

"I don't know. I don't want to go into all of that now. Dani can fill you or Alden in." He glanced up at the clouds coming in. "You need to load those two up and get going before it gets dark or more snow comes down."

"I don't like leaving you out here alone." Tad shoved his book in his pocket and pulled out his own radio.

"I'm not alone, I have Dog and Horse."

Tad shook his head. "When are you going to give them proper names like Prince and Marvin?" His friend laughed.

Hawke grinned. "I think they like the names they have." He walked over to where they'd transferred Dani onto a sled attached to one of the snowmobiles.

She put out a hand. "You aren't coming with us, are you?"

He grasped her hand and shook his head. "I have to lead Horse down. By himself, he won't walk out like

Jack did with Dot. They'll get you to the hospital and get that leg looked at. I'll call you as soon as I get reception."

She whispered, "What about Kieran?"

"I want you to tell Tad and Deputy Alden everything we know. The body, how Kieran ran, I brought him back, everything from when you two were alone." He leaned down and kissed her cheek. "Don't worry about me. I'll be right behind, just slower." He released her hand and motioned for the snowmobiles to get going.

The machines moved out slower than when they'd approached. They had a medical emergency in the sled.

Hawke glanced down at Dog. "Well, boy, it's just you and me and Horse. Let's see if we can get to the bottom of this mountain by daybreak."

# Chapter Fifteen

As the snow grew less and less, Horse's pace increased. Hawke finally gave up leading and crawled up on top of the mule. The lulling motion rocked him to sleep. He was glad the packs wouldn't allow him to fall off.

Barking woke Hawke. He raised up to see what Dog was barking about and realized the mule had stopped.

"Sleeping Beauty, why don't you slide on down and I'll get you home."

Hawke scrubbed his eyes and stared in the direction of the voice.

Herb Trembley, his landlord, had a hold of Horse's lead rope.

Dog was barking and running around them.

"I'm glad to see you. How did you know when I'd get here?" Hawke dropped down off the animal and just about fell when he couldn't feel the ground, only his buzzing legs. His feet and lower legs were asleep.

"I took Jack and Dot home. Darlene is spoiling them. Trooper Ulman called and said they had Dani and a man, and you'd be down with the mule and Dog eventually." Herb helped him over to the passenger side of his pickup. "I waited for Darlene to put together sandwiches, cookies, and coffee, and then I came back up here and slept in the truck waiting for you."

Hawke hugged Herb. "Thank you. This has been one hellacious week."

"We called Spruel when you didn't show up on Thursday, but they said another storm was headed to the mountains and they couldn't send anyone up until yesterday. Then I got the call from Ed Green. He'd found your horses and the notes. I hightailed it out here to find Search and Rescue getting ready to go out. That was smart of you to send the horses down with notes."

"I didn't have a choice. The snow up there was so deep it made trying to get anywhere with them take twice as long, and Dani was hurt and alone with someone I suspected of murder."

Herb lowered him onto the seat. "Eat a sandwich while I load up Horse, then I want to know what all happened."

Hawke nodded.

Dog jumped up on Hawke and over into the back seat, then leaned over his shoulder drooling.

"Yes, you get something good to eat, too." Hawke found a sandwich in a container, broke off part of it, gave it to Dog, and then took a large bite. Ham and Swiss. His favorite. Leave it to Darlene to send his favorite sandwich. And he bet her oatmeal cookies with apricots pieces would be the cookies she'd sent along.

Herb slid in behind the steering wheel. He started the vehicle, grabbed a sandwich, and said, "What's this about Dani hurt and a murderer?"

Hawke spent the drive home telling Herb about how Dani was hurt and finding a body. As they pulled up to the barn where his apartment sat over the indoor arena, Darlene walked out. It was now 8 a.m. and life on the farm was beginning a new day.

"You look terrible!" she exclaimed when Hawke stepped out of the vehicle.

"Thank you for the food. I needed it." He walked over and gave the woman a hug.

"I've got Horse. Go take a shower and get some sleep," Herb said.

Hawke shook his head. "I'll get a shower, but I promised Dani I'd check in on her as soon as I was down here."

"Nonsense. I'll go check on her. She would be the first to say you should rest. She'll just be relieved you are in your own bed." Darlene grabbed his arm, leading him to the stairs up to his apartment. "Go on. Sleep. I'll go see her and let her know you are tucked in your bed."

He started to object but the stubborn set to the woman's jaw and her narrowed eyes revealed it would be best to do as she said. "Tell her I'll see her this evening."

Darlene smiled. "I'm sure she'll like that."

Hawke sighed, caught his landlord grinning at him, and walked up the stairs to shower and sleep. Dog trotted up the stairs ahead of him. His roommate wanted his own bed as well.

When Hawke woke at 5 p.m., he was greeted by

Darlene as he walked down his stairs.

"Dani is fine. They kept her in the hospital overnight even though she called Sage to come get her." Darlene stared at him. "She has an awful lot of your traits. Are you sure you two are a good match?"

He laughed, and said, "That's why we get along so well. I'll grab some food and go visit her." His phone buzzed. A glance showed Sheriff Lindsey's name.

"Thank you for checking on Dani and letting her know I made it off the mountain." He walked over to his personal pickup. The space where his work pickup and horse trailer usually sat looked empty. He'd have to get someone to take him to the Moss Springs Trailhead and retrieve them.

Once he was headed toward Alder, the only town in the county with a hospital, he dialed the sheriff.

"Lindsey," the man answered.

"It's Hawke. What did you need?"

"We need your statement, and we have a name for your suspect, who by the way, is denying everything you told Ulman, and Dani Singer told Alden."

Hawke narrowed his eyes as anger sizzled in his veins. The man had used them to get off the mountain and now was denying everything. "What's his name and is he connected to any money laundering organizations?"

"He's Kieran Gilmore. He owns a pawn shop in Boise. The police there have been keeping an eye on him. They say they saw him leave with a Patrick Barclay the day the first storm hit. They were both carrying suitcases and boarded a private airplane. One that they discovered was owned by a corporation. They are still working out who actually owns the corporation."

Hawke entered Alder. "Are you at the office?"

"No. Just got home. Why don't you come by in the morning? I'll catch you up on everything and get your statement."

"I'll do that. Thanks." Hawke drove through the Shake Shack, ordering two burgers, two fries, and two chocolate shakes. Once he had his order, he headed to the hospital.

He'd woke, wondering if the man he'd tied to the tree was still alive. He hoped someone had flown up there in a helicopter and retrieved him. Or even his buddy found him and let him loose.

At the hospital, he inquired which room was Dani Singer's. The nurse directed him, and he found Dani sitting up, playing a game of solitaire.

She glanced up. Her gaze traveled over his face. "It's good to see you looking rested."

He walked over and kissed her. "It's good to see you being taken care of." He held up the bag. "I brought dinner."

"The MREs we had were better than what they fed me at lunch." She shoved the cards into a pile.

Hawke placed the burgers, fries, and shakes on the table and sat on the side of the bed, facing her across the long narrow table.

"What did they say about your leg?" he asked.

She patted her thigh. "That whoever put the bone back together did a wonderful job."

"I was lucky."

She shook her head. "I was impressed with how you stayed calm and did what had to be done. Even if it meant pain for me."

He took her hand and peered into her eyes. "I may have looked calm on the outside, but inside, I hated hurting you but knew you would never want to see me if the injury made it so you couldn't fly again."

"You thought that?" She squeezed his hand.

"I did. I know how much flying means to you. It would be like taking away my horses and telling me I couldn't go on a mountain again." Hawke held onto her. The connection was only their hands, but he could feel the warmth and empathy emulating from her hand and her eyes.

"Well, according to the doctor, I'll be able to fly in four to six months, depending on how quickly I heal." She frowned. "It has to be four. Any longer and we'll lose out on a month of registrations."

"I can get something from my mom that will help your body heal faster." Hawke released her hand and picked up his hamburger. It was cold, but it was better than anything he'd eaten in over a week.

The nurse came in to check on Dani. "Visiting hours will be over in an hour."

Hawke nodded.

When the woman left, Dani asked, "Did they figure out who Kieran is yet? And what about the two men on the mountain?"

Hawke filled her in with what little he knew from the sheriff. "I'll meet up with him in the morning." He picked up the bag and papers from their dinner and deposited them in the trash. "I could come by and break you out of here after I meet with him."

"When do you have to be back to work?" Dani asked, patting the bed beside her.

He sat back down, and they clasped hands. He was glad he hadn't lost her, and he had a feeling she was happy he had made it off the mountain alive as well. "I'm going to see if I can get another week off, since I didn't really get a vacation, having found a body and transporting the suspect off the mountain."

She grinned. "I could use a nurse for a week."

# Chapter Sixteen

Hawke called Spruel when he was on his way to Alder the next morning.

"You want to take another week off? You've already been gone a week and a half. But I understand it was one hell of a week. The weather has kept the hunters and fishermen at home," Spruel said.

"Has anyone gone up to retrieve the body? I put it in Dani's hidden room in the barn." Hawke didn't want the party getting up there and not be able to find the body.

"They're talking about sending in a helicopter day after tomorrow. The weather is supposed to stabilize."

"What about the man I tied to a tree? Anyone going after him?" Hawke felt bad that the man could die from exposure.

"Tad is doing a flyover this morning to see if he can locate the man and retrieve him." Spruel cleared his throat. "Why exactly did you tie the man to a tree?"

Hawke told the story of the two men coming after them.

"You left a woman you care about with someone you suspected of murder?" The disbelief in his voice made Hawke cringe.

"She had a gun, and he didn't."

"But she had a broken leg," Spruel said.

"She can handle herself." Hawke didn't like Spruel making him think he'd acted wrong when the two men were after them. "I'm in Alder, I need to give my statement to the county."

Before he exited his pickup, Hawke called Deputy Alden.

"Good to hear you made it off the mountain," Alden said.

"Yeah. And thanks for getting Dani to the hospital and looked at." Hawke had a question, but he didn't want to butt in since he'd just asked for a week off. "I heard someone is going in a couple of days to retrieve the body."

"Yeah. I'm going with the team."

"Any chance you'd have room for me? I put the body in a hidden room in the barn. Dani'd have my hide if you go in there and tear up her barn looking for the body." Hawke wasn't going to say anything about staying on the mountain to look for the plane and two suitcases.

"If you can get it okayed by the sheriff and your sergeant, I don't mind you tagging along."

"Thanks." Hawke ended the call and entered the Sheriff's Office to give his statement.

Sheriff Lindsey met him in the lobby and ushered him back to his office. "Gilmore is saying you said he killed the other man in self-defense, and he should be released."

Hawke studied the sheriff. "I told him the scenario I figured out from the evidence I'd found appeared to be self-defense to get him to tell me what had happened. But I never felt like he was telling me the truth about anything."

Lindsey nodded. "He's not good at lying. He's changed his story twice now. We let him make a call this morning. Ralph said it didn't sound like he called a lawyer. There was talk about suitcases and Arlo and Jerome."

"Arlo was the name of the man I tied to the tree," Hawke volunteered. "Jerome must have been the other man."

"Did he tell you his name?" The sheriff was writing down everything Hawke said.

"No. I took the radio he had with him, and someone called twice trying to get him to reply. That person mentioned he'd let the woman go and later said he was going back for the woman and mule." Hawke went on to tell Lindsey about spotting the helicopter, it putting down, and the men who were trailing them.

"What is odd, is that the men split up. I'm guessing they thought they were after two people, yet the one left Dani, and headed out after me and the other man. There is no way they found the body and if the other man, Patrick, radioed them, they should have been looking for both men." Hawke shook his head. "It just doesn't make sense."

"Are you sure Gilmore hadn't contacted them? Maybe told them he'd killed Patrick and to pick him up?" Lindsey watched Hawke.

Paty Jager

Shaking his head, Hawke said, "I don't know. He seemed genuinely scared when I caught up to him. And he was the one who brought up there would be men coming for him and he wanted off the mountain before they arrived." Hawke scrubbed a hand over his face. "I think he knew there was money in the suitcases he and the other man carried onto the plane. They wouldn't have left them on the plane. I bet they are hidden somewhere in or around the lodge." Now was his chance to ask. "I'd like to ride up to the lodge with the retrieval team and take a look around."

"If they have room, I don't have a problem with that. But you better clear it with Spruel. I'm sure he wants you back to work." Sheriff Lindsey didn't look up from where he was writing on a notepad.

"He gave me another week off." Hawke stood. "I believe you have everything."

"Want to interview Gilmore?"

Hawke thought about that. Did he want to talk to the man? "No. Not until I can have a look around and see if I can find the suitcases. Though you might tell him the Boise Police were on to him and see if he tries to wiggle out of that."

Lindsey smiled. "I like that idea."

Hawke left the Sheriff's Office and headed to the hospital. It was after ten and he had a feeling Dani would be waiting at the front door of the building for him.

He pulled up to the entrance and grinned. Dani sat inside the glass doors in a wheelchair with aluminum crutches across her lap.

When he entered the hospital, the nurse standing behind the wheelchair sent him a strained smile. "We've been waiting here for nearly an hour."

"Sorry, she can be a bit pushy," Hawke said, stepping back to avoid getting hit by a crutch. "Did she sign everything and collect everything she needs?"

"Yes. I have it all. Let's get out of here. I want to go home." Dani started to push up out of the chair.

"You have to ride in the chair to the car," the nurse said, putting a hand on Dani's shoulder, forcing her back down into the wheelchair.

Hawke took the bag sitting on Dani's lap and the crutches and led the way out to his pickup. He lifted Dani into the passenger seat and thanked the nurse.

"You're going to be a bad patient, I can tell," Hawke said, reaching over her to fasten her seatbelt.

"I just don't like all that antiseptic smell. Reminds me of my visits to a pilot who lost his legs in a crash." She shuddered.

"You'll be home in no time. I just have to stop by the Trembleys' and pick up Dog." Hawke closed her door, walked around to the other side, and slid in under the steering wheel.

When they were pulling out of the parking lot, Dani asked, "Did you learn any more about Kieran?"

"Not really. I think the answers may still be up at the lodge." He glanced sideways at her.

"You're planning to go back up there, aren't you?" Her voice was reproachful but also resigned.

"They're going up tomorrow to retrieve the body. I'll catch a ride up with them and look around." He told her about the Boise Police seeing the two men carrying suitcases onto the plane.

"That could have just been clothing." Dani shifted.

"If it was clothes, don't you think they would have layered up on clothing after the plane crashed?" Hawke believed they were suitcases with either counterfeit or real money hidden somewhere around the lodge.

"He didn't seem to have common sense. It was stupid of him to take off like he did without proper clothing. He could have rummaged around and found Tuck's clothes or even some of mine to add layers." Dani didn't tolerate needy people. "And he didn't take any food. Did he want to starve to death on the mountain?"

Hawke turned into Trembleys' lane and stopped the vehicle. He stared at Dani. "He hadn't planned to go anywhere until we showed up. I bet he only took off to hang out away from the lodge and wait until we left. Only he walked so far, he became cold and disoriented."

Dog was running toward them. Hawke opened the door, and the animal leaped into his lap, licked the hand Dani held out, and sat in the middle between them.

"That saves you having to visit with Darlene and Herb." Hawke turned the pickup around.

"I like Darlene. She knows everything about you." A smile tipped the corners of Dani's mouth.

"I've told you everything about me. What could she possibly know?" Hawke didn't like the idea Dani thought Darlene knew everything about him. She didn't. He'd told Dani nearly everything that he felt was necessary for the woman to know.

"That your favorite sandwich is ham and swiss, you love her oatmeal cookies, and you like shepherd's pie." Dani pet Dog. "I've made oatmeal cookies and sandwiches before, but she'll have to show me how to make the pie."

Hawke glanced around Dog as they slowed through Winslow. "You don't have to become a chef to make me happy."

"That's good because I've never liked cooking. But I don't mind whipping up something now and then."

They visited about how she was going to manage while he was gone. He parked in front of her apartment, located over a garage, which was going to be inconvenient with her crutches.

Hawke stared at the apartment. "You have to promise me that you won't try going down those stairs unless someone is with you." He glanced over at the stubborn woman.

Dani sighed. "I won't attempt them alone for a month. I want to heal and be able to fly by May."

He hurried out of the pickup and around to her door. "Do you want me to carry you up?"

She laughed and said, "No. We're both too old for that kind of foolishness. It will just take me a bit." She placed the ends of the crutches on the ground, slid down, with her armpits on the crutches, and swung toward the stairs.

Hawke gathered her stuff and closed the door. Dog raced around Dani and up the stairs, waiting at the top. Hawke stayed two steps below her to give her room to work the crutches.

They didn't have to worry about her landlords coming out and wondering what was happening. They had gone to Arizona for the winter.

Ten minutes passed and Dani arrived at the top of the stairs. Her face was red from the exertion. Hawke could see her arms and leg trembling. She was exhausted.

He took the key out of her hand, unlocked the door, and swept her up in his arms, carrying her to the couch and placing her on the cushions. "I'll get water and pain pills."

Kicking the door closed, he placed the bag he carried on the table and dug through it to find the pills he'd heard rattling around. He noted they were just extra strength ibuprofen. That was good. Dani would have refused anything stronger.

He filled a cup with water and handed both to the woman he'd risk his life for.

Dani took the cup and the water and swallowed. She closed her eyes. "I need to rest." Her eyes fluttered open. "I'm going to be boring company."

"Can I get on your computer?" He had an idea of what he could do while she rested.

"Sure." She rattled off the password, and he kissed her forehead and pulled a throw over her.

When her breathing was even and he knew she'd fallen asleep, he walked into the combo kitchen and dining room and opened her computer. First, he looked up all he could find about Kieran and his pawnshop, then he went to the Wallowa Valley Realty website and started browsing the properties for sale. He'd talked it over with Dani last month and she'd agreed to them purchasing land and living together when she wasn't up on the mountain.

He tagged three places that met their criteria and sat back, wondering what they were going to do for dinner.

# Chapter Seventeen

Hawke sat shoulder to shoulder with Deputy Alden and Dr. Gwendolyn Vance, a local doctor who was the county medical examiner, in the back of the helicopter being flown by Newell Norton out of La Grande.

"I heard you were the one who found the body," Dr. Vance said as they started their descent to land in front of the barn at Charlie's Lodge.

"Yes. I moved him into an area where no one else coming along would find him." Hawke smiled at the woman. "That's why I came along. To keep Deputy Alden from tearing up the barn looking for the body."

"If that was all you were doing, you wouldn't have brought along a pack with snowshoes hanging off of it," the deputy said, pointing to the pack sitting in the front passenger seat. "And we wouldn't have been crammed in here together."

"You'll just have the body in here with you on the

way back and that seat will be open for Dr. Vance." Hawke winked at the woman, and she smiled. He'd liked the doctor since the first time she'd shown up at a crime scene. She was all business but also knew how to make people at ease.

"Does the sheriff and your boss know you plan on hanging around up here?" Deputy Alden asked.

"They will when you get back."

"What if something happens? You said the radio up here is broken." The deputy sounded as if he cared that Hawke was putting his life at risk.

"I have a radio and parts for the broken one. I won't have anything else to do at night. I'll mess with the radio and see if I can get it working." Hawke was relieved when the rotors stopped moving and they could exit the helicopter. He'd never been one for being smashed up against other people.

The deputy hopped out, commenting on the depth of the snow.

Hawke grabbed his pack and dropped out. His legs sunk in the drift to mid-thigh. There had been more snow since he'd left.

"Why does Dani have that funny flag and bear on the porch roof?" Deputy Alden asked.

"I put it there when I thought there might have been a helicopter flying over." He turned to their pilot who helped the Fish and Wildlife biologists fly in and out of the wilderness. "If you had flown in with Search and Rescue, would you have realized that was a sign from me?"

Newell stared at the flag and bear. "I would have definitely known it was new or unusual. That's a Native American flag. Was that supposed to tell me you left a message?"

"Yeah."

"And since I heard you came out Bear Creek, the bear and the way it is pointing was significant."

"Yes. I wanted whoever saw this to know I was headed to Bear Creek." Hawke smiled.

"I would have had to have talked it over with several people, but we probably would have come up with that scenario." Newell grimaced. "Can we get out of this snow? It's cold on the family jewels."

Newell was about five-five and the drift was up to his crotch.

"Dr. Vance, stay put until we dig a path." Hawke put his hand up to keep the woman in the helicopter. She was dressed for cold weather, but he didn't think she needed to swim through the snow to the barn to see a man who had been dead for nearly two weeks and had been moved.

The other two men followed the trail Hawke broke to the barn. They found shovels and started clearing a path two feet wide from the barn to the helicopter. It was about thirty feet. They were sweaty and thirsty by the time they arrived at the helicopter.

Dr. Vance handed them each a bottle of water, climbed out of the aircraft, and walked to the barn. Alden grabbed the body bag and the men followed with the shovels over their shoulders.

Once in the barn, Hawke grabbed the flashlight hanging inside the entrance and handed it to Alden. "Hold that while I open the door."

The barn was dark since the only door they could open was the man door, which opened inward. The large double doors that took up most of the front of the building would need snow cleared away to be opened and allow the sunlight in.

Hawke strode over to the hidden access to Dani's parts room. It had halters and lead ropes hanging on bent horseshoes nailed on the wall. He twisted the horseshoe farthest on the left and tugged. The door opened.

"That's interesting," Norton said. "Why does a barn need a hidden room?"

"Charlie made it that way so he could keep items he didn't want someone walking off with out of sight." Hawke stepped into the room, barely large enough for the four of them and the body. "As you can see, Dani keeps all her aircraft parts in here. Valuable things she doesn't want to have disappear when they aren't up here in the winter, and so no one who is here in the summer knows about them." He peered at Norton. "You didn't see this."

The man nodded. Hawke knew Deputy Alden and Dr. Vance would never say anything. But he'd only met Norton a time or two and wasn't sure if he knew when to keep quiet.

"You said you moved the body?" Dr. Vance asked.

"Yeah." Hawke pulled out his phone and scrolled to the photos he took before moving it.

The doctor grasped his phone and studied the photos. She nodded her head and knelt beside the now frozen body. Hawke was glad he wouldn't be riding back in the helicopter with them. Once the body started to warm up, he imagined it would begin to build up gases and smell bad.

Once Dr. Vance had examined the victim and made notes, they carefully picked up the frozen corpse and placed it in the long black bag.

Alden zipped it closed. "What do you think caused his death?" The deputy straightened and studied the doctor.

"Like Hawke said, the blow to the head from what I can tell here. You'll know more when it goes to autopsy." Dr. Vance walked to the door of the small room.

Hawke, Alden, and Norton picked up the bag and followed the woman out to the helicopter. Once everyone was settled in for the ride back to the county, Hawke walked back to the barn. He turned and watched them take off, then strode into the barn, closed the door to the secret room, and picked up his pack.

It was going to be lonely up here without Dog or Dani. He only planned to take a day or two to poke around looking for the suitcases. Then he'd head down the Moss Springs Trail and drive his work vehicle and horse trailer home.

He hung the flashlight back by the door, put his snowshoes on, and exited the barn, taking his pack and a shovel with him. At the lodge, he opened the door and dropped his pack inside. Then he went around to the back and dug a path from the back door to the outhouse. When that was finished, he went in, leaning his snowshoes against the back wall.

It was late afternoon when he melted snow and ate one of the sandwiches he'd brought with him. There was only another hour of daylight. He'd start the fire in the fireplace and see if he could make any sense of the pieces that had once been a radio. Tomorrow at first light, he'd start looking for places the suitcases could have been stashed. If he couldn't find them around the lodge, he'd see if he could pinpoint where the plane might have gone down.

Hawke had searched all through the barn, lodge, shower house, and cabins. He was headed to the bunkhouse as the sun peaked over the mountain to the east. It would make sense they might have left the suitcases in the building they'd slept in. But it would depend on if the money was hidden before the man Patrick was killed or after. If after, Kieran could have hidden them anywhere. Even out in the trees.

Hawke stomped the snow off his snowshoes and left the webbed footwear at the door as he entered the bunkhouse and began a thorough search. When he came up empty, Hawke sat on a chair and forced himself to remember when he and Kieran were in here rummaging about for warm clothing for the man to wear. Had he seemed overly anxious when Hawke had gone near any spot in the building?

The door to the cupboard on the floor under the small counter had been partially open. Hawke stood and walked over to the cabinet. He swung the door open. The items on the shelf were scattered as if the board had been moved or struck. He placed his hands underneath the shelf and it moved. He lifted it out and pulled a flashlight from his pocket. He shined the light into the cupboard and stuck his head in. That's when he smelled fresh sawn wood and noticed sawdust.

How long had it taken the two men to find this cupboard that the shelf could be removed to make a hiding spot underneath? Which had him circling back to the fact, how did the person who smashed the radio know it was there? Had Patrick been to the lodge before and scoped it out? How else would they have known it was even on the mountain after the plane crashed? Dani hadn't seen the body. He would get a photo from the man's driver's license and have Dani, Tuck, and Sage all see if they remembered him as a guest.

Hawke raised the boards. A whoosh of cold air blasted his face. The bunkhouse was set up on two-foot stilts to keep the spring melt from filling the building with water. He shined his light down in the hole and spotted a suitcase. He pulled it out and fished around with his hand and arm and caught hold of the handle on another one.

When the two suitcases sat side by side, he pulled out his phone and took photos of the cupboard, boards, and suitcases. He replaced the boards and stood. Picking up a suitcase, he placed it on the table and opened it. The luggage was filled with money in tens, twenties, fifties, and hundreds.

Hawke picked up a bill and looked at it. He couldn't tell if it was real or counterfeit. He put one of each denomination into an evidence envelope and closed the suitcase. Then he picked up the other suitcase and did the same with the contents in it. Once he'd slid the evidence envelope into the inside pocket of his coat, he grasped the suitcases and carried them to the door.

Once the luggage was securely stored in Dani's hidden room, Hawke went in the lodge and gathered up his belongings. He made sure the fireplace was banked and would go out soon and that all the doors were securely closed.

Buckling on his snowshoes, he sensed something was off. It was quiet except for the occasional thump of snow falling off tree limbs. Earlier there had been birds singing, the far-off sound of an elk bugling, and the yip of a coyote in pursuit of prey. At this moment, it was dead silent.

Something was out there.

Something that didn't belong.

Hawke quickly pulled on his pack, held his shotgun in front of him, and hurried around to the back of the lodge. It was easier to get lost in the trees leaving from this direction. Though if they were halfway observant trackers, they would see his prints in the snow.

# Chapter Eighteen

Hawke kept a steady pace through the trees up the ridge. He was off course to follow the trail to Moss Springs. The plan was to get up Jim White Ridge and follow along the top, staying in the tree line, and then down the other side, still keeping hidden in the pines the best he could. He'd stay off the trail until he was close to the trailhead where his vehicle was parked. After two hours of uphill hiking, he stopped to get a drink and see if he could get a radio signal. The birds were singing and the sounds in the forest before he broke out near the top of the ridge had been normal. There hadn't been the hush of danger.

He opened a bottle of water, drank, and pulled a high-power radio out of a side pocket on his pack. The closest frequency it might get would be the county dispatch. He dialed that in, listened to the crackling, and pushed down on the button.

"Dispatch this is Hawke, can you hear me? Over." He waited. Repeated and listened. Nothing but crackle.

He dialed in the frequency the State Police used. "Hello, anyone. This is Hawke, can you hear me? Over."

"Hawke? Where the heck are you. I can barely hear you. Over."

He thought it was Trooper Shoberg. "Is that you Shoberg? Over."

"Yeah. Where are you? Over."

"I'm headed to Moss Spring bu—" The crack of a gun and the sting of a bullet ripping through his arm ended the conversation.

He dropped the radio into a coat pocket and took off as quick as he could toward a mound of snow that had to be a tangle of huckleberry bushes.

Two more shots echoed across the canyons on both sides.

Hawke dove behind the snow mound. He shoved two MREs into his smaller hiking pack that was inside the larger pack. He hated leaving so much survival equipment behind, but he needed to travel lighter to stay ahead of the people after him. Dumping all the shotgun shells into the smaller pack, he thrust his arms through the shoulder straps, grabbed the shotgun, and took off as fast as he could jog in snowshoes headed down the other side of the ridge. He had to make it to the trail. It was the only way he'd get help. Shoberg knew where he was headed and had to have heard the rifle shot during their exchange.

Snowshoes were the fastest way to travel in the deep snow and made less of a trail to follow than if he'd been trying to wallow through the three feet of snow without the shoes, but they still left tracks.

Stopping to catch his breath, Hawke checked the bullet wound. It left a hole for cold air to seep into his coat sleeve but had barely grazed his arm. The blood was already freeze-drying. He used his knife to cut off a long thin fir branch with full smaller branches. Using a piece of the climbing rope in his pack, he tied it to the back of his pack to drag the branch along the ground behind him and hopefully make the people following him have a harder time.

He didn't jog, but he kept a fast pace down the hill. Hawke avoided brushing against trees and bushes to not leave any broken twigs or branches to be used to follow him. An area ahead looked like a good place to make his prints disappear. The wind had swept the snow off the top of a rocky mound. As he approached, Hawke noticed the bushes in front of the small hill looked darker behind. There was a small cave. There wasn't any sign of an animal having gone in or out.

Continuing up over the mound, making his prints disappear, he followed the basalt formation until he came to more trees and walked into those. He stopped long enough to remember the location of the cave in case he found himself having to circle back.

Another hour and it was going to be dark. He planned to keep on going through the night. Moss Springs was only three to four miles as the bird flew but a bit longer going up and down the ridges in between him and the trailhead. Dropping down into the canyon below would be faster and easier traveling, but that would leave him more visible and an easier target for the people following him. By morning he hoped to either be at the trailhead or have run into someone from law enforcement coming up the trail to look for him.

Darkness fell. An owl called out a soft question of "Who-who-whoo?"

"I wish I knew who was following me," Hawke said softly. As quickly as the gunmen had come upon him, they must have seen him carry the suitcases into the barn. When they couldn't find the money, came after him. They had to have been watching the lodge since Search and Rescue had picked him, Dani, and Kieran up. "Had they expected Kieran or Patrick to come back for the money?" It hadn't looked like anyone had been searching for the suitcases.

He kept on walking but stopped talking to himself. The sound his snowshoes made on the snow was loud to his ears and he didn't want anyone to hear his voice.

On crisp cold nights like this, without wind to carry sounds in all directions, he could be pinpointed fast. It was how the horned owl hunted. By sight and sound.

He pushed on until the moon was directly overhead. The moonlight on the white world lit everything up, except the darkness hidden under the trees. It would be easy to keep on traveling through the night. As tenacious as the people after, or with Kieran, had been so far, he didn't for one minute think they would stop for the night either.

Opening an energy bar, he ate as he walked. Another hour and he would be working his way up the last ridge between him and his vehicle. Hawke had veered to the right of the small valley where the actual trail meandered through. The thought of walking through the open area hadn't appealed to him. He preferred scaling the ridges to being a sitting duck.

His toes had become numb an hour ago. He knew he chanced frostbite by continuing and not warming himself, but all he had was the emergency blanket and the pair of toe warmers that had run out of heat. His thirty below sleeping bag and two more sets of toe warmers were in his pack leaning against a tree miles behind him.

He kept his fingers warm by pulling them out of the fingers of his gloves and balling them in his palm, while the other hand held the shotgun.

Hawke's body pushed on, but his mind started wandering as the cold began to seep up his legs.

Something moved in the trees.

He whipped his head to the left, holding the shotgun against his chest because he'd balled both hands up in his gloves and he couldn't hold the weapon as he should.

Peering into the darkness, his heart didn't pump adrenaline. His movements were slow, clumsy.

"Who-who-whoo?" The soft call of the owl sounded like a voice questioning his presence.

It wasn't until he sunk in the snow that he realized he'd gone down on his knees. He shoved to the side, rolling deeper into the white cold cushion. The frozen crusty top remained glistening over him as he peered up at the faint glimmer of moonlight shining through the pine trees.

This wouldn't be a bad place to end his life. He was surrounded by the mountains, the spirit of his ancestors, and, as if he knew Hawke's thoughts, the owl asked again, "Who-who-whoo?"

He wasn't alone. The owl would keep him company until his body shut down. He thought of Dani and her strength to endure getting off the mountain with a broken leg. She was tougher. Hell, he'd learned at a young age watching all his mom endured, that women were tougher than men. That's why they statistically lived longer.

His eyes started to close….

A bark echoed through the trees.

"Dog? Are you here?" he whispered.

Another sharp bark and he realized it wasn't Dog. A wolf?

The sound came again, closer.

Hawke opened his eyes and peered into the yellow eyes of a large owl leaning down in the hole examining him. The bird barked again.

Warning! That was the sound owls made when they were warning of danger. But what danger? That he was willing to lay here in the snow and die? Or were the men gaining on him?

If he were already dead the men wouldn't get the chance to beat him to discover where their money was hidden. He started to giggle thinking about that and the owl barked again.

"What am I to do?" he asked the bird, staring into its big golden eyes. His feathered guardian didn't move, just continued to gaze down at him.

Hawke thought he saw a warrior in the shiny orbs. He wasn't ready to stop protecting his ancestor's land. He pushed to his knees and worked his way up to his unfeeling feet.

The owl hopped back three times and sprang up in the air, soundless as the large wings spread and carried it up four feet off the ground. It circled and came back as if it wanted Hawke to follow.

Keeping his gaze on the bird, he followed, thinking about what all he had to live for. A small farm with Dani, Dog, and the horses. Perhaps an earlier retirement than he'd once thought. Or at least a less grueling schedule than he'd kept the last twenty years.

The bird circled above what looked like a cave made of large rocks tumbled together. Hawke walked up to the entrance and dropped to his hands and knees. Shining the flashlight inside, he checked for signs of wildlife. It appeared to have been a spot where a wolf or cougar had eaten a deer. The bones were scattered around inside.

He entered the tight space, shoved the bones to the side, and wrapped his legs and feet in the emergency blanket. Then he pulled out an MRE and used the heating packet to not only heat up his food but to warm his hands.

He'd replenish his body and try to warm up before tackling the descent of the last ridge, cross Little Minam River, and then he'd have only a couple hundred feet to the trailhead.

The food warmed his insides and made him realize he'd been close to giving in to hypothermia before that owl arrived and made him want to go on. To do better by his mom, Dani, and their people. He couldn't do that if he were dead. Giving into the cold would have been a cowardly way to die. He may not have had the chance to participate in ceremonies, wear the paint, or learn the ways of a warrior, but he was going to act like one.

He pulled his boots off and began rubbing his feet, getting the blood to circulate. It hurt like a son-of-a-bitch, but he needed to have his feet to get him to the trailhead and get to the bottom of the homicide and the suitcases of money.

# Chapter Nineteen

The sound of gunfire woke Hawke. He sat up and hit his head on the rock ceiling. "Ouch!" he hissed and rubbed a hand over the top of his head.

There it was again. It sounded as if a gunfight was happening not that far from him. He quickly folded the blanket, shoved his belongings into his pack, and crawled out of the rock den. His legs were stiff, and his feet still hurt, but he could feel them. That was more than the night before.

He stood, registered where the sound was coming from, and strapped on his snowshoes, heading in the direction of the gunfire.

Forty yards south, a man crouched behind a rock. He had an AR rifle pointed down toward the trail.

That's when Hawke realized the owl had led him close to the trail. He hadn't been on top of the ridge as he'd thought.

Had there only been one person following him? He pulled out his pair of small binoculars and scanned the area beyond the first man he'd spotted. There was another man. The one he'd tied to a tree. It appeared his friend had gotten to him before Trooper Ulman had.

Scanning the area down the trail, he spotted Shoberg, a deputy, and two other people. They were hiding behind snowmobiles.

Hawke made his way toward his rescue party.

"We're the police. If you don't drop your guns we will return your fire," Shoberg shouted.

The man closest to Hawke tossed his weapon out and raised his hands. "I'm not shooting a cop," he said, loud enough for the other man to hear.

Glancing around, Hawke spotted the man he'd tied to a tree. He also tossed his weapon out in front of where he hid.

"There are only two," Hawke called out.

"Is that you, Hawke?" Shoberg replied.

"Yeah. Thanks for coming."

Hawke waited for Deputy Novak to traipse across the snow and put cuffs on the man. Once the man was restrained, the deputy smiled at Hawke. "I'm glad to see you. It took Steve all day yesterday to get clearance for us to come look for you. Even when he said he'd heard a shot and lost you on the radio."

"I'm glad you came. My feet have frostbite, and I could use a ride back to my vehicle." Hawke followed the deputy and suspect back to the snowmobiles.

Shoberg had the other man handcuffed. "Good to see you. After hearing the shot yesterday, I thought we'd be bringing your body back out of here."

Hawke pointed to the hole in his sleeve. "It just

missed me." He studied the two men.

The one he'd tied to a tree glared at him. "I should have shot you when you came back to the lodge."

Hawke grinned at him and pulled his badge out from under his shirt and coat. "You're lucky your bullet barely grazed me. Was the money Patrick and Kieran hid stolen from your boss?" He studied the man.

The man's jaw might well have had a lock on it. He clenched his teeth and didn't say a word.

"Max, take Hawke on your machine and get him down to Moss Springs." Shoberg studied Hawke. "And drive him home. I'll get someone to pick you up at Trembleys."

Hawke was relieved he wouldn't have to drive. He wasn't sure if once he warmed up, he'd be able to stay awake.

The ride to the trailhead took only thirty minutes. Once Max had Hawke tucked into the OSP vehicle, he put his snowmobile on the trailer and came back over to drive Hawke home. The drive took over an hour but felt like five minutes.

"Hawke, wake up." Herb Trembley's voice roused Hawke from a dream about an owl.

"I've got him from here. My wife can take you wherever you need to go."

Opening his eyes, Hawke saw the barn and arena. Dog was whining. A wet nose touched his hand. He glanced down at Dog, wiggling and licking his hand. "Hey boy. I could have used your help and company."

"You think you can get up the stairs to your place?" Herb asked.

"If you help me. I can barely feel my feet." He gingerly slid out of the passenger side and looked around. "Where'd Max go? I wanted to thank him."

"Darlene already drove off with him. Come on."

As they walked into the barn, nickering and the bray of Horse met him.

"In case you can't tell, your trio missed you."

"I've only been gone for three days," Hawke said as they passed the three geldings.

Dog ran up the stairs ahead of them. Hawke grabbed the handrail and winced as he pushed off each step to move up to the next.

"Maybe you should have a doctor look at your feet," Herb said as Hawke opened the door to his one-room apartment.

"I'll warm them up and take care of them." He sat on the one chair in the room. "Have you talked to Dani? How is she doing?"

"Darlene has gone over every day to check on her. Sage has been spending the nights with her."

Hawke laughed. "I bet that is all going over well with Dani. She likes her privacy like I do."

Herb grinned. "That's what Darlene said. I'll get some warm water in a bucket to soak those feet."

"I'll just take a hot shower and then put a heating pad on them. Thank you." Hawke pushed back up onto his stinging feet and headed to the small bathroom. "I'll call Dani when I get out of the shower."

"Sure you don't want me to stick around until you get out?" Herb stood by the small kitchenette. He poured water into the coffee pot and started it brewing.

"I'll be fine. Thanks." Hawke walked into the bathroom and closed the door. He didn't want anyone around when he came out of the shower. He wasn't even sure what kind of shape his feet were in.

Staring at the growing blisters on his toes, Hawke placed his feet on a heating pad set on low and loosely draped a fluffy blanket he'd received from Kitree for Christmas over the top. He picked up his phone and dialed Dani.

"Hello, Darlene called and told me you were back," she answered. "Why did you go back up there? You could have told the deputy how to find the body in the barn."

He knew she'd be mad about his staying on the mountain by himself, but hadn't expected her to lead with that. "I also wanted to find the suitcases."

"Did you?" she asked, the angry tone slipping away.

"Yes. They are now hidden with your helicopter parts. The two men who were after us were staking out the lodge waiting for someone to come back for the money."

"Did you get shot?" Reprimand sizzled in her tone.

He sighed and told her everything that happened while he was on the mountain.

"Now we're both crippled," she said.

"Yeah, I won't be able to work until these blisters go away." He grimaced as he slid his feet farther apart under the blanket.

"Can you drive? You could recuperate with me. I'm tired of Darlene and Sage hovering."

Hawke chuckled and said, "You don't think I'll hover?"

"Not if you can't stand on your feet for very long."

They both laughed at her joke.

"I'll check in with Spruel and see if Herb can take care of the boys for a few more days and then I'll be over." He also planned on calling Sheriff Lindsey to see if he could sit in on the interviews with the two men and talk to Kieran.

"See you in an hour."

"Make it two. I'll grab some food from the Rusty Nail on my way through Winslow."

"Make mine the chicken strip basket."

"I'll do that." Hawke ended the call and dialed Spruel.

"What's this I hear of you going back up in the helicopter and not coming out?" Spruel answered.

Man, he really needed to keep his boss up to date on his whereabouts before he was given desk duty. Hawke went on to explain why he'd stayed and that he'd found what he was after. But he hadn't realized he was being watched.

"You put your life on the line for something we could have sent a team up to locate." Spruel reprimanded him.

"I wasn't sure there would be any suitcases with money. I was just going by what Sheriff Lindsey learned from the Boise Police and a hunch." Hawke wondered if Shoberg and Novak were back with the two men yet.

"You only have three more days of vacation left," Spruel said.

"About that." Hawke went on to tell him about being shot at and having frostbite in his feet.

"Hawke, go to a doctor and get a letter stating you aren't fit to work, or I'll make you come in and do desk duty." The call ended.

Looked like he'd better go see Dr. Vance before he went to Dani's. He called and made an appointment for 2 p.m. and then called Dani to let her know why he'd be late getting to her place.

Since he was going to be in Alder to see the doctor, he might as well stop by the Sheriff's Office and talk to Lindsey in person.

# Chapter Twenty

Hawke loosely wrapped his feet with Telfa gauze and slowly pulled on a stretched-out pair of wool socks. Then he eased his feet into an old, large pair of moccasins. Dog watched him hobble over to the door.

"Are you going with me?" Hawke asked, grabbing a coat and a hat.

Dog ran to the door, waiting for him to open it. The animal bounded down the steps, while Hawke cautiously moved from step to step. Only the bandages and thick socks buffered his blistered feet from the hard wood stairs. The moccasins he wore were a pair his mom had made for his father years ago. The cushion between his feet and the ground were bandages, socks, and tanned elk hide.

When he walked out of the barn, Herb hurried over. "Where are you going?"

"Spruel said I need a medical release to get out of

work. I'm headed to Dr. Vance's office." He opened the door of his personal vehicle.

"I can drive you," Herb offered.

"I'll be fine. I'm going to Dani's afterward. Can you take care of my geldings for a few days? I'll be staying with Dani until my feet are healed."

Herb grinned. "This might be interesting to see how the two of you get along when you are both tied down by medical issues."

"Very funny. Just because we both don't like to be idle doesn't mean we'll have problems." Hawke held out his hand.

Herb grasped it.

"Thanks for always being willing to step in and help me out." Hawke meant it. And again, wondered what he was going to do when he and Dani purchased a place.

"Darlene and I think of you as family. You always help family."

Hawke nodded, extracted his hand from Herb's, and slid into the pickup. Yeah, thinking about moving away from the Trembleys was what had him dragging his feet about getting property of his own.

Dog sat in the passenger seat, a smile on his face, and ears held high. He was excited to go for a ride.

Hawke's stomach started growling as he entered Alder's city limits. There was time to swing through the Shake Shack, grab something to eat, and check-in with Sheriff Lindsey before his doctor's appointment.

Sitting in the parking lot of the drive thru, Hawke ate his food, sharing with Dog and thinking about the two men who had been well equipped to survive on the mountain for a week. Or had they? How big was the operation he and Dani stumbled into? That helicopter had been expensive and new. What kind of illegal endeavors would need to be covered up at such a high cost?

He finished the burger, fries, and shake, drove up to the garbage can, and tossed the empty sack, wrappers, and cup into the trash. The best place to try and find answers would be the Sheriff's Office.

All the parking slots in front of the Sheriff's Office were full. He pulled around behind the building and found one close to the back doors. He'd have to walk by the jail, but to get to Lindsey's office would be about the same distance as if he'd walked through the front door.

"You guard the pickup," he told Dog, scratching the animal's head and easing out of the vehicle.

He walked through the back door, taking care to step lightly.

Yelling came from inside the jail. Listening at the door, Hawke could make out Kieran's voice. The man was chewing someone out. Could he be the mastermind of whatever Hawke and Dani had stumbled into?

The door opened as Hawke reached out to grasp the handle.

Ralph, the youngest jail guard, nearly ran into Hawke. "Hey! Hawke, what are you doing back here?"

"Headed to see the sheriff. I heard yelling and wondered if you needed help." He'd act as if he didn't know the men in the cells.

"It's been a madhouse ever since I walked the two new prisoners past the guy you brought in. He's been calling them all kinds of names and telling them he should have gone with another outfit."

Gone with another outfit. What had he hired those men to do?

"Let me know if you need any earplugs." Hawke slapped the young deputy on the back and continued on down the hall to the main part of the building.

His feet were burning when he knocked on Sheriff Lindsey's door. When no one responded, he opened the door and peeked in. Empty.

Continuing down the hall, he found Sheriff Lindsey and Deputy Novak in one of the interview rooms.

"Mind if I join you?" Hawke asked, carefully walking in and sitting down at the end of the table.

"What are you doing here?" Novak asked. "The last time I saw you, I figured you'd sleep for a week."

"Just all the way back from Moss Springs. I'm glad Max was willing to drive me home." Hawke pointed to the folder in front of the sheriff. "What have you learned?"

"That you're on medical leave." Lindsey looked him up and down. "I heard you were shot."

"Just grazed my arm. It's more like a barbed-wire fence scratch." Hawke rearranged his aching feet under the table.

Lindsey closed the file, laid an arm over it, and peered at him. "Spruel said he wasn't expecting you to be on your feet for a week."

"Feet! You said your feet had frostbite," Novak piped in.

Hawke scowled. "Yes, I'm headed to see Dr. Vance, but had some free time and wondered what you knew about the two who shot at me, and you." His gaze landed on the deputy.

Sheriff Lindsey continued to study him. "You aren't going to con your way onto any more helicopters so we have to go out and rescue you again?"

Hawke held up his hands. "I won't be going any distance anywhere until my feet heal. But my brain still works." He tipped his head toward the door. "I came in past the jail and heard Kieran Gilmore yelling at the two men that were brought in. It sounded like he hired them."

Lindsey and Novak exchanged a glance.

The sheriff opened the folder. "Kieran appears to be someone higher up in the money laundering scheme than the Boise Police first thought."

Hawke pulled the sheets of paper the sheriff slid over to him closer and began reading. It did appear that Kieran might well have been taking the money to flee the country. Which reminded him. Hawke reached into his pocket and pulled out the two evidence bags holding the money he'd taken from the suitcases. "These are bills I took from the suitcases I found. I couldn't tell if they were counterfeit or real, but thought someone else might be able to."

Novak picked them up, opened one, and peered at it. "If they are fakes, they are damn good ones."

"Take those over to the OSP lab in Pendleton. They should be able to tell us," Sheriff Lindsey said.

Novak stood. "I'll go now." He left the room and Hawke studied Lindsey.

"I'm getting a different scenario in my head. I thought Kieran killed the victim out of self-defense. But I think the bullet that shot him was the victim's attempt at trying to steal the money and once he was dead, Kieran called the two that are now in jail with him, to come get him. The storm and Dani and I arriving at the lodge threw his plans off." Hawke had been leery of the man from the beginning, but he hadn't seemed like a killer. Which was why he had the two men for hire coming to get him and must have told the man who found him and Dani not to harm her. Because she knew nothing about the money.

"It wasn't until I found the money that anyone tried to harm me." Hawke thought on that. "I don't think Kieran is a killer, but he is greedy. Has he called a lawyer?"

"I don't think he's asked for one." Sheriff Lindsey shoved all the papers back in the folder.

"He may want a phone call now that the two people looking for his money are in jail with him." Hawke grinned. "It will be interesting to see if he calls a lawyer or someone else to retrieve the money." He glanced at his watch. "I need to get to my doctor's appointment. Give me a call if you learn anything new."

"Stay off your feet," Lindsey said.

"That's the plan after I see Dr. Vance." Hawke walked back down the hall. The prisoners had calmed down. Either Kieran had run out of words, or he was plotting how to get his money back.

Dani opened the door to her apartment. Dog ran by her, and Hawke slowly climbed the stairs. He'd stopped at the Rusty Nail as he'd promised. He carried their dinner, Justine had graciously brought out to his pickup for him, gently putting pressure on his feet as he shoved from one step to the next.

Dr. Vance had been sympathetic, doctored his feet, rewrapped them, and told him to take ibuprofen if they hurt too bad. She told him all the things he already knew. When he walked into the room, he'd asked for a slip to give to Spruel. She'd insisted on unwrapping, checking, and rewrapping them before writing out the note saying he wasn't to work for a week.

"I think you climb those stairs slower than I do," Dani joked.

He narrowed his eyes. "You aren't supposed to be going up and down these stairs."

She shrugged. "I only did it yesterday. I felt sorry for the birds hanging around the feeder looking for something to eat."

Hawke stopped at the top of the stairs. His feet stung. "I'll fill it the next time."

Dani swung away from the door on her crutches. "If you're going to tell me not to do things like Darlene and Sage, you can go back to your place."

He grinned. He'd known the two women would make Dani behave. While Dani was used to giving orders in the Air Force, she knew when to back off when her quiet cook pressured her to be still, and he had no doubt Darlene had used her *mom* ways to get Dani to cooperate.

Placing the bag of food on the small table in the kitchen, he sat down. "I dropped off my doctor's note stating I wasn't to work for a week at the office when I went through Winslow."

"I'm glad she told you a week. You have to be exhausted from all the walking in snow and not sleeping the last two weeks." Dani placed a plate in front of him and one across the table. She plunked down silverware and opened the fridge door. "What do you want to drink?"

"Beer if you have it." He'd been thinking about how good a beer was going to taste with the pulled pork sandwich he'd ordered. It was the special for the day and he never shied away from Marilee's specials. Her cooking was the best he'd ever had. Though he wouldn't tell his mom or Darlene that.

Dani set two bottles of beer on the table and eased down onto a chair. "Have you learned anything interesting about our friend Kieran?"

While they pulled the food out of containers, Hawke told her about finding the money and the new information Sheriff Lindsey had dug up.

She stopped with a fry halfway to her mouth. "You think Kieran killed the other man in cold blood?"

"Yes and no. I think he is a greedy man and when the other person attempted to take the money, he killed him." Hawke picked up the sandwich and took a bite. Chewing, he closed his eyes. Marilee made the best barbeque sauce. Even Justine, who had waitressed at the Rusty Nail for as long as Hawke had been going there, couldn't tell him what ingredients were in the older woman's recipe.

"But what about Kieran being shot?" Dani picked up a chicken strip.

"I think he was shot by the man he killed as he, Kieran, swung the board that killed him." He dug in the pocket of his coat that hung on the back of his chair. "I want to know if this guy looks familiar. If you didn't recognize Kieran, I want to know how they knew about the lodge and that there was a radio locked in your room?"

He scrolled through his photos and found the one of the man's face he'd taken when he'd first found the body.

Dani blinked hard when she first glimpsed the photo and then stared at it. "I'm not sure. He looks a little bit familiar. But I can't be certain he's been to the lodge."

"I'd like Tuck and Sage to take a look." He sat the phone down on the table.

"I need to call and tell her she doesn't need to stay overnight." Dani pulled her cell phone out of her sweatpants pocket.

"Ask her if she and Tuck can come over for a bit. Kitree, too." Hawke ate over half of his sandwich while Dani spoke with Sage.

She ended the call. "They'll be over around seven."

Hawke nodded and finished off his dinner and beer. He put the trash in the garbage and dishes in the dishwasher while Dani went in and sat on the couch. He'd had to argue with her that her medical condition was worse than his. His was just uncomfortable for now, she could lose the use of her leg if she didn't heal correctly.

At a quarter to seven, Dog sat at the door whining. Hawke opened the door and the dog stepped out onto the landing, looking down at the parking area.

"Go greet them," Hawke said, and the animal shot down the stairs. He heard Kitree squeal with delight and knew Dog must be giving her kisses. The two had become friends when Hawke was keeping the girl safe. Only Kitree called Dog, Prince. She thought it suited him better than Hawke's name for the animal.

Dog and Kitree were the first ones up the stairs. Both bounded up and stopped in front of Hawke. Dog's tongue hung out, and Kitree wrapped her arms around Hawke's waist.

"It's good to see you!" she said, staring up into his face.

His heart always swelled when this child was around him. He'd never have children of his own but this one would always hold a spot in his heart. He hugged her back. "It's good to see you, too."

Sage stopped in front of them a smile on her face. "She's been wanting to see you ever since we came down last month."

"I've been busy or else I would have come by for a visit." Hawke released the child. She and Dog hurried into the apartment.

"Good to see you." He gave Sage a hug and shook hands with Tuck.

He followed the family into Dani's living room. Kitree was already seated on the couch beside Dani telling her about what she'd been learning in school. Hawke smiled. The child had become embedded in Dani's heart as well.

After Sage brought drinks out from the kitchen and everyone was seated, Hawke cleared his throat.

"I won't go into details of what all Dani and I have been through the last couple of weeks, but I have a photo I'd like you to look at. I want to know if this man has ever been to the lodge." He pulled out his phone and found the less gruesome photo and cropped it to just show the man's face.

Tuck took the phone and studied the photo. "He does look familiar." He handed the phone to his wife.

"He was there this summer. Only for a couple of days, I think."

Kitree took the phone. She bit her lower lip and blinked her eyes. "That was Mr. Pat. He and I went for a walk to find mushrooms." She peered over at Hawke. "Is he…dead?"

"I'm afraid so. That would answer how he knew where to find the radio and the lodge." Hawke eased the phone away from the child.

170

# Chapter Twenty-one

Dani rose off the couch. "Kitree, come help me get my things ready for bed." The child followed her down the hall.

Hawke turned his attention to the husband and wife studying him. He told them how he'd found the body, about the smashed radio, and finding money stored under the bunkhouse. "Do either of you remember if this man was in the bunkhouse? I know the two, the dead man and the man we brought back, spent a night, possibly two, in the bunkhouse. The beds were rumpled."

Sage shuddered. "I'll be sure we have clean sheets and blankets put on before we climb into those beds."

Tuck rubbed a hand across the back of his neck. "I hate to say it, but I think he spent the most time with Kitree. That's who you need to be asking questions."

Hawke nodded. He hated the thought of asking the twelve-year-old questions about a man she knew was dead. But she seemed to be the logical person.

Sage stood. "I'll go help Dani and send Kitree out."

When the woman walked into the small room off the living room, Tuck turned to Hawke. "Are you and Dani safe?"

Hawke studied him. "We should be. The only three people who know about me finding the money are locked up in jail. And I'm sure Sheriff Lindsey will send someone up to get the money tomorrow. I told them where I hid it."

"In Dani's secret parts room?" Tuck grinned.

"Yes. The same place I hid the body until law enforcement could collect it." He picked up the coffee Sage had handed him. He sipped. It had grown cold while they talked.

"That room has turned out pretty useful," Tuck said, picking up his glass of water.

"Old Charlie, Dani's uncle, had that room built so he could hide items he didn't want walking away." Hawke thought of how excited the old man had been to show the hidden room to Hawke when Charlie had discovered Hawke was also Nez Perce.

"How many people know about it? It has been there a lot of years." Tuck put his glass back on the table.

"All of us in this apartment. Now Deputy Novak, Dr. Vance, and a helicopter pilot from La Grande. And the only other person is a man who worked for Charlie for four decades and you took over his job. He would never tell anyone about the room."

"What about the pilot from LaGrande?" Tuck asked in a tone that had Hawke studying him.

"Why do you ask?" Hawke watched as Tuck tapped a finger on his knee and peered back at him.

"If you found two suitcases full of money, that would be a pretty good incentive for someone who knew about a secret room to try and either get the money or tell someone who would pay him well how to get it." Tuck shrugged. "But what are the chances he would know how to get ahold of the person the money belongs to. Or that he would find out about it."

Hawke had an uneasy feeling. If Tuck came up with that scenario this quickly, so might the helicopter pilot. If he knew about the money. "I need to make a phone call. When Kitree comes back in here let her know I want to ask her some questions." Hawke hobbled into the kitchen and called Sheriff Lindsey.

"What the heck are you doing calling me, Hawke? You're on medical leave."

"I wanted to make sure no one gets wind of the money up at the lodge." He didn't want word of the money stirring up trouble. There could be more than a pilot headed up to find it.

"We're not that stupid. Do you know how many people would want to find that money?"

Hawke sighed. "Good. I was talking with Dani, and we thought it would be a mess if that happened." He wasn't going to mention he'd told the Kimbal family. "What do you know about the helicopter pilot who took Novak and Dr. Vance in for the body retrieval?"

"Newell Norton? He just started working with the Fish and Wildlife. He went to helicopter school and signed contracts to do county and state work. Why?" Suspicion warbled in the sheriff's voice.

"He saw the hidden room in the barn. I want to make sure he doesn't run his mouth off about it."

"So did Novak and Dr. Vance," Lindsey countered.

"I trust them. I don't know this Norton."

"I'll have Novak have a talk with Norton. Now go rest those feet." Lindsey ended the call.

Hawke thought about Tuck's concerns. They were well-founded. Back in the living room, Kitree and Sage were sitting on the couch next to Tuck.

"Did Dani go to bed?" Hawke asked.

Sage nodded. "She won't admit it, but she's been going to bed early every night. I think the leg bothers her more than she's letting on. She toughs it out all day and then finally takes pain pills at night."

"I'm glad she isn't being stubborn and not taking the pills. That will help her heal faster." Hawke smiled at Sage. "Thank you for looking out for her while I was gone."

She smiled back at him. "You know I'd do anything for Dani and you. The two of you are like family to us." Sage grasped her husband and Kitree's hands.

"And we feel the same." Hawke moved his gaze to Kitree. "I don't want to upset you, but I'd like to know everything you can remember about Mr. Pat."

The girl swallowed and clung to Sage's hand. "He was nice. He said he had a daughter about my age at home. I asked him why he didn't bring his family. He said he was checking it out for his boss who was thinking about bringing his people here." She picked at a flower on her shirt with her free hand. "He stayed in one of the cabins. When I'd said I was going to pick mushrooms at lunch, he said he wanted to go. So when I was ready, I went to his cabin. I was going to knock on the door, but it was open. He was talking on his phone. I thought it was weird because you can't use a phone at the lodge."

"Was he talking to someone? Like a call?" Hawke

asked.

"No. When he saw me, he turned it off. I think he was recording what he was saying."

"Did you hear any of it?" Hawke didn't want to pressure the girl, but it was interesting that he had been sent up there to check the place out.

"Only that he said there were two rooms in the lodge, three cabins, and a bunkhouse. And he said something about easy air access." Kitree glanced at her parents and then back at Hawke. "It sounded to me like he was trying to sell the lodge. I asked him that when we were picking mushrooms. He said, no, he was just making sure he told his boss everything that was available." She shook her head. "I told him guests don't stay in the bunkhouse, that was where my family lived. He just stared at me and talked about something else."

Hawke glanced at Tuck and Sage. "Does any of this make you remember anything more about the man?"

They both shook their heads. It was obvious the man hadn't thought a child would remember what he'd said. He had underestimated Kitree. She was older than her years, having spent her life before her parents' deaths and living with the Kimbals fending for herself and her father. Her mother had been too caught up in the business that killed her parents.

"Thank you for coming over. This has all been helpful." Hawke stood.

Everyone else stood and grabbed their coats off the hall tree by the door.

"Tell Dani if she needs anything to call," Sage said.

"I will. And thank you again for all your help." He hugged Sage and Kitree, shook hands with Tuck, and closed the door behind them.

Hawke walked through the small apartment, though larger than where he lived, turning off the lights. Dog followed him into the bedroom.

The light on his bedside table gave off a subdued glow. He undressed, climbed into bed, and lay on his back listening to Dani's breathing and wondering how the dead man fit into the equation. Was he working for Kieran? Was that who sent him to check out the lodge? Or was there someone else out there looking for the money and anyone who knew where it was?

The following morning, Hawke sat at the table with Dani eating breakfast and discussing when he'd be well enough to take them both to Mission to see his mom. She'd enjoy a visit from them.

Dani stirred her tea, staring into the cup. "I'd like to go to the next Tamkaliks Powwow."

Hawke stopped spreading jam on his toast and studied her. "Why do you want to go?" Not that he minded. He'd been thinking about participating more in the ceremonies and powwows.

"This is stupid and not at all like me, but I want to learn more about our ancestors. Th-that owl. The way it looked at me and…I'm sure it talked to me. I just feel like I need to learn more about my heritage. The side that I've ignored most of my life."

Hawke reached across the table and grasped her hand. "The owl came to me, too. I was cold. Exhausted. I wanted to lie down and go to sleep."

"Hypothermia," she said.

He nodded. "The owl landed next to me, forced me up with his stare, and led me to shelter. Those mountains, the ones I patrol, are the same ones our ancestors hunted and fished. They buried their old and sick there. It is in our blood. It's no wonder you were willing to take over the lodge and I can't seem to stay off the mountain even when I'm not working." He squeezed her hand. "I'd be honored to experience the Tamkaliks Powwow with you."

"You don't think I'm crazy?" She peered at him over the rim of her cup.

"No crazier than I am." He winked and picked up his cup of coffee.

His phone buzzed. Hawke picked it up. Lindsey.

"Hello."

"Hawke, Gilmore contacted a lawyer. He'll be bailed out tomorrow morning. Can you come up with any proof he killed Barclay?"

# Chapter Twenty-two

Hawke shoved to his feet. "I don't have proof. The two-by-four he slammed into the victim's head was too rough for fingerprints. All I know is they were the only two at the lodge. One ended up dead and the other had a bullet wound in the arm and was wandering around in the forest." He stared at Dani as he continued going through everything with the sheriff on the phone. "You need to send someone up for that money today. If he gets out, that's the first place he's going to go, and he'll tear that place apart looking for the suitcases."

"I know you don't trust Norton but I'm sending Novak and a trooper up there today with him to get the suitcases. I just wanted to let you know." Lindsey ended the call.

"What was that all about?" Dani asked.

Hawke repeated what the sheriff had told him.

"Do you think Kieran will come looking for us?" she

asked.

"I don't see why. We helped him off the mountain. Granted he would have rather stayed with his money, but we did keep him alive."

"You also found the money and hid it," she said.

"He doesn't know that." As soon as the words came out, he realized Kieran did know that. The two men they'd brought in would have told him they saw Hawke carrying the cases to the barn, but they couldn't find them.

"I need to call Herb and Darlene. He may go there looking for me." He picked up his phone and dialed his landlord's landline. No answer. He glanced at the clock. They were probably both out doing chores. He dialed Herb's cell phone.

"Hell-lo," he answered.

"Hi Herb, it's Hawke. I just wanted to give you and Darlene a head's up. The guy Dani and I brought down off the mountain will be getting bailed out tomorrow. He may come looking for me. I'd appreciate it if you didn't tell him where I am. Just say I'm on medical leave, I packed a bag, loaded up Dog, and left. That's all you know."

"I can do that. Do you think he's dangerous?"

"Not to you or Darlene, but make sure she tells him the same thing." Hawke didn't believe Kieran would hurt the Trembleys. They would have no reason to know where the money was hidden.

"Okay. You and Dani still getting along?" The older man chuckled.

"Yes. Are you hoping we can't get along?" Hawke joked.

"Nope. Just would like to be a fly on the wall when

you two start butting heads." The line went dead.

Hawke shook his head.

"What was that all about?" Dani asked, pushing to her foot and shoving the crutches under her arms.

"Go on into the living room and get comfortable. I'll clean up breakfast and come tell you." Hawke stood.

"You know, I might get used to having you wait on me. I might not want to go back to being domestic." She swung her way into the living room, smiling.

Hawke shook his head. He didn't mind sharing the household chores. As a kid he'd done his fair share with a working mom and an alcoholic stepfather. Someone had to take care of his younger sister and take the burden of household work off his mom when she came home from working two jobs, only to have his stepfather go through her purse and take any money he found and get drunk. Those were thoughts he didn't like to dwell on. The stepfather died long ago. His mother was in good health, a positive role model to the youth she babysat, and doing well by herself.

If Marion would just give her a call once in a while, his mom's life would be complete. But his younger sister went off the rez for a college education and took the first job offer farthest from Oregon. She had only been home twice since graduating college twenty years ago.

The dishes were easy to rinse and put in the dishwasher. Hawke walked into the living room and found Dani typing away on her laptop.

"You planning on writing a book about being cooped up with a broken leg?" He sat in the chair closest to the couch since she had her legs stretched out the length of the furniture.

Her lips tipped up at the corners. "No. I'm googling

Kieran Gilmore. We might as well see how much we can get on him."

"I should have brought my computer. I could access law enforcement records." He was mentally thumping himself. Pulling out his phone, he called Herb back.

"I told Darlene what to tell anyone looking for you," Herb said when he answered the call.

Hawke chuckled and said, "I didn't think you'd forget. If you or Darlene happen to be headed this way today, could you bring my work computer? It's in my OSP vehicle. You know where I keep the keys."

"I'm sure Darlene would like an excuse to come see how you two are doing cooped up." The man laughed and ended the call.

"I'm sure glad Herb is getting a kick out of us being cooped up together."

Dani looked up from the computer. "What do you mean?"

Hawke explained how his landlord thought they would be fighting before the week was out.

She smiled. "I don't see that happening. We've been slowly easing into being around one another for longer and longer periods. When we get that property together, you'll still be working and I'll still spend most of the year up at the lodge. I think we'll have enough breaks from one another that we can make it work."

He stared at her. She made their relationship sound like a partnership where she would relish the time away from him. He'd have to think about this a little more. His view of their purchasing property was so they would be able to spend more time together.

"The Boise Chamber of Commerce page said that Riches Pawn is owned by Kieran Gilmore. When I went to the website it says they are a pawnbroker and financial services." She glanced at him. "Do you think that money came from the pawnbroker side or the financial services?"

"I think we need to learn more about Kieran and his business." Hawke stared down at his feet. He couldn't drive that far and walking around doing the leg work would only make his feet worse, not better. "Darlene is bringing my work computer over sometime today. That might help us dig up more information."

"It says the business is part of a string of stores in the Pacific Northwest." Dani typed some more. "The first store started in Seattle and is still run by the family. Patrick Barclay, a great- great-grandson, is the family member now running the chain of stores."

"Kieran killed the owner of the chain of pawnshops?" Hawke peered into Dani's eyes. "I wonder if he was next in line?"

"If he was, does that make him family, or just someone who worked his way up in the organization?" Dani dropped her gaze back to her computer. The keys clattered as she typed.

"I wonder why Patrick told Kitree he was checking out the lodge for his boss? He was the boss."

"What about Kitree and Patrick? He's the dead man, right?" Dani stopped typing.

Hawke told her everything that Kitree told him the night before.

"That's interesting. It says here that the Barclay family came to America in eighteen-fifty-five to escape the starvation happening in Ireland. The family tried a hand at farming and the husband, Patrick's great-great-grandfather, started bartering with people and soon started a shop where people could purchase used items and get money for items they wanted to sell. The beginning of the pawnshop. In the nineteen-thirties, his great-grandfather started giving loans. And his grandfather started the chain of businesses." Dani looked up. "It looks like the business won't be in the Barclay family anymore if Kieran takes it over."

"What were Kieran and Patrick doing with two suitcases of money?" Hawke scratched his head and stared at the photo on a shelf of Dani standing beside an impressive-looking helicopter.

"We need to discover if they were enemies or friends," Dani said.

Hawke pulled out his phone. "What's the phone number for Kieran's pawnshop?"

Dani rattled it off, and Hawke poked the numbers on his phone.

"Riches Pawnshop and Financial Services, Boise," a female voice answered.

"Hi, I'd like to speak with Kieran," Hawke said.

There was a pause. "He won't be in today."

"Can you tell me how I can get ahold of him?"

Again, a pause. "What is your name?" The woman's voice wasn't as cheerful as her greeting when she'd answered the phone.

"I'm a friend he met in the Eagle Cap Wilderness. I wanted to give him some information he'd asked me about. When will he be in?"

"Eagle Cap Wilderness? His plane went down there. Who are you?" Suspicion dripped in her voice.

"I'm a friend. Who *are* you?"

"What is your name and number? I'll have him call you when he gets back." All business as if she hadn't moments before slipped she knew where he had gone and what had happened to him.

"I'll call back later." Hawke ended the call.

"What was that all about?" Dani asked, setting her laptop on the coffee table.

"A woman at the pawnshop knows he left on a plane and that it crashed." He studied Dani. "She wouldn't give me her name." He stood. "I'm making us some more coffee. I hope Darlene gets here with my computer soon. I need to see if Kieran is married or has a female partner."

Darlene arrived at the same time as Hawke's phone started ringing. He left the door open for her to come in and took the call in the bedroom.

"What have you found out?" Hawke asked Sheriff Lindsey.

"There is an FBI Agent here who says he knows you. He'd like to come talk with you. I didn't want to send him over if you didn't want to talk to him." The sheriff said this as if he didn't think Hawke would be willing to work with the FBI.

"Is it Special Agent Pierce?" That was the only FBI Agent he could think of who would ask for him. They'd worked a human trafficking ring on the Umatilla Reservation a year before.

"Yeah. How did you know?"

"He's the only FBI Agent I know. Is he interested in Kieran Gilmore?" Hawke had a feeling with the pawnshops being spread over several states, the FBI had been keeping tabs on them if they were doing illegal activities.

"Yeah. Want me to send him over?" Lindsey asked.

"Give him my phone number and I'll tell him how

to find me." Hawke wasn't going to give the sheriff or anyone else in law enforcement anymore gossip about him than they already had.

"Sure." Sheriff Lindsey sounded disappointed.

Hawke ended the call and waited in the bedroom. Pierce would call him as soon as he was given the phone number.

His phone rang—a restricted number. That had to be Pierce.

"Hello?" Hawke answered.

"Hawke, it's Quinn Pierce with the FBI. I have some questions for you regarding the man you brought down off the mountain several days ago." The commanding voice was the same as when they'd last met. He was a good agent and a good man, but he tended to take things a bit too serious for Hawke's liking.

"That's fine. I'm not at home. I'm staying with a friend who has a broken leg." He rattled off the address and directions to get to the apartment.

"How far is that from the Sheriff's Office?" Pierce asked.

"About thirty minutes."

"I'll bring lunch."

"Bring it for three."

The line went silent.

Hawke walked out into the living room and found Dani and Darlene working on a puzzle on a board that sat across Dani's lap.

Darlene glanced up. "Get your phone calls finished?"

"Yeah." His gaze landed on Dani. "We have a guest coming over. He's bringing lunch."

"Anyone I know?" She pushed the board with the

puzzle onto the coffee table.

"You met briefly about a year ago."

He could see she was trying to figure out who it might be.

"I'll be on my way. I set your computer on the kitchen table." Darlene stood. She stopped in front of Hawke. "I thought you were supposed to be healing and not working."

Hawke grinned. "I'm doing leg work without using my legs. Digging up information on a computer isn't going to hurt my feet."

"As long as you remember that and stay put. No running around." Darlene picked up the empty cups from the coffee table, carried them into the kitchen, and returned with her coat and purse. "Let me know if you two need anything else."

"Thank you for making the trip to bring me the computer," Hawke said, hobbling alongside her to the door.

"I had to come down here and visit Selma anyway. She isn't making any headway on what to call our quilt show at the church." Darlene waved to Dani and opened the door. "You two be good."

Hawke laughed and closed the door behind the woman.

Dani met his gaze when he stepped from the entry hall into the living room. They both laughed.

"She knows you too well," Dani said.

"Yeah, it's scary how well she knows me. One of the reasons I want to get a place of our own. Get away from Herb and Darlene and them knowing so much about me…us."

"But they are good people. I'm sure they don't share

everything with everyone they see." Dani studied him. "Do they?"

"To my knowledge, they only share the embarrassing stuff." He grimaced thinking about some of the women Darlene had tried to fix him up with over the years.

Dani laughed and asked, "Who is the guest coming over?"

"Special Agent Quinn Pierce. Remember him? He helped with the human trafficking ring at the casino." Hawke wondered how Dela Alvaro was doing. She had been tenacious about finding the missing women. He'd also learned it was because she had lost a friend as a teenager.

"Oh yeah. The person who said it would take months to get that young woman out of Qatar." She raised her eyebrows. "Will it take him months to discover what Kieran is up to?"

Hawke smiled and shrugged. "I don't know what he wants. But I'm thinking it has something to do with our friend we found on the mountain."

# Chapter Twenty-three

Forty-five minutes later, Dog barked at the door. Hawke hobbled over. He'd already helped Dani to the kitchen table and had a fresh pot of coffee brewing.

Opening the door, he found the same smartly dressed man, wearing sunglasses that he'd met while hunting down the traffickers. He held a computer bag in one hand and a brown bag that emitted the scents of greasy fries and burgers in the other.

"Hawke." Pierce shifted the brown bag into the hand holding the computer bag and extended his empty one.

Hawke shook hands. "Pierce. What brings you to Wallowa County?" He led the way into the kitchen.

"You look like you're hobbling. What happened?" Pierce stopped short at the sight of Dani sitting in one chair and her cast resting in another. "Shit, no one said anything about the two of you being hurt." Pierce placed the brown paper bag on the table and his computer bag on the floor by the chair he lowered onto.

While Hawke poured coffee for all of them, he told the agent what had transpired on the mountain. Ending with, "I'm on medical leave, and Dani is recuperating from her broken leg."

Pierce opened the bag and handed out burgers wrapped in paper and small bags with fries. "It sounds like you spent a good deal of time with Gilmore on the mountain."

"Is that who you really want to talk about?" Hawke asked, unwrapping his burger and studying the items between the buns. These had to have come from Al's Café in Eagle. They were still warm and looked like one of their burgers.

"Yes. There's been buzz that the Barclay family was losing their good reputation. For over a century their financial side of the business was legit. But the last ten years or so word has been going around that if borrowers don't pay their loans bad things happen to the people around them. Their money resources seemed to triple about the time your friend Gilmore made connections with the OMG, Outlaw Motorcycle Gangs."

Hawke exchanged a glance with Dani. "What about Patrick Barclay? Did the feds or anyone else see him with a biker gang?"

"As far as we can tell, he was keeping things legit in Seattle and the other Washington state stores. Half of the Oregon stores are legit. All of the California stores and the Boise store are laundering money. We think for one of the OMG gangs, Brother Speed. Your friend Gilmore is the one who started all the illegitimate practices from the intel we've collected." Pierce bit into his burger.

Hawke thought about this. "How is the Seattle store

doing? Do you think Barclay was borrowing money to keep it afloat? Maybe Gilmore let slip where the money came from, and Barclay wasn't going to have that store tarnished?"

"Word has it that the Seattle store is doing fine and running clean. We've been wondering about those suitcases of money you found. I'll be happy when the helicopter gets back here with them. The bills you had sent to the lab came back as legal tender. Nothing off about them." Pierce sipped from the cup of coffee Hawke had placed on the table in front of him. "They had some trace of drugs, but this day and age unless they're bills fresh off the press, there's going to be a trace."

Hawke nodded, nibbling on a fry.

"Do you know if the two were friends before they took the flight they did? And why that flight, that day? If Patrick—" Dani stopped when Pierce gave her a quizzical look. "If Barclay and Kier-Gilmore were friends, why would one turn on the other? And we know it was Pa-Barclay who knew the mountain and the lodge."

Pierce stared at Dani and then at Hawke. "How do you know Barclay had prior knowledge of the lodge?"

Hawke told him about the man visiting the lodge the past summer.

"We haven't found the plane. I've had a helicopter buzzing around trying to locate it." Pierce rolled up the empty burger wrapper and picked up a fry. He pointed it at Hawke. "You have any idea where they might have gone down?"

"Was Barclay the pilot?" Hawke countered.

Dani and Pierce both stared at him.

"Gilmore kept saying the pilot was dead. I think the

pilot was Barclay. He crashed the plane on purpose. I think he was trying to get rid of Gilmore. Maybe he didn't like what the other man had brought to his family's legacy?" Hawke wadded up his wrapper and fry bag, tossing them into the open brown bag on the table.

"You think the flight had been a way to get rid of Gilmore and it backfired on Barclay?" Pierce's tone said he didn't quite buy the scenario.

"It makes more sense than anything else I've come up with." Hawke picked up his coffee mug and drank half the cup.

Dani leaned back in her chair. "But why did they have two suitcases of money if it was just a way to get rid of Kier-Gilmore?"

"I think that needs to be asked of the only person who would know." Hawke studied Pierce.

He nodded. "I haven't spoken with Gilmore yet." The agent wiped his hands on a napkin. "I suppose you'd like to be in on this since you know all the particulars?"

Hawke grinned. "If you don't mind driving me there and back."

"I'll set it up for tomorrow morning."

"Sheriff Lindsey said Gilmore was being bailed out tomorrow morning." Hawke wondered why the Fed hadn't been told that already.

"I see." Pierce pulled out his phone and walked into the other room.

"What do you think he's going to do?" Dani asked, picking up the brown bag, wadding it in a ball, and tossing it at the garbage can in the corner of the room.

Hawke wasn't surprised when the paper ball landed in the can. "He'll either set it up to talk to him tonight or he'll find a way to postpone the bail hearing."

"I'll be here at seven a.m. to pick you up. The bail hearing has been postponed due to the judge being called out of town." Pierce didn't smile, but his eyes glinted with humor.

"I'll see you at seven." Hawke followed the man to the door.

"What do you know about the two men that shot at the party that came to rescue you?" Pierce asked when they were standing on the landing outside the apartment.

"After hearing Gilmore chewing them out in the jail, I'd say they are thugs for hire. You might be able to make a deal with them that will get them to rat out Gilmore. It makes me wonder if they knew what was in the suitcases and if they would have given them back to Gilmore? It looked like a lot of money. Enough for the two men to change identities and live a nice life in another country." Hawke eased his butt onto the handrail to take pressure off his feet.

"Care to take a run at them tomorrow as well?" Pierce asked.

Hawke grinned. "I'd love to visit with them."

Pierce walked down two steps and turned back around. "I know Gilmore has only had one phone call, but be careful. You and your friend," he nodded to the apartment, "thwarted something that must have been a big moneymaker for him."

"I'm taking precautions. See you tomorrow." Hawke watched until the FBI Agent slid into his SUV and drove away.

He didn't see how Gilmore could have contacted anyone to retaliate for him, but he and Dog would be on alert to anyone prowling around.

At 6:45 a.m., Hawke began his descent of the stairs. He'd called Tuck the night before and asked him to arrive at seven and stick around until he returned. Tuck had arrived at 6:30. He said Kitree had wanted to come with him, but he'd talked her into going to school.

The dark SUV pulled up to the garage as Hawke stepped from the last stair. He walked over, opened the passenger door, and settled into the seat. The aroma of strong coffee filled the interior.

"Did you bring me a cup?" he asked.

Pierce grinned. "Can't figure out who is going to be good cop and who is going to be bad cop without coffee." He pointed to the cup closest to the passenger seat in the cupholder.

"I'm always the good cop. Someone has to sympathize with them." Hawke grabbed the cup and sipped. "You picked this up at Coffee and Cream, didn't you?"

"How can you tell? They have plain cups."

"They are the only place in the county that makes coffee so strong they have to add the cream." Hawke took another sip. He didn't like things in his coffee, but this particular brew was enhanced by the sweet cream that was added.

"Dela and I both wondered how you hadn't become a detective or gone higher up the State Police ranks." Pierce glanced over at him and back at the road as they drove through Eagle.

"Dani and I were wondering about Dela. How is she doing?" He avoided the prying into his not moving up the ranks with a legitimate question.

"She's doing well. She's head of security at the casino now."

"That's good. She was the one to realize the former head of security wasn't doing his job." In fact, the man had been helping human traffickers take women from the reservation. That was the lowest form of human in Hawke's estimation. One who preyed on his own.

"She's helped solve a couple of murders since then. She would have made a good FBI agent." The sympathy in the agent's words had Hawke glancing over at him.

"Why can't she still be an FBI agent if she wanted to?" Hawke had never understood the need for someone to be limited by their lack of mobility. That had nothing to do with their ability to figure things out and the mental fortitude it took to put up with morons like Pierce every day.

"She'd never make it through the physical tests. You know, not that long ago she jumped into a domestic fight between her neighbors and she didn't come out looking very good." Pierce drove through Winslow. "Do we need to stop at your office for anything?"

"No." Hawke didn't want his boss to see him out moving around when he was supposed to be on medical leave. "I think it was brave of her to help the woman. How did the man she protected the woman from end up? Was he arrested or did he get away?"

"He was arrested. Dela had him tied up with a dog leash."

"Then I would say she did exactly what should have been done. Did the woman survive? Were their children involved?" Hawke knew what it was like to be a child watching your mother be beaten by the man whom she'd married. It was the worst kind of helplessness.

"The woman survived. She's been removed from the reservation to somewhere new and reunited with her son." Pierce now sped up for the ten miles to Alder and the County offices.

"Then it sounds to me like Dela would make any law enforcement agency a good officer." Hawke stared out the window as they drove past the road to the Trembleys'. He wondered if Dela would like to work anywhere other than the casino. The next time he and Dani visited his mother, they'd take her to dinner at the casino and try to bump into Dela. He'd liked the young woman. She was smart and didn't back down from anything. He chuckled. She was a younger version of Dani.

"What's funny?" Pierce asked.

"Just something I thought of. It has nothing to do with why you're driving me to talk to Gilmore." Hawke stared ahead, wondering how the FBI Agent planned to handle Kieran.

# Chapter Twenty-four

Hawke and Pierce sat in the interview room at the Sheriff's Office. The door opened and Deputy Alden walked Kieran Gilmore into the room. The man was wearing the orange jail overalls.

Gilmore's gaze landed on Hawke. He glared and sat down. "Are you the reason I'm not getting bail this morning?"

"That would be me." Pierce drew Gilmore's anger to him.

"Who are you?"

"Special Agent Pierce with the FBI."

Gilmore narrowed his eyes and peered at Hawke. "Why did you bring the FBI in? You said it was self-defense."

"He didn't bring me in. We've been watching you and your business for some time now, Mr. Gilmore." Pierce opened the file in front of him. "You've had several visits from Bear Callaghan. A known member of the Brother Speed Outlaw Motorcycle gang based out of Boise."

Gilmore didn't say anything. His gaze was cast down on his handcuffed wrists.

"Kieran, did you get into something you couldn't get out of?" Hawke asked, deciding to have the man think he was still on his side.

Gilmore raised his head and studied Hawke. "What do you mean?"

"We know that the man you killed was Patrick Barclay, a descendent of the Barclay family who founded the Riches Pawn and Loan businesses. We know you own one of those businesses. What were you and Barclay doing with two suitcases of money?" Hawke held the man's gaze.

"You know about those?" He said it as if he hadn't learned from the other men that Hawke had found the cases. The person Gilmore was showing them was the soft-spoken scared man he'd been while with Dani and Hawke. Not the man Hawke had heard yelling at the other two men in the jail. That bossy, take-charge person was the man they needed to bring out of Gilmore. The man who had the guts to go into a partnership with the Brother Speed.

"You know I do. You talked to the two men who saw me find them and carry them into the barn. I'm wondering if that is your money or money that needs to go to Brother Speed before they decide your death would be just as satisfying." Hawke studied the man sitting across from him.

Gilmore didn't flinch or bat an eye at the mention of the motorcycle gang perhaps wanting him dead.

"Who are the two men in the cells? Someone you hired to help you get the money off the mountain?" Hawke didn't wait for an answer. "I'm not sure how you managed to contact them after Barclay smashed the radio. But I'm pretty sure he'd planned to kill you and leave you on the mountain. He didn't like you bringing the motorcycle gang into business with his family's legacy, did he?"

A corner of Gilmore's mouth tweaked up as if he thought it was funny he'd brought shame to the Riches Pawn and Loan businesses.

Or was the comment about the family legacy what had him smirking? "Are you related to the Barclays?"

Pierce pulled out his phone and started texting.

Hawke was surprised the FBI Agent had stayed quiet and let him talk to Gilmore. For all the good it was doing. The man was keeping his mouth shut. Which gave Hawke an idea. He motioned to the door with a tip of his head.

Pierce nodded. "We'll be right back."

When the door opened, Deputy Alden stepped into the room.

"Keep an eye on him until we get back," Pierce said, walking down the hall to another interview room. "What was your idea?"

"We need to talk to the two men that shot at me and the rescue party. We need them to tell us more so we can catch Gilmore in some lies. And if you happen to have someone who can talk to the Brother Speed in Boise, it would be interesting to know if that money is theirs or not." Hawke's gaze landed on the room where Gilmore sat. "I say we put him back in jail and let him see us take the other two out. See if that gets him fidgeting."

Pierce grinned and said, "I like the way you think. By the way, the way you were talking to him, like you were friends, that's the best tactic you can take when interviewing."

"It's not a tactic. If you treat people with respect, they will return it." Hawke walked into the other interview room. "I'll be in here waiting for one of the prisoners."

Hawke settled himself in the seat, wishing his feet would heal quicker so he could be out talking to people who weren't trying to hide things from them.

Ten minutes later, Pierce and Arlo, the man Hawke had tied to the tree, entered the room.

Arlo lunged at Hawke. Pierce detained him, shoving him down in the chair across from Hawke.

Making sure his feet were tucked under his chair so the irate man couldn't bump or stomp on them, Hawke smiled. "We meet again."

"I could have froze to death on that mountain," Arlo spat.

Hawke motioned with a hand in an up and down motion. "You're alive. I didn't tie you to the tree to die, only to detain you so I could get my injured friend down the mountain to help."

"Like you'd come back for me." Arlo's face grew redder with each accusation he tossed at Hawke.

"No, I sent another State Police Trooper to get you. But your friend had found you first." Hawke tipped his head. "How did your friend find you? I had your radio."

The man leaned back in his chair, a smug smile on his lips.

"All of that doesn't matter," Pierce hopped in. "We ran your prints, and you aren't connected to any Outlaw

Motorcycle gang."

Arlo's eyes widened. "Why would you think that?"

"Because the man you were helping is connected to the Brother Speed gang," Hawke said, drawing the man's attention back to him.

"Shit!" Arlo became agitated. "Fuck! If my boss finds out we were working for a motorcycle gang he'll jam us up good. I told Jerome this didn't feel right. We were to pick up Barclay and two suitcases. That's all he hired us for. When we couldn't get him, the boss asked if we had the suitcases. Which we didn't, and went back to find them. Then you showed up and we saw you carry them to the barn." He studied Hawke. "Where did you hide them? We looked all over that building. We even looked behind the barn thinking maybe you shoved them out somewhere when we were watching the front."

Hawke just smiled and then sobered. "Did you ever see the man who hired you in person?"

Arlo shook his head. "No. Our boss talked to him and set up the extraction. I thought it was weird that we'd been told to pick up a man and two suitcases at a lodge in the middle of the Eagle Cap Wilderness. But we go where we're told and get paid good money."

"That was all you were told?" Pierce asked.

"Yeah."

"Then why did you shoot at law enforcement when you came across them?" Pierce stared at the man.

Hawke didn't think Pierce's stare would break the man, but it was fun to watch.

"We didn't know they were law enforcement. For all we knew they were more people coming to steal the suitcases we were told to get. We always finish our assignments." He ended with pride in his voice.

"What if I told you the man who hired you is dead? I found his body when my friend and I arrived at the lodge. You would have been picking up the wrong man if he hadn't taken off at our arrival."

Arlo shook his head. "No, the boss received a call from the man's secretary saying he was still waiting for us. We couldn't get in to find him until the storm let up. Then we arrived at the lodge, and no one was there. We saw tracks, but it was more than one person. We weren't sure if he'd been taken hostage or what."

Hawke locked the information about the man's secretary away. He had a pretty good idea he knew who that could be. The woman he'd talked to at the Boise pawnshop yesterday.

"I need the name and phone number of your boss," Pierce said.

While the man rattled off the information, Hawke stood and hobbled to the door.

"What's wrong with you?" Arlo asked.

"You were worried about dying. So was I. Trying to get away from you, I dropped my pack, leaving my extra foot warmers. My feet have frostbite." He continued out the door, down the hall, and into the other room with Jerome.

This man wasn't as thick and muscular as Arlo. He did look fit and ready for any job he was given.

Hawke sat down at the table across from the man. They studied one another until Pierce arrived.

Pierce pulled out his notebook and tipped his head toward Hawke as if saying, start asking questions.

"Jerome, we just finished talking to Arlo. We understand the job of extracting Patrick Barclay and two suitcases from Charlie's Lodge in the Eagle Cap

Wilderness was a mission given to you."

Jerome nodded.

"The man you were to pick up was dead when I arrived at the lodge. The other man with me said there were people after him. That's why we took him with us. I want to know what happened when you approached the overhang where the woman, the mule, and the man were hiding." Hawke sat back and waited.

Jerome took in everything Hawke said, his eyes widening at the part about a man being dead and another one saying he was running from people. "When I approached the overhang, the man popped up, with a finger to his lips. He showed me a piece of paper and put it in the snow. Believing he was the man I was after and he was the one paying the bill, I pretended I believed the woman and walked away. I hid out of sight until they left. Then I went back and picked up the note he'd left. He said to get the suitcases at the lodge and bring them to an address he'd send our boss."

That was why they hadn't been pursued. Hawke wondered at how quickly Gilmore could think on his feet. That was a ballsy assumption that the men knew about the suitcases. And what business would he have told the boss to have the money delivered to?

"How did you find Arlo so quickly?" Hawke asked.

The man grinned. "We have GPS. We can keep track of each other at all times. When he didn't answer the radio and hadn't moved from the same spot, I went looking for him. Once he was loose, we headed back to the lodge to find the suitcases."

"Did you know what was in the cases?" Hawke asked.

"No. We just knew it was part of the job."

"Worth shooting at law enforcement over?" Pierce asked.

Jerome's face reddened. "Hey, we didn't know he," the man pointed with his chin toward Hawke, "or the others were law enforcement. For all we knew it was someone trying to take the suitcases we'd been paid to protect. Why else would so many people be up on the mountains in those snow conditions?"

"Have you ever done business with the Brother Speed?" Pierce asked.

Jerome's gaze landed on the FBI Agent. "No. They're a motorcycle gang that's into all kinds of illegal shit."

"The person you thought you were working for? The one who yelled at you when you were brought into the jail, he deals with Brother Speed. Those suitcases may have had something to do with the gang. You might want to ask your boss for a vacation for a while. Especially if that man, Kieran Gilmore, gets bail tomorrow. Because I'm sure he'll tell the gang you two screwed up." Hawke watched Jerome's eyes as he slowly realized that the person in the jail wasn't the man they'd been working for and the one they'd let yell at them wasn't even paying for their time. He was working for a gang.

Jerome's face screwed up in rage. "Any chance we can get put in the same cell as that S.O.B?"

Hawke didn't smile on the outside, but he thought that would be something fun to watch, given all the trouble Gilmore had caused him and Dani. And all the lies he'd told. Gilmore had to be a pathological liar. Nothing that came out of his mouth was the truth.

Hawke again nodded toward the door. He and Pierce walked out into the hall.

"Now what?" Pierce asked.

"I don't think these two know anything about the relationship between Barclay and Gilmore or the OMG. It is evident they didn't know they were shooting at police. I didn't hear anyone announce they were law enforcement until after those two fired their first rounds. But then it was the shooting that woke me up. Jerome and Arlo thought they were protecting their mission and didn't know their client was dead." Hawke glanced at both interview rooms. "And they need to let their boss know what happened and have him decide what he wants them to do regarding the Brother Speed."

"I have their boss's information and can contact him and fill him in." Pierce walked down the hall to Sheriff Lindsey's office. He knocked.

"Come in," called out the sheriff.

They entered the office. Hawke sat in the chair in front of the desk. Pierce stood to the side of him.

"Have you figured any of it out? Who are we charging with what?" Lindsey looked up from the folder in front of him on the desk.

Quinn gave a rundown of what they thought about Arlo and Jerome.

Lindsey's face reddened and he started up out of his chair. "They shot at law enforcement!"

Hawke put up a hand, signaling for the man he'd known even before Lindsey became sheriff, to settle back in his chair. "From talking to them, they didn't know we were law enforcement. They'd been sent to do a job. They thought Gilmore was Barclay, the person who had hired them." Hawke went on to tell the sheriff what they'd learned about Gilmore pretending to be Barclay and telling the men to get the suitcases.

Sheriff Lindsey studied Hawke. "Do you still think he killed Barclay in self-defense?"

Hawke shrugged. "If Barclay had faked a crash on the mountain in hopes of killing Gilmore, then, yes, he could have killed Barclay in self-defense. However, I believe both men were out to get rid of one another, thinking the other didn't realize it." He held up both hands. "If we can find solid evidence that Gilmore was trying to take over the Riches legacy, then we can call it murder, whether it was or wasn't, and make a jury believe it."

Pierce stepped forward. "I have agents digging into the Barclay family tree and others who are checking out how deep Gilmore is in the Outlaw Motorcycle gang and Brother Speed."

"How do you propose we keep him locked up until you get all the information?" Lindsey asked, glancing at Hawke then Pierce.

"As soon as the money is picked up and put in evidence, we can let him loose. It might be fun to see who he visits and what kind of reception he receives," Pierce said.

Hawke nodded. "It would be interesting to see how scared Gilmore is of the gang and if he tried to muscle into the Barclay business." He asked Pierce, "Who is second in command in the Barclay family?"

Pierce held up his phone, tapped keys, and scrolled. "It appears to be a sister. Patrick was divorced and has a child living with his ex-wife and the parents are both gone."

"Has the sister been active in the business? Is she married?" Hawke wondered if Gilmore had been working that route as well to get his hands on the Barclay family business.

"The sister has been working in the Seattle store and isn't married but has been dating several different men." Pierce studied Hawke. "What are you thinking?"

"Any chance you can find out if Gilmore was one of the men she's been seeing?" Hawke had learned a long time ago that no one had a perfect family or a perfect relationship.

# Chapter Twenty-five

Pierce dropped Hawke back at Dani's around one. Hawke had asked the FBI Agent to stop at the Rusty Nail while he'd purchased two of the day's special for him and Dani. They could eat them for lunch, or dinner if she'd already eaten.

"Are you and Dani in a serious relationship?" Pierce asked as they pulled up in front of her rented apartment.

"We're talking about purchasing land and a house together." While her apartment was cozy, there wasn't any room for his horses and mule, and he liked to have room to wander outside without walking across a neighbor's land.

"That's serious. And marriage?" Pierce turned the vehicle off.

"Why are you asking these questions?"

"Just curious. She seems to know a lot about your job and helps you come up with answers. Doesn't it bother her that your job is dangerous?" Pierce wasn't looking at him. His steadfast gaze studied the stairs to the apartment.

"She spent twenty-five years in the Air Force flying planes and helicopters in and out of dangerous situations. She understands duty and that I have a responsibility to do my job." He shrugged. "As for marriage, I was burned before and she doesn't seem to need to be legally attached to anyone."

"What about children? Little Hawkes running around?" Pierce asked.

Hawke laughed and said, "Have you been talking to my mom?"

Pierced chuckled and shook his head.

"Dani is getting too old to have a risk-free pregnancy. I'm too busy to deal with raising children. Neither one of us feels the need to be a parent. We are talking about setting up a couple of camps on the mountain to teach teens outdoor survival. We like to work with kids, just don't have the time to raise one right." It was Hawke's turn to study Pierce. "Why are you asking all of these personal questions?"

"Trying to figure out what I want. I was married before, too. It didn't work out. I don't want to screw up again, but I'm getting older and would like to have some kids. You know that old clock ticking that everyone talks about. But the person I'm interested in isn't ready to settle down. I'm afraid when she is, it will be too risky for her to have a child." He sighed. "I don't know why I'm telling you all of this. I haven't said this to anyone else. Just keep knocking it around in my head."

"I'm honored you felt you could talk to me. Now you need to unburden yourself to the woman you have in mind." Hawke opened the door as Dog bounded down the stairs and Tuck stood at the top landing.

"I'll let you know who Gilmore meets up with." Pierce started the vehicle as Hawke eased out onto his feet.

"Thanks. And I'll let you know if I learn anything new."

Pierce studied him for a second and nodded.

"Let me help," Tuck said, standing beside him. "You know you should stay off your feet."

Hawke handed Dani's wrangler the bag with the food and then held onto the railing to help take pressure off his feet as he climbed the stairs. "I plan to spend the rest of the day off them as much as possible."

Inside, using her crutches, Dani stood by the kitchen door. "I hadn't expected you to be gone so long." It wasn't a reprimand, more a question about what all had transpired.

"Have you had lunch?" he asked.

"Yes."

"Tuck, you can put that in the fridge then." Hawke eased his way over to the chair and sat.

The refrigerator door closed, and Tuck walked back into the room. "You want me to stay a little longer?"

"No, we'll be fine. Thank you for staying with Dani." Hawke held out a hand to shake.

Tuck grasped his hand. "If you need me to stay or come back by this evening, I can."

"We should be fine. Any threat that might come our way, won't be until tomorrow."

Dani sat on the couch propping her cast on pillows. "You think Kieran will do something to us?"

"I don't know. I learned some more about the

situation today, but until we really know more about him and his relationship to the man he killed, we won't know what he is truly capable of." Hawke waved at Tuck. "Go home and give your wife and Kitree a hug from us."

Tuck smiled. "That's an easy order. But call if you need anything."

"We will," Dani said.

Tuck walked out, the door closed, and then opened again, and he stuck his head in. "One of you needs to get up and lock this."

Hawke raised a hand in acknowledgment and stood. He hobbled over to the door and snapped the deadbolt into place.

After gathering a sandwich and glasses of iced tea for him and Dani, Hawke sat back in the chair and propped his feet up on a pillow on the coffee table. In between bites, he relayed what they'd learned that morning.

"Right now, your FBI friend is trying to discover information about the Barclay family and learning all he can about Kieran's connection to the motorcycle gang?" Dani asked.

"That's pretty much it." Hawke had finished his sandwich and sipped his tea.

Dani pulled her laptop onto her lap. "I discovered the dead man's sister this morning and have been going through her social media."

Hawke heard the note of satisfaction in her voice. "And what have you discovered?"

"She likes to go out partying and drinking. One of her favorite places is..." Dani spun the computer around for Hawke to see the photo. A tall thin blonde woman in her thirties had her arms around the neck of a man dressed in a black leather jacket sitting on a motorcycle outside of a bar called the 9lb Hammer.

"I take it the tall blonde is the sister?" Hawke studied the man she had her arms around. He was beefy with a scruffy beard and a bandana tied around his long dark hair. He appeared to be about her age, but it was hard to tell in the dark lighting.

"Cecelia, or as she prefers, CeeCee Barclay. Thirty-three. Studied business at Stanford and came back to help run the family businesses. From what I can tell, Patrick was private and liked to acquire money and not spend it. CeeCee is the opposite. She believes if you are making money, you should spend it. And have a good time doing it."

"It's pretty safe to say she might have helped Kieran get in with the Outlaw Motorcycle gang, seeing this photo of her hanging out at a biker bar." Hawke glanced at Dani. It was evident she enjoyed digging up this information. "Any chance you can go on the Boise Riches Pawn and Loan site and see if you can discover the name of the woman who seems to be second in command at the store? I think she's also in with the bikers."

He set his plate and glass on the end table beside his chair and leaned his head back, closing his eyes. It was rare he took a nap during the day but since returning to the valley, he'd been taking a nap every afternoon and still sleeping all night. It was evident his last trip up the mountain had taken more out of him than he'd thought. The tapping of the keys on the laptop lulled him to sleep.

<><><><><><>

Dani glanced over at Hawke. He was sound asleep; his mouth open and soft snores broke the silence in the room once she'd stopped typing. Spending the morning digging up the information she had on CeeCee Barclay had been almost as thrilling as flying. Not quite the same level but discovering more and more about another person's life had been exhilarating. Especially if it could help them get to the bottom of the man's death in her barn and make sure no one came after her and Hawke.

She had the information about Zariah Young, the woman who was listed as assistant manager for the Boise Riches store. Dani had dug around on the social media sites and discovered she also liked biker men and had appeared in a photo with CeeCee Barclay. Both women sat on the back of motorcycles their arms around the men in front of them.

Maybe Kieran had been pulled into helping the motorcycle gang by the women and he and Patrick were trying to get out when the plane went down.

Dog whined at the door.

"Coming." Dani slid the laptop onto the coffee table and settled her feet on the ground. She grasped her crutches and swung her way over to the door. "Don't go too far. We can't come get you out of trouble," she said to Dog, turning the deadbolt and opening the door.

Dog rushed out.

She closed the door and swung her way into the kitchen to make a cup of coffee and grab a cookie that Darlene had brought with her one of the days she'd spent here. A glance at the clock showed her why her stomach was growling. It was nearly 6 p.m. She'd spent several hours on the computer looking up information she hoped would help Hawke and the investigation.

A thought came to her. She hadn't looked up Kieran on social media.

# Chapter Twenty-six

A loud bang brought Hawke out of the dream he'd been having and to his feet. Pain shot up his legs as he tried to remember where he was and why the sound had caused him to panic.

"I'm fine. Everything's fine!" Dani called.

Hawke hobbled into the kitchen and found Dani standing by the stove, a pie tin on the floor at her feet. "What happened?" He shooed Dog back and knelt to pick up the—"Ouch!" hot tin.

"I put the food you brought from the Rusty Nail in the oven to warm up. When I pulled the first one out it slipped and landed on the floor."

"You put this foil on here tight enough it just spilled some sauce." Hawke used a towel to pick up the tin. "Dog, clean."

Dog went to work licking the sauce off the floor.

"Sit down. I'll get the other one," Hawke said, moving so Dani could go by him and collapse on a chair.

She handed him the thick oven mitts she had on her hands.

Once they were seated and enjoying the meal, Dani said, "Want to know what else I learned this afternoon?"

Hawke set his fork down and picked up his glass of iced tea. "Whose life were you digging around in?"

She smiled. "First Zariah Young. She's Kieran's assistant manager."

Hawke nodded. "What did you find out?"

"She also likes bikers and knows CeeCee Barclay."

Hawke stopped sipping his tea and set the glass down. "Interesting." He picked up his cell phone sitting on the table.

"What are you doing?"

"Seeing if Pierce knows this." Hawke scrolled through his contacts.

"Wait. I also discovered that Kieran is a member of the Brother Speed. Or at least he shows up in some photos of the group outside of biker bars. I also found him in a couple of photos with CeeCee sitting on his bike, with her arms around his waist."

Hawke narrowed his eyes and studied her. "How can you tell it was the two of them? Wouldn't they have helmets on?"

"They are sitting on a bike in front of a biker bar, no helmets, staring at the camera. As if they were saying, look at us." Dani picked up a chicken leg. "I would think whoever has been watching the motorcycle gang would have photos of all three of the people somewhere."

"Yeah." Hawke pushed Pierce's name and the call icon. The phone rang four times. His finger hovered over the off icon when Pierce answered.

"Hawke, what's up?" The Fed sounded frazzled.

"Did you know that Kieran, Patrick's sister, and Kieran's assistant were all part of the biker culture?" Hawke watched Dani pick at the chicken leg as she listened.

"We knew about CeeCee. Who is Kieran's assistant?" The phone made scratching noises and he heard muffled voices.

"Zariah Young." Hawke asked Dani, "Can you bring up an image of her so I can describe her to Pierce?"

Dani shoved up on her crutches and went into the other room.

"Boise is shorthanded. I'm out in the field helping to apprehend a wanted felon."

"I can call you back or you call later."

Dani set the laptop on the table and thumped down onto the chair.

"I'll try to call you in a couple of hours. I'm interested in knowing why that woman's name hasn't come up. Later." The connection ended.

Hawke stared at his phone. "That was an interesting comment."

"What?" Dani asked.

Hawke relayed the conversation to Dani.

"It sounds to me like someone has been keeping Zariah's name out of things," Dani said, picking up her drink.

"I wonder why?" Hawke finished off his meal and cleaned up the table. He slid his chair over next to Dani's. "Show me the photos you found."

They spent an hour with Dani going back through the photos she'd saved and the sites where she'd found them so Hawke could study other photos as well.

By the time his phone rang, they had settled onto the

couch and Hawke had discovered that Zariah was only ever photographed with the same man on the same motorcycle. They were in front of different bars in different poses, but something felt off about the photos.

"Did you get the bad guy?" Hawke answered, seeing Pierce's name.

"Yeah. He was being a dick and had taken his girlfriend hostage." Pierce sighed. "We managed to get her away and take him out. Not the way legal wanted it to go. They were hoping for the man to be caught and confess to several killings."

Hawke nodded. "There are families out there looking for closure."

"That's why we do what we do, right?" Another deep sigh. "That's over. Now tell me what you found out."

"You want to wait until morning? You could use a quiet night after what you've been through." Hawke knew how hard it was to calm yourself after you'd had adrenaline pumping for hours while trying to defuse a situation.

"No. I'd rather think about this."

"Okay." Hawke went on to tell him about the images Dani found of the three people, but also his feeling the photos of Zariah felt off.

"Have Dani send me what she found, and I'll ask about Zariah Young."

"She's sending them now." Hawke had handed Dani Pierce's business card when they'd started talking. He'd figured the man would want the images sent to him.

He heard an intake of breath. "Is the first photo she sent of Zariah?"

Hawke asked Dani.

216

She nodded.

"Yes."

"I'll go talk to her tomorrow, while I'm still in Boise. Thanks for the photos." Pierce ended the call.

"What was that all about?" Dani asked.

"I think Pierce knows Zariah and she may be undercover."

The next morning Hawke and Dani had just settled into the living room after breakfast when there was a knock at the door. Dog stood by the door, his tail wagging as Hawke hobbled over. The animal probably either heard or smelled whoever was out there and they were friends.

Hawke opened the door.

Herb and Darlene stood on the landing, smiling.

"I brought you some fresh muffins," Darlene said, pushing by him and into the living room.

Herb shrugged. "She insisted we had to come over and check on you two."

"I'm sure it was just her," Hawke said sarcastically, following his landlords into the living room.

Darlene had already moved into the kitchen. From the sounds coming from the room, she was making coffee.

"How's the leg?" Herb asked Dani.

"Good. It hurts less and less each day." She'd turned to sit with her foot propped up on the coffee table.

Hawke sat down beside her on the couch. That way they were a solid front for whatever questions the older couple bombarded them with.

Herb sat in the chair Hawke had vacated when the couple arrived.

Darlene bustled out of the kitchen, carrying a tray of muffins and four small plates with napkins. "We might as well enjoy these while they're fresh and we visit."

A glance at Dani's face and Hawke wanted to laugh. The woman who wasn't used to having her space invaded was working hard to be genial.

The older woman disappeared into the kitchen.

"Hasn't been anyone around asking about you," Herb said, picking up a plate and napkin and placing a muffin on it.

"There may be no one. However, if they do show up, you don't know where I am." Hawke followed his landlord's actions, putting a muffin on a plate and handing it to Dani before putting a muffin on a plate for himself.

Darlene returned with four mugs and a pot of coffee. She placed the mugs on the coffee table on the opposite end of Dani's cast and filled the cups. Then she handed one to each person.

"How's the leg coming along?" she asked, handing Dani a cup.

"Fine. It's starting to itch." Dani sipped the coffee.

"The horses are doing fine. They don't get as spoiled when you're away, but they aren't starving. I let them out in the arena last night to run around." Darlene sat down in the last available chair.

"Thank you. Even if I were home, I wouldn't be hobbling up and down the stairs to take care of them." Hawke would have to come up with something good to thank these two for taking care of Jack, Horse, and Dot.

"Yes, you would be," Herb said. "I think this is the best way for you to heal quicker. If you were at our place you'd be going up and down the stairs and probably even driving around when you shouldn't be."

"He has a point," Dani said, staring at Hawke.

He sighed. They all knew him too well. "I agree this is the best place for me."

Darlene's smile grew wider and her eyes lit up.

"I don't suppose there's anything you can tell us?" Herb said.

Hawke's phone rang. It was still sitting on the kitchen table.

"I'll get that." Darlene bounced up off the chair as if it were a trampoline and headed into the kitchen. She returned and handed the phone to Hawke as it continued to ring.

"Hello," he answered, seeing that it was Pierce.

"I was just beginning to think I needed to send someone to check on you," Pierce replied.

"The phone was in another room." Hawke stood and headed to the bedroom. He didn't need his already nosey landlords hearing more than they needed to hear. A glance at Dani left him with a searing gaze that said, don't leave me alone.

He walked into the room and closed the door. "My landlords came to check on us. I'm in another room now. What did you learn?"

"Zariah Young is undercover DEA. I recognized her photo from an operation I had with the agency several years ago. She's the one who's been feeding information about Gilmore and the Brothers Speed to us and DEA. Right after Gilmore was locked up, she received a visit from the gang. She doesn't think they discovered her true identity but to keep her alive and able to give evidence, she was pulled and put in a safe house."

"What about the sister? The photos of her with

219

bikers didn't look photoshopped. And the one with her and Zariah." Hawke wondered how this whole thing went from him finding a body in Dani's barn to money laundering and biker gangs.

"The sister is in over her head with the Outlaw Motorcycle Gang according to Zariah. She is the one who approached Gilmore to start laundering money. She thought Bear Callaghan, the leader of the Boise gang, was going to marry her. He dumped her right after they started using Gilmore's business."

"What about Gilmore? Is he okay with it or was he coerced?" Kieran hadn't looked like a man who feared for his life the last time they'd talked. He'd been too smug. As if he thought someone would bail him out of everything.

"According to Zariah's reports, Gilmore is in love with CeeCee. He became a biker because she liked the bad boys." Pierce said the last two words sarcastically.

Hawke could hear the murmur of voices in the other room. "Did Zariah know why Barclay and Gilmore had the two suitcases of money and where they were going?"

"She said, what she'd overheard of the conversations between the men, Patrick had learned of the gang's takeover of his businesses and was hoping to buy his way out of what had happened. But Zariah said she'd heard Gilmore talking on the phone to someone about how they'd have enough money to disappear. She wasn't sure who he was talking to. When she tried to get his phone to see who he'd called, he caught her. That was one of the reasons she was pulled, along with everything else that has gone on."

"Has anyone confirmed with the sister that it's her brother who is dead? I've not seen an official photo of him. For all we know the body I found may not even be him." Hawke didn't think Barclay was a very smart businessman if first the outlaw gang took over his franchises and then he thought he could buy them out with two suitcases of money.

"It is Barclay. The sister does know. She's been hiding inside the Barclay estate outside of Seattle since she received the news of her brother's death."

"Who's minding the business?" Hawke wanted to know who would be next in line to take over if something happened to the sister.

"The local one is a long-time employee. The corporate offices, according to an agent who went there asking questions, looks like a morgue. He said everyone is just sitting at their desks, not moving or talking. It seems no one knows what to do without Barclay giving orders." Pierce let out a long breath. "I'm glad I don't have to question them."

"I think we need to visit with Gilmore again," Hawke said.

"Can't. He was released on bail today."

"Who bailed him out?" And Hawke wondered where the man had gone. Back to Boise, or continued on his way out of the country to avoid the bikers.

"It looks like it was a lawyer that is on retainer to the OMG."

"Is anyone following Gilmore? I'd be curious to see if he pays his respects to the sister or he asks for forgiveness from the gang." Hawke had sat on the bed to relieve his feet. He wished they'd heal faster so he could be out doing some leg work.

"We have someone keeping an eye on him. You should be safe."

"I'm not worried about me. I want to know where he goes and who he sees. I want to know whose money is in the suitcases. Gilmore's, Barclay's, or the gang's."

"We're working on that, too. Just stay put and I'll keep you up to speed on what's going on. I'll talk to you later." Pierce hung up abruptly.

Hawke wondered if the agent had tried to stop him from asking more questions or if Pierce had been called away by something. He shoved his phone in his shirt pocket and walked back into the living room.

Herb and Darlene grinned at him. Dani raised an eyebrow.

"These muffins are delicious, Darlene. Is this a new recipe?" Hawke asked to show them he had nothing to discuss. At least not until his landlords left.

# Chapter Twenty-seven

As soon as Herb and Darlene cleared the door, Dani started asking Hawke about the phone call. He told her what he'd learned from Pierce.

"So, you think Kieran is either heading to Seattle to see CeeCee or he's fleeing the bikers?" Dani asked.

"That's what would be logical. He's either checking to make sure the woman he loves is okay or he's trying to save his ass." Hawke studied her. "Which do you think?"

"Save his ass. He never once acted like a man who was in love with anyone other than himself." Dani said it with such confidence Hawke believed her. "He was most likely just using her to get more claim to the family business."

"You were around him more than I was. I'd go with your gut reaction." He thought about that for several moments. "The money he needs to leave the country is sitting in evidence at the county office. Unless he has more stashed somewhere…" Hawke pulled out his phone. "I think we need to have a realtor come over and show us some property."

Dani stared at him as if he'd said he was going to behead someone. "What?"

"I know a woman who just became a realtor and who knows her way around a courthouse and property records. She could look into whether or not Kieran has property other than his business and house. Someplace that he might be hiding more money." Hawke scrolled through his contacts and found Wallowa County Realty.

"Wallowa County Realty, how may I direct your call?" a voice he didn't recognize answered.

"I'd like to speak to Gail Wexmen, please."

"She's out with a client. May I have her call you back?"

"Yes." He left his name and phone number.

He relayed what he'd learned when Dani continued to stare at him.

"Is she the woman who has been supplying you with the places you've been showing me?" Dani asked.

"Yes. She only recently received her realtor's license, but she was a big help in a murder last year and I like her honesty." He walked into the kitchen. "What can we make for dinner?"

It was close to six when Hawke's phone rang. They had just sat down to eat.

"Hawke," he answered the call.

"This is Gail Wexmen. You left a message for me to call you."

"Yes, Gail. It sounds like you've had a long day. I was going to ask if you could come show my friend and

I more photos of a couple of the places you'd sent links for." Hawke wasn't going into detail over the phone about what he really wanted.

"Oh, wonderful! Which ones are you thinking of?" Her enthusiasm made him wish he hadn't used their interest in property as a ruse to get her here.

"Can you bring your computer, and we can look at everything you have?" Hawke caught Dani staring at him. They hadn't completely discussed whether or not they were ready to do this and here he was getting the young woman's hopes up.

"Sure. How about tomorrow morning at nine? Where do you live?"

Hawke gave her Dani's address. "Come up the stairs alongside the garage. We're in the apartment above."

"I'll see you then."

He ended the call and shrugged. "We're looking at property tomorrow at nine."

Gail was punctual. She knocked on the door at ten till nine. Both he and Dani had showered, eaten breakfast, and were sitting in the living room waiting. Pierce hadn't called with anything new. Hawke had talked to Sheriff Lindsey to confirm that Kieran had been released the day before. They needed more evidence that he had actually killed Barclay, or it would go down as self-defense. They hadn't found the airplane.

Hawke was just about to ask Dani how a crashed plane could remain hidden from the sky when Gail arrived. He walked to the door and let her in. He'd swung his feet out of bed this morning and had only minor discomfort. They were on the mend.

"Mr. Hawke, it is good to see you." Her gaze

scanned the small apartment as he led her into the living room.

"Gail, this is Dani Singer. She and I are the ones who will be purchasing the property." Hawke motioned for Gail to sit on the couch next to Dani, who had her leg propped up on the coffee table.

"How did you hurt your leg?" Gail asked.

"The horse I was riding fell in the snow and I landed on a rock," Dani said, as though she'd been asked the question a million times, when in fact she hadn't.

"Ouch! I'm glad all you came away with was a broken leg. It could have been worse." Gail pulled her computer out of her bag. "I'm assuming Mr. Hawke—"

Dani snickered.

Hawke interrupted. "Just Hawke. Don't put a mister in front of it, please."

"Oh, all right. Did Hawke show you the properties I'd sent him?" Gail asked.

"A couple," Dani replied.

"Did you like any of them?" Gail watched Dani as attentively as Hawke watched suspects when he questioned them.

"I kind of liked the one that had the smaller house," Dani said.

Hawke was surprised. She hadn't said one thing good or bad about any of the places he'd shown her. Had she thought he hadn't been sincere in his desire to get a place?

"The Myer place. That house is cute!" Gail tapped on her keys and soon was showing them both the property lines via a satellite image and more photos of the barns and the house.

Hawke had to admit, it was a pretty place with

Hurricane Creek winding through it. There was a field that could be hayed to feed the animals through the winter and several pastures to keep his horses year-round and keep the lodge horses in the winter.

"I had a new listing this week. I haven't had time to make up any pamphlets yet, but I can show you the aerial photos and the photos that have been taken. Mind you it is December and things aren't green and pretty." Gail tapped the keys on her laptop and up popped a newer house but in the style of an old farm house. There was one barn, some corrals, and only perimeter fencing. They'd have to build cross fences.

"I don't think this is what we want," Hawke said, thinking about all the fencing he'd have to do and the large house was more than he and Dani needed.

Dani leaned forward. "The other place is pretty because of all the trees and the small house. But this place has more open area. I could actually land the helicopter here and store it off the mountain in the winter."

As Dani spoke Hawke took a harder look at the property. His lips quivered as he recognized the land. The listing was to the east of Herb and Darlene. "What's the address of this place?"

Gail rambled it off and Hawke grinned. Close enough the Trembleys could help him take care of the animals when he wasn't around.

Hawke glanced at Dani. "This is next door to Herb and Darlene."

Dani's gaze flicked up from the photos to him. "Is that good or bad?"

Hawke laughed and said, "Good. It means when you are at the lodge and I have to work overtime, they can check on my horses and Dog."

She smiled. "Is that why you've been dragging your feet? No one to take care of your animals if we moved and were both busy?"

He nodded.

Gail smiled and started to shut her laptop. "I can get you a showing today or tomorrow."

Hawke stalled her hands. "I have a favor to ask of you."

She studied him. "What is it?"

"Can you look up records for other states?" Hawke knew he was asking her to do something he should have asked Pierce to check. But once they discovered if Gilmore had other property, he could give that information to Pierce along with his theory.

"I can. What do you need?" Gail pushed her laptop open and waited with her hands over the keyboard.

"I would like to know if Kieran Gilmore owns property in Oregon, Idaho, or Washington. And the addresses, please." Hawke stood. "Would you like something to drink?"

"Hot tea if you have it. With sugar." Her fingers were tapping away as he walked into the kitchen.

His chest hummed with happiness that Dani had liked the piece of property next to the Trembleys. He couldn't believe their good luck that the property was even available. The only downfall was the fact they hadn't talked about moving this soon. But if the place was perfect, and it was given the location, they needed to move on it. Knowing Herb was next door, he would help Hawke with the fences, and they could hire him to put up the hay with his equipment.

A smile spread across his lips as he carried a tray

with two cups of hot water, a small dish Dani kept various teas in, and a sugar pot into the living room.

Dani scribbled on a notepad as Gail read off her screen.

"You must be having some luck," Hawke said, placing the tray on the end away from Dani's cast.

"I started in Oregon because those are the quickest for me to get into." Gail studied the teas in the dish, picked one, and placed it in a cup of hot water.

Hawke handed Dani the dish of teabags.

She plucked her favorite tea and he handed her a steaming cup.

"Does that mean he has property in Oregon?" Hawke asked.

Dani nodded. "He owns the Riches Pawnshop building in Springfield."

Hawke wondered if he would have stashed skip money there. It seemed too likely someone working there would come across it.

"I'm digging through the Washington records now. So far, nothing." Gail sipped her tea and scrolled with her right hand.

He pointed to Dani's laptop. "Did you learn anything about where he grew up when you were checking him out on social media?"

"I saw he went to high school in Hailey, Idaho." Dani pulled her computer onto her lap. "I didn't see anything about family, but I can look in the census and see if he still has family there."

Hawke nodded.

"I can't find anything in Washington. I'll look in Idaho." As Gail typed, she asked. "Does this have anything to do with the body they found at Charlie's

Lodge?"

Dani and Hawke exchanged a glance.

"Why would you say that?" Hawke asked.

"I've heard rumors that a plane crashed and bags of money were hidden at the lodge, but no one can get in because of all the snow." Gail stopped typing. "If no one can get in, how did they haul a body out?"

"I'd appreciate it if you'd help stop the rumors," Dani said. "I own Charlie's Lodge and would prefer the place is still standing when I go back up in the spring."

Gail studied Dani. "You own the lodge? I didn't know that." She glanced at Hawke. "And you? Do you own it too?"

Hawke shook his head. "It's all Dani's. I'm only a State Trooper, looking to get out of the apartment I live in over an arena, and Dani wants a place bigger than this to stay at in the winter and when she's down here picking up clients."

"I see. No wedding in your future?"

Hawke and Dani must have both given her a disgruntled look because she quickly dropped her attention to her laptop.

He glanced at Dani. She just grinned and continued typing on her computer. Hawke wandered into the kitchen and made himself a cup of coffee. His phone rang. Pierce.

Sitting in a chair, he answered, "What have you found?"

"Right to the point. I like that about you," Pierce said and chuckled. "At the moment, Gilmore seems to be hiding in his house outside of Boise. According to surveillance on CeeCee Barclay, she's not left her home either."

"And the Brother Speed? What are they doing?" Hawke wondered that they hadn't made a move to find a way to get their money back. If assuming it was their money.

"They seem to be business as usual. I'm starting to think that money wasn't theirs. There hasn't been any of them seen around either the business or Gilmore's house. We've also been monitoring Gilmore's calls. He hasn't called anyone."

"Unless he is using a phone you don't know about?" Hawke went on to tell Pierce about how he and Dani didn't think Gilmore really had feelings for CeeCee and might have just been using her to get to the Barclay fortune.

"We thought of that. Zariah is at the Barclay mansion visiting with CeeCee to see how involved she thought she was with Gilmore and if she was knowingly and willingly bringing the Outlaws into the business."

"I have something?" Gail called from the other room.

"Who was that?" Pierce asked. Suspicion rang in his voice.

"Dani and I are looking into purchasing a place. Our realtor is here going through listings." He wasn't lying but he was leaving out information he knew Pierce would be interested in.

"So this means you two are getting married?"

Hawke let out a deep sigh. "No. It means we are living together. Neither one of us wants to be legally bound to the other."

"I get it. That way you can walk out whenever you want, but having property together, will still be messy." Pierce talked to someone. "Gotta go. They say Gilmore came out of his house and got in his car."

Hawke wanted to say, he was probably headed to Blaine County since he grew up in Hailey, Idaho but kept his thoughts to himself. He stood and walked into the living room. "What did you find?"

Gail glanced at Dani who motioned for her to go first. "I found a Gilmore with property in Custer County, outside of Stanley. It's up in the mountains."

Dani raised her hand with a finger pointing up. "Delwin Gilmore homesteaded the property, and it has passed down to each generation after his death. Right now, it is in Kieran's father's name, but I'm guessing Kieran is the only one who uses it."

"Why do you think he is the only one to use it?" Hawke asked.

"Because he is an only child with three female cousins who no longer live in Idaho." Dani grinned. "Though if they came to visit, they might go up there for a mini-vacation."

"This property is secluded?" He pulled out his cell phone and opened his Maps app. "Looks like it's three hours to Stanley and then however long it would take to get to the property. I'm sure with the storms we had there has to be more than the usual amount of snow over there as well." Hawke stared at the small screen. He needed to call Pierce back and let him know what they believed.

He scrolled and pressed the FBI agent's name.

"Special Agent Pierce."

"It's Hawke. Is Gilmore headed north?"

"Yeah. How did you know?"

"We discovered his father has property up outside of Stanley. He's either going there to hide or pick up traveling money he stashed there." Hawke waited for

Pierce to tell him this was up to the FBI.

"We know about the property. From what I've been told there isn't any way into it, with all the snow. But thanks." Pierce ended the call.

Hawke growled.

"What's wrong?" Gail asked.

Dani knew not to ask.

"Nothing." He sat in the chair opposite the couch. "How about we set up a time tomorrow for us to look at that property."

# Chapter Twenty-eight

Gail left after using Dani's copy machine to print out pages on the property they would look at the next day.

"Are you sure you're ready to purchase property?" Dani asked when they sat down to eat a sandwich in the kitchen.

"No. But I've been dragging my feet because I worried about the horses and Dog on days when I might be detained. Having Herb and Darlene next door makes me think this is the right place. And you liked there would be space for the helicopter to land and room to build a hangar." The more Hawke thought about it, he didn't see any downside to them purchasing the land.

"It's an awfully large house," Dani said.

He could see she wasn't up to taking care of that much house. Neither was he. "We can get someone to come in and clean. I'm sure Darlene knows a young woman who could benefit from cleaning the house once a week."

Dani studied him. "You don't mind having a stranger in the house? They'd have to clean in the summer when no one is around."

"I can do background checks on the people we're considering." But Hawke was sure Darlene would only suggest people of good character.

She smiled. "I would like to get out of this cramped apartment."

He grasped her hand as she picked up the bag of chips. "After spending so much time with me lately, you think you could handle me full time?" Peering into her eyes he saw the answer.

"We haven't killed each other yet. Not even an argument. I think we'll be fine."

"Me too."

His phone rang.

Sheriff Lindsey.

"Hawke."

"It's Lindsey. We received more reports from forensics on the body. You want to come take a look at them?"

Hawke glanced at Dani. "Sure, I'll be there in an hour." He ended the call. "Want to go for a ride to Alder? After we can run by and see the Kimbals."

Dani smiled. "It would be nice to get out of here for a while. That was one of the things I was looking forward to most tomorrow. Just getting out of here."

"Now you can go somewhere two days in a row."

Dani said she'd just keep Dog company in the pickup while Hawke read the reports. He swung through the Shake Shack and bought her a milkshake and Dog an ice cream cone before parking his vehicle in front of the County building.

Inside, the deputy at the front desk told him he could find a print copy of the reports in the small office reserved for visiting law enforcement. He entered the room and found the folder with a note from Lindsey.

*Check out the toxicology report.*

Hawke turned the pages in the folder until he found the blood test results. There were traces of Vicodin in Barclay's system. Reading further, the pathologist had asked for the victim's medical records. Barclay had never been prescribed an opioid.

It was a drug that was misused but why would a pilot take Vicodin before or during a flight?

He texted Dani. *Is there any reason a pilot would take Vicodin before flying?*

*Only if they wanted to crash.*

It appeared Barclay may not have planned the landing on the mountain. Someone had given him a drug that would mess with his reflexes, vision, and perception. Yet the two men had walked away from the crash and made it to the lodge. Only to argue and attack one another.

Hawke really wanted to find the aircraft. He decided to hire Hector Ramirez to fly him over the area southeast of the lodge. Returning his attention to the report, he read that the Medical Examiner believed the Vicodin had accounted for unusually rapid blood loss due to the blow to the head.

Now Hawke wondered about the timing of events when Barclay was struck, and Gilmore was shot. Nothing about this made any sense. Not the homicide, the flight, the suitcases with money, and the motorcycle gang being involved. They were missing something.

He took a photo of the blood results and the stomach contents and closed the report. At the front desk, he told the deputy he'd left the file in the room. He walked out to his pickup and opened the door.

Dog had ice cream on the end of his nose and Dani was laughing. She swung her leg with the cast down to the floorboard.

"This is a nice welcome," Hawke said, sliding in and starting the vehicle. "I need to make a detour before we go to Tuck and Sage's place."

"We're just along for the ride," Dani said, buckling her seat belt.

Hawke drove out of Alder toward Prairie Creek.

"Does this have anything to do with what you just read?" Dani asked, shoving her napkin in the shake cup.

"Yes. I want to find the plane that supposedly crashed, leaving the two men on the mountain." Hawke stared ahead, trying to figure out if they hadn't been in a plane, why or who had dropped them where they did.

"Did anyone think to check if either of the men had pilot's licenses?"

Hawke glanced over at the woman staring back at him. "I haven't heard of anyone doing it." He pulled over to the side of the road and pulled out his phone. Scrolling he found Sheriff Lindsey's number. It rang.

"Lindsey."

"Sheriff, did anyone verify if either Barclay or Gilmore had a pilot's license?"

"Hawke, did you read the report? See the toxicology results?"

"Yes. That's why I'm asking. I'm also going to have Hector take me up in his helicopter tomorrow and see if we can find the plane." Hawke was studying Dani. Her scrunched-up face said she wished she didn't have a broken leg so she could fly him.

"I'll check and get back to you." The call ended.

Hawke pulled back onto the road and continued.

"Hector is a good pilot," Dani mumbled.

"I'd rather be flying with you, but under the circumstances…"

"Yeah. And I'm pretty sure I won't fit in his helicopter with three of us." She was quiet until they turned onto the road that would take them to the airport.

"When my leg is healed enough, he could fly me in to get my helicopter. I could still get repairs done before I'm able to fly." She relaxed in the seat.

Hawke turned into the small airport and up to the grungy building with a crooked sign that said: Office.

"Can I come in?" Dani asked.

"If you feel up to it." Hawke opened the back door of his extended cab pickup and pulled out her crutches. He opened the passenger door and she slid out, settling the crutches under her arms.

Dog stood on the seat, sniffing.

"You can get out but don't go very far," Hawke said.

The animal jumped down and Hawke closed the door.

Dani had already made her way to the office. Hawke walked in behind her.

"Dani girl, what brings you here, and what happened to you?" Hector Ramirez dropped his feet to the floor and set down a can of soda. The ever-present cigar remained clamped between two fingers. He was a retired Army and ODFW pilot.

"I had an accident with a horse," Dani said, sitting

in the folding chair in front of the vintage metal desk.

Hector shook his head. "The only thing to put between your legs and be safe is a joystick."

Dani laughed.

Hawke stared at them. It must be a pilot joke. "What is a joystick?"

"It's the lever between a pilot's legs that moves a helicopter from side to side and forwards and back," Dani said.

"You're out of uniform and hauled this young lady in here in a cast, what's up?" Hector asked, easing back in his chair.

"I want to hire you to take me up the Minam River beyond the lodge. Supposedly, a plane crashed up there two weeks ago. But so far no one has been able to find it." Hawke saw the older man's eyes dart to Dani.

"It wasn't you who crashed, was it?" Hector's gaze dropped to Dani's cast.

"No, I told you, I received this from riding a horse. We were headed up to the lodge so I could fly my helicopter out for the winter."

"Your bird didn't make it out?" Hector asked.

"No. I'm hoping when I get this cast off you can fly me up and I'll bring it out then."

"There will be a lot of snow to remove to get it off the ground." Hector watched her close.

"I know. I'll take help." Dani smiled at Hawke.

Hector slapped his hand on his desk, making them both jump. "When do you want to go looking for this crash?"

"Tomorrow afternoon," Hawke said.

"I'll have the bird fueled up and ready to go. Should be back before dark. My eyesight's not what it used to be."

Hawke held out his hand.

Hector clenched his hand.

"I appreciate this. If I felt this one would behave herself, I'd have hiked in and looked for it." Hawke released the man's small hand.

"This way is warmer and quicker. What time tomorrow?"

"I'll be here at one." Hawke glanced at Dani. She nodded.

"I'll be ready and waiting."

Hawke waited for Dani to get to her feet and he opened the door. "Thanks, Hector."

The man waved as he watched Dani swing her way out of the building. He motioned for Hawke to close the door.

Hawke did and faced him. "What's up?"

"That little lady is going to be able to fly again, right? I've seen the glow she gets landing and taking off. She'll be lost if she can't fly."

"Her doctor said everything is healing just fine." Hawke hadn't realized how much the older man thought of Dani until today.

"Good. Good. Go on, she's going to need help getting into that beast of a truck you have."

Hawke grinned and exited the building. Dani already sat in the passenger seat. Her crutches leaned against the back door.

"What was that all about?" she asked.

"Hector wanted to make sure you were going to be able to still fly." Hawke closed her door, grabbed the crutches, and opening the back, placed them inside. "I told him you were going to be as good as new when the cast came off."

"I hope so."

Hawke closed the door and climbed into the driver's side. "What do you mean? You heard the doctor. It is healing nicely and everything should work as normal once you get the cast off and do some physical therapy."

"I've had a reoccurring dream where they take the cast off and my leg has shrunk." Dani didn't look at him. She stared down at her clenched hands.

"Hey. The doctor was optimistic. You should be, too. Come on. Let's go visit with Kitree."

# Chapter Twenty-nine

The next morning, Hawke drove Dani over to the property next door to the Trembleys. He'd called Herb the night before asking questions about the property. It didn't surprise Hawke to see Herb chatting with Gail when they pulled up to the house.

Hawke helped Dani out of the pickup while Dog whined and begged Herb to pet him.

"Do you want to look at the house first or the property?" Gail asked. "It will be warmer in the house if you want to take a spin around the property now."

"Should I have stayed in the pickup?" Dani asked.

"No. I brought over our ATVs." Herb waved a hand and Hawke spotted the his and hers version of ATVs his landlords had purchased five years ago.

"I'll ride behind Herb and you two can use the other one," Gail said.

"You should have brought over my horses," Hawke said, not liking the idea of bumping around on the small four-wheeled contraption.

"Dani wouldn't have been comfortable on a horse," Herb said, swinging a leg over the more worn vehicle.

Hawke stepped on the other one and threw his leg over. Then he patiently waited for Dani to pull her body up onto the seat behind him with her good leg next to his and the one in the cast sticking out straight.

Herb drove slow, and Gail shouted comments while pointing.

"This is a pretty place," Dani said, holding him around the waist.

"I have always liked Herb's place, but I hadn't thought about there being a place in the same area available." Hawke caught Herb smiling at them. His landlords would be busting their buttons if he and Dani moved in next door.

Gail had been right. After riding the ATVs through the three inches of snow, it was a relief to walk into the warm house.

Hawke scanned the empty rooms. "When did the owners move out?"

"Last week. The husband inherited his uncle's place in southeast Washington and the wife found a job at a hospital up there." Gail spread a notebook out on the kitchen counter. "Sorry, there isn't anywhere for you to sit," she said.

Hawke walked over, grabbed Dani around the waist, and sat her on the counter next to Gail's book.

The younger woman giggled.

Dani rolled her eyes and Hawke chuckled.

"Do you want to look at more places?" Gail asked.

Dani and Hawke said, "No," at the same time.

Herb grinned.

Hawke never tired of looking at the Eagle Cap Wilderness from horseback or from the air. As he and Hector flew up the Minam River canyon, he enjoyed the view of the ragged rock mountain tops, cloaked in snow. Below the white tops, pine, fir, and lodgepole limbs dipped from the weight of snow. He could see tracks where a herd of elk had forced their way through the drifts, headed down the mountains. The snow was so deep they could only eat the moss on trees to survive. They would move down to the lower country to forage. The large amount of snow so soon in the mountains would make all the wildlife change their usual patterns. However, all the moisture was a good omen that the farmers and ranchers would have plenty of water for their crops this summer.

"Do you have any idea where this plane is?" Hector asked.

"I figure it must be southeast of Charlie's because they were flying from Boise. And it shouldn't be that far away, because they didn't appear to have been out in the cold long enough to get frostbite considering how they were both dressed." Hawke didn't glance at the pilot. He kept his gaze on the white landscape below.

Hector dipped the helicopter downward, dodging trees and checking out the areas he thought would make a good place to land in an emergency. "If we go much farther, it ruins your idea they weren't far from the lodge."

Hawke agreed. "Go a little farther then turn around and head back this way. Sometimes things look different from a new direction."

"Roger." Hector continued for another mile, then

did a circle and headed back higher up, where they could see farther in all directions. "Was the storm before or after they landed?"

"Either after or when they landed." Hawke spotted something. "Circle around." He pointed. "Over there. It looked like a mound I don't remember." He'd patrolled these mountains the last seventeen years and knew nearly every inch of them.

Hector circled and Hawke caught sight of the spot. "Just to the right." He pointed.

He pulled on his coat as Hector hovered about thirty feet in the air above the spot.

"What are you doing?" Hector asked.

"Can you get closer to the ground? I'll drop out and see if it is the plane." Hawke was strapping on the snowshoes he'd brought with him.

"I wondered why you had those things. Don't take too long. It's going to get dark and be harder for me to navigate with my vision." Hector slowly lowered the aircraft to about six feet off the ground.

Hawke jumped out, landing on his feet, and found himself buried in the snow up to his thighs. Struggling to pull his snowshoe-bound feet out of the hole, he finally stood and walked over to the mound. Using his hands, he probed into the frozen whiteness. Under a foot of crusty snow, he felt something hard and smooth. He rapped and heard a hollow knock. He'd found the plane. With all the snow it was hard to tell what damage had been done during the landing.

The thump of the helicopter hovering overhead had him wishing he had more time to dig and see what he could learn from the aircraft. There was too much snow to dig through to even find a way into the plane. The men must have survived the crash with little physical trauma, opened the doors, climbed out, and walked away carrying the suitcases.

Hawke reluctantly moved away from the mound and motioned for Hector to pick him up. The only thing he'd learned was where the plane had landed. Without being able to get inside, he hadn't really advanced the investigation. Already, his brain snapped and flashed thinking of a way to get back up here and take a look in the aircraft.

Hector lowered the helicopter, hovering four feet off the top of the snow. Hawke was glad the top layer was crusty and didn't blow around from the rotors. He ducked and headed to the aircraft, opening the door and crawling in. He'd barely settled in the seat when the helicopter rose, heading over the mountains faster than when they'd been looking for the plane.

"Now what are you going to do?" Hector asked.

"Borrow a snowmobile and come have a look at it." Hawke stared out the window. The aircraft had to hold some answers. The pilot had been drugged. When had that happened? Was that what caused the emergency landing? And who had done it?

Walking into Dani's apartment, he found her seated at the kitchen counter scribbling numbers on a piece of paper.

"What's this?" he asked.

"I'm figuring out how we can make that place we looked at this morning work." She glanced up and raised her empty mug. "Could you pour me more hot water?"

He smiled and filled her cup.

"What did you learn?" she asked, shoving the paper

to the middle of the table.

"We found the airplane. It was about four miles from the lodge." He poured himself a cup of coffee and sat down across from her.

She studied him. "Did you learn anything else?"

"No. It's covered in over a foot of snow. It's going to require digging to get in and see what I can find."

Her eyes narrowed. "You're going back out there, aren't you?"

"We can't wait until spring to get answers to solve Barclay's homicide. If we can determine where he ingested the drugs and follow that to what he ate or drank, it might point us toward the killer."

"I suppose you've already set up the trip?" She continued to watch him.

"I called the sheriff on my drive back here. He's rounding up three snowmobiles and a deputy and state trooper to go with me tomorrow. We'll dig until we can open a door, and we'll bag everything up as evidence."

She held a hand out to him. "You're still on medical leave."

He grinned. "Which is why I can go. If I were back working, Sergeant Spruel would make me stay down here."

"You don't need to expose your feet to more cold weather and what if you all get stuck up there?"

Dani never second-guessed any of his decisions or told him what to do. He stared at her, wondering what had caused this change.

"Why are you worrying? I'm going up there with two other lawmen. We'll go in, remove the snow, collect evidence, and ride back out."

"Before I was used to you coming and going. I knew

247

you'd be back when you had a mind to. Now that we've been spending so much time together and I've witnessed the chances you take…" she stopped, massaged her temple. "I'd like you to be in one piece when you retire."

"I dig for the truth. It's who I am. It's why I'm good at tracking. I don't like to leave anything that doesn't make sense unanswered. You're going to have to trust me. That I'll come back to you in one piece." He squeezed her hand. "If I can't find the answers, I can't stay still."

She dropped the hand massaging her temple. Her gaze scanned his face. "You're saying that if you aren't allowed to follow and find the answers you won't be able to stay or live in one place with me?"

He held her gaze. "I'm saying. If my mind isn't free of questions about something, I'm not content."

# Chapter Thirty

Hawke, Deputy Novak, and Trooper Shoberg throttled down their snowmobiles as they arrived at the crash site. Hawke had led the group from the time they left Moss Springs to this point. He'd barely used the usual trail as they made a more or less straight line for the downed aircraft. Going around thickets of brush and groves of trees that were too close to allow the snowmobiles through.

They donned snowshoes and ate a quick lunch along with hot coffee from thermoses.

"Do you really think we're going to find anything of importance here?" Novak asked. "Not that I mind a day out on a snowmobile when the sun is shining."

"If Barclay was drugged, which made him drop this plane on the mountain, there might be something in there that will prove it. And prove his death was premeditated. Which will help to convict Gilmore." Hawke bit into the sandwich he'd brought, thinking about how Dani had been quiet this morning when he'd made his lunch and left. He'd made Dog stay behind with her. He would give her company and let her know if anyone came to visit.

Shoberg uncapped his thermos. "I read the report about there being Vicodin in Barclay's system. Are you hoping to find traces of it in something in the plane?"

"Yes. And there might be something to tell us what the two men were doing together or if one had planned for the other not to make it off the mountain." Hawke was still unclear who had been in charge of the flight and where the men were going. The only person who could answer that wasn't talking.

They put away their lunches and pulled out the shovels they'd brought along. An hour later, they had the snow removed from the area around the cockpit and cargo doors. Hawke turned the handle and raised the cockpit door. The inside of the aircraft smelled new. "Do we know if one of the men owned the plane or if they rented it?" he asked.

"From what we learned, Barclay and two other businessmen in the Seattle area own it," Shoberg said.

"I'll grab some photos." Novak leaned into the cockpit, snapping photos while Hawke opened the cargo door and leaned in. This is where the suitcases would have been on the flight. The men hadn't had any bags with clothing in them. It made sense that Barclay wouldn't if he'd flown over, picked up Kieran, and they were flying back to Seattle. But Kieran would have been spending the night or a couple of days. Why didn't he have a packed bag?

Novak backed out of the cockpit and Shoberg leaned in, pulling on latex gloves. He handed everything that wasn't attached, out to Hawke who dropped the items in evidence bags. Novak photographed the cargo hold. Hawke wrote the pertinent information on the bags and shoved them in a backpack. Once the cockpit was cleaned out, Shoberg moved to the cargo hold and Novak used a small handheld vacuum to pick up unseen evidence from the seats and floors in the cockpit and then the cargo area. When he was finished, he bagged the vacuum and added it to the pack.

"That looks like everything that might have any type of evidence," Shoberg said, shouldering the pack.

Hawke stuck his head in the cockpit one more time. "I want to dust for prints and check the seats."

Shoberg took the pack off and handed Hawke a print kit.

Hawke leaned in, dusting the throttle handle on the near side of the cockpit. He knew if there were prints, they would be on the underside of the handle. He used a tape and grabbed what he could from there. Then he dusted the lever in between the seats, capturing more prints. He also did the dash on both sides and the throttle on the righthand side of the cockpit. And any buttons on the control panel that were flat and might give an imprint. Once he'd labeled each card of prints with where he'd acquired them, he unstrapped his snowshoes and climbed into the seat on the left. It was perfect for him. Barclay had been just about his size. Kieran was shorter. He noticed the seat on the other side was sitting the same distance from the control panel.

Grunting as he pulled himself out of the cockpit, Hawke was satisfied they'd gathered all they could from the plane. He picked up his snowshoes and wallowed through the snow to his snowmobile. "Let's get out of here before dark."

Shoberg and Novak were already settled on their machines. They took off following the trail they'd made on the way up. Hawke strapped his snowshoes on the back of his snowmobile, swung a leg over, and turned the key. The machine roared to life, and he set off after them.

Dani and Dog sat in the kitchen. She'd made soup for dinner after a long conversation with Dog about possibly trying to drive to Winslow for one of the Blue Elk's burgers. Dog had been up for the drive, but Dani didn't think she could work the pedals with one foot. That had her turning to the cupboard and pulling out the can of soup.

She'd tried to call Hawke checking if he'd be back by dinner. He'd left before dawn, stating they needed all the daylight they could get to go up to the downed plane and back. She knew she'd been a bit cool to him last night and this morning after she'd told him how she felt about him always putting himself in danger and then his response.

Sighing, she handed Dog a cracker. "At least he left you here, so I had someone to talk to."

The animal crunched up the cracker, licked his lips, and winked at her.

She laughed. He was good company. And a good listener. She'd talked things out with him during the day and she now felt she could explain herself better to Hawke.

Dog's ears went up and his nose pointed toward the other room.

"What do you hear?" She sat still and listened. There

was the sound of a vehicle. It wasn't Hawke's truck. Nor was it Tuck's pickup or Sage's Jeep. It rumbled, like a motorcycle.

"Do you think Hawke asked someone to check on us?" Dani asked quietly.

Dog rose to his feet and walked into the other room.

Dani rose up on her crutches and swung out of the kitchen, through the small living room and into the bedroom. She grabbed the Beretta M9 she kept in her bedside table, shoved the magazine into the receiver, put the weapon on safety, and tucked the weapon into her waistband at the small of her back.

Back out in the living room, she swung over to the door. Dog's hair was up along his spine, and he had a low growl rumbling.

"Easy, boy," she whispered and pulled the Beretta out of her waistband. She flipped off the safety and chambered a round, aiming the weapon at the door.

The creak of the stairs outside tightened her muscles. Dog's growl became more menacing. It wasn't the first time she'd wished there was a window on this side of the apartment so she could see who was approaching.

The landlords had made it that way, so they had privacy from whoever lived in the apartment over their garage. But it was damned inconvenient when you may have unwanted guests.

Hawke wouldn't have left them alone if he'd thought they were in danger, but whoever was coming up the stairs was being careful and quiet. Anyone who was a friend wouldn't be so careful. They'd want her to know they were coming.

The doorknob moved.

She heard the scritch of someone picking the lock. That solidified this wasn't a friend. Her training kicked in and all she thought about was the invader.

Dani squeezed the trigger, shooting the door at head height. The wood cracked and someone yelled.

The pounding of feet going down the stairs had her releasing her breath.

She needed to call for help. But what would she say to the cops? I shot at someone trying to break in. She backed up into the living room holding the gun in her hand as she grasped the crutch and moved over to where she'd left her phone. Dialing Tuck, she kept her eyes on the door.

"Hey, Dani, what's up?"

"Hawke is gone, and someone tried to break in." She was surprised at how calm her voice sounded. Her heart was pounding in her chest and her throat felt dry.

"I'm on my way. Keep this line open so I can hear."

She heard gravel crunching. "Dani's in trouble. Call the police." Tuck's voice sounded urgent.

"You still there?" Tuck asked as Dani started to put the phone down.

"Yes. I shot at them, and they ran down the stairs. But I haven't heard their vehicle leave." She moved to the kitchen with one crutch, holding the phone and the beretta in one hand.

Dog had his head cocked, listening as well.

"Where's Hawke?" Tuck asked.

"He went up to the plane crash with other officers today. He should be back soon. He wanted off the mountain by dark." She wondered if she should at least text Hawke and let him know what was going on.

The sound of the garage door going up startled her.

"I think they're in the garage. But I don't know how they got in. It's locked all winter when my landlords go to Arizona."

"I'm almost to Eagle."

Dani heard the frustration in his voice.

Dog started howling.

"What's that?" Tuck asked.

"Dog. Something's wrong." Dani moved to the window on the side opposite the stairs in the living room. She didn't see anything. She swung into the kitchen and looked out that window, facing the driveway. There were two motorcycles and smoke coming out of the garage.

"Shit! They're trying to burn down the garage!"

"I'm close."

"Be careful. There are two of them because there are two motorcycles sitting out front." She started coughing as smoke seeped into the living quarters.

"I've got my shotgun. I see flashing lights behind me. Sage must have called the police. Hold on. I'm going to tell her to call the fire department."

The line went quiet but not dead.

Dani swung into the bedroom, grabbed two bandanas, and returned to the living room where Dog was whining and pacing back and forth.

"We can't go out. They'll grab us or shoot us. Here." She tied a bandana to Dog's collar, so it hung over his nose. Then she put one around her nose and mouth to keep from inhaling too much smoke before Tuck and help arrived.

Pounding on the door, spun her around. The crutches went out from under her and she landed on the floor. Dog lay down beside her, licking her face.

"I'm fine."

"Fire! You need to come out!" Shouted a male voice she didn't know. But had a good idea it was the person wanting her out of the apartment.

A siren shrilled, and she heard feet pound down the stairs. A motorcycle started up and tires screeched.

Dani struggled to her feet, swung over to the door, unlocked it, and stepped out onto the landing, sucking in fresh air.

She saw lights, people running, and shouting. Dog quivered at her side as if he wanted to join the chase. But she kept a hand on his collar. "I need you here," she said.

Tuck appeared at the bottom of the stairs. "Are you okay?" he called up.

"Yes. Get the fire out and I'll throw some clothes in a bag. I can't stay here tonight. It's too smokey." She returned to the apartment, opening all the windows. Once that was done, she threw pajamas, a couple of sets of her clothes, and her toiletries into a backpack. She added her phone, her gun, and her computer along with Hawke's work laptop. She slung that onto her back and swung her way back out to the landing.

She tucked both crutches under her left armpit and grasped the railing with her right hand. The wail of a firetruck approached along with flashing lights.

By the time she arrived at the bottom of the stairs, Tuck was by her side.

"They tried to burn the place down to get you to come out." He waved a hand at the blackened garage.

"My landlords aren't going to be happy about this." She studied the damage and knew she'd not be staying in the apartment anymore. It looked like they would need to close the deal on the place she and Hawke looked at sooner rather than later if she wanted a place to live.

She heard her phone ringing in her backpack. "Can you fish my cell out?" Dani turned so Tuck could unzip the pocket.

He pulled phone out and answered it. "Hey, Hawke." Tuck paused. "Dani's fine. She's right here with me. The cops are trying to catch the guys who were here and the fire department is putting out the fire."

He smiled and nodded. "I'm taking her and Dog to my place." He nodded again. "Yes. You can come by no matter what time it is. See you then." He shoved the phone back into her pack and took it from her. "Come on. Sage will have the spare room ready for you."

Dani studied the man she'd hired as her wrangler at the lodge two years ago. He, his wife, and Kitree had become family to her. She was so grateful for them. "Thank you. Was Hawke upset?"

"Yeah. He'll come straight to our house when he gets back in the county. He said they were off the mountain and headed this way."

"Good. I won't have to worry about him."

A county deputy walked up to them. "Ma'am, we caught up with one of them and can get information on the other from the motorcycle plates. But I need to take your statement."

Tuck spoke before she had a chance. "I'll take her to my truck, and she can sit down while you ask her questions."

The deputy backed up allowing them to walk by. "Isn't that Hawke's dog?" the deputy asked.

"It is." Dani shoved up into the passenger seat of Tuck's truck as he opened the back door, tossing in her pack and allowing Dog to jump in.

The deputy eyed her and said, "I'm Deputy Alden. I

didn't think Hawke left that dog with anyone but his landlords."

Dani wasn't sure what the man was fishing for. "He left Dog with me today because he feared someone would come around, as they did." She held the man's stare, offering no more than that. Dog put his head over the seat and laid his head on Dani's shoulder. "He let me know someone was coming. When I watched and heard them trying to pick the lock, I fired a round at them."

"Do you have the gun?" the deputy asked.

"Yes. It's in my pack. I have a carry permit and carried my berretta for twenty years in the Air Force. I know how to use it and shoot someone if need be." She used her officer tone that she'd perfected over the years of going up the ranks in the Air Force.

"Then what happened?"

She went on to tell him about the sound of the garage door and noticing the smoke.

The deputy turned to Tuck. "Why are you here?"

"I called him when I realized someone was breaking in."

"And who are you to this woman?" Alden asked Tuck.

"She's my boss. My wife and I have been helping take care of her since she broke her leg. When she called, I headed straight here, keeping her on the line while my wife called the police." Tuck stood beside the closed back door of the truck.

Alden turned his attention back to Dani. "Do you have any idea why these men wanted in your apartment?"

She cleared her throat and said, "I'm sure it has to do with the body that was found at Charlie's Hunting

Lodge. I own the resort and was with Hawke when he found the body."

The deputy's eyes widened. "You're the new owner of the lodge." He said it as if he were putting pieces of a puzzle together. "Now I understand why you have Dog."

Alden scribbled in his notebook. "And you think this has something to do with the body found in the barn?"

"Yes. The Outlaw Motorcycle Gang is mixed up with the man we found on the mountain and who was with the man who was killed." Her throat burned. "Tuck, can you find me some water or anything that will put out the fire in my throat."

"Oh, yeah. Sorry." He ran back to the stairs and up into her apartment.

She cringed thinking it wasn't safe for someone to walk around up there.

"I'll let you go as soon as he gets back. How much did you know about the man who was killed?" Alden studied her.

"Pretty much everything Hawke has dug up. He's been staying with me since we came back from the lodge." She wondered if that would get him in trouble.

"I see. Do you think the men who tried to break in wanted information from you?"

She shrugged. "I guess. Who knows what they were after? They may have thought Hawke was in there and wanted to kill him. I don't know. You'll have to ask them."

Tuck appeared with a bottle of water.

Dani took it, unscrewed the top, and drank.

"Can I take her?" Tuck asked.

"Yes. But what's your address?"

Tuck told him.

"And your phone number?" Alden asked Dani.

She recited it for him.

"Thank you. If we need any other information I'll be in contact."

Dani nodded as Tuck slid in under the steering wheel.

"Let's get out of here. They still haven't caught one of the men but his bike is still here so he can't follow us." Tuck started up his vehicle and they drove away.

Dani stared at the smoldering, black inside of the garage. She hoped the apartment floor wasn't compromised so much they couldn't go in and get her stuff out.

# Chapter Thirty-one

Hawke called Sheriff Lindsey to see what had happened at Dani's as soon as he hung up from talking to Tuck. He should have been at the apartment with Dani. But his gut also told him he'd needed to take Novak and Shoberg to the plane crash. There had to be something in what they gathered to help them sort things out about Barclay's homicide and where Gilmore and the motorcycle gang fit in. Because after tonight it was evident that they did fit into what had happened.

"Lindsey," the sheriff answered with a weary voice.

"Sorry to bother you, Sheriff, this is Hawke. What can you tell me about what happened at Dani Singer's place?" Hawke tried to make it sound like an official call. However, his gut was still twisting, and his chest remained tight from fear and uncertainty. Not for himself but for the woman he'd brought into his life.

"I'm still trying to get all the information. A call

came in about someone breaking into the residence at…" he rattled off the address of Dani's apartment. "About fifteen minutes later another call claimed the same place was on fire. I know this is the woman who owns Charlie's Lodge. Why was anyone interested in hurting her?"

"Dani is a good friend. I've been staying at her place while she is recuperating from a broken leg and I'm on medical leave. She's helped me dig up some of the information I found on Gilmore and Barclay. I think whoever went there was looking for me." He glanced at the two men in the vehicle with him. "Shoberg and Novak picked me up at her place this morning before we went up to the plane crash. My pickup is parked there."

"You think they were trying to quiet you? But why you and not the other officers on the case?" Sheriff Lindsey asked.

"I don't know. Did they catch anyone?" He wanted to know why he was targeted as much as the sheriff did.

"They caught one of the men. One got away. But we have his motorcycle and Alden is checking with Idaho DMV."

That made sense if the two men had come from Idaho, that they would be part of the Boise gang. Something was definitely going on in Boise.

"Thank you. I'll check in with you tomorrow morning." Hawke ended the call.

"What are we missing?" Shoberg asked.

Hawke told him about the pair of men who tried to get to Dani, possibly thinking he was in the apartment.

"Is she okay?" Novak asked.

"I didn't talk to her, but Tuck says she's fine. He took her to his place. Once you drop me off to get my vehicle, that's where I'm headed."

"You sure it's a good idea for you to go there if one of them is still loose?" Shoberg asked.

"You'll just drop me off, and I'll get in my pickup and drive away." Hawke really wanted to look around but realized that would be putting himself in jeopardy. He didn't want to put Dani through anymore tonight.

They talked about the case the rest of the way to Dani's.

Shoberg turned onto the road that went by Dani's place. He made a loop to be headed back out before stopping and letting Hawke out. "I'll get this evidence over to Pendleton in the morning."

"Thanks for taking me along," Hawke said, opening his door.

The two men laughed.

Novak said, "We had to. You were the only one who knew where to find the plane."

Hawke waved, closed the door, and walked over to his vehicle, sitting to the side of the black open hole of the garage. He slid into the vehicle, started it, and took in the sight his headlights illuminated. His hands shook as he backed up. Dani and Dog could have died if she and Tuck hadn't stayed calm and acted quickly.

He broke the speed limit driving through Eagle to get to the Kimbals' house outside of Winslow. His foot eased up on the accelerator as he turned into their lane and saw the lights burning bright.

He parked beside Tuck's truck as the door opened and Dog bounded out followed by Kitree. Dog yipped and jumped up on him when he stepped out of the vehicle. "Hey, boy. I'm glad you're okay." He scratched the dog's neck and ears, his tension slowly easing.

"Dani's staying the night with us. Are you?" Kitree asked when she stopped a few feet from him.

He gave the girl a one-armed hug. "We'll see." They walked up to the house, and he entered behind the girl and Dog.

Dani sat in a chair. He walked over, knelt beside the chair, and put his arms around her. He whispered in her ear. "I'm sorry I left you alone."

She pushed him back and peered into his eyes. "You didn't know anyone would try to harm me. Besides, you left Dog. He warned me that something wasn't right." She grasped one of his hands. He felt her slight tremors. She was scared but didn't want to show it around the others. He gave her hand a squeeze and stood, holding a hand out to Tuck. "Thank you for getting there so quickly and keeping calm."

Tuck shook his hand. "No problem. You know how we feel about both of you."

"Dani is settled in our spare room. You're welcome to stay too, if you like," Sage said.

Hawke smiled at the woman. "Thank you. I'd like to visit with Dani and then see how tired I am. If I can stay awake long enough to go home, that's what I'll do. I don't want to put more people at risk."

"I'm going to turn the camera on at the gate and my brother's two dogs will be prowling around all night. They'll let us know if anyone shows up." Tuck put his arm around Sage's shoulders. "You're safe here."

"Thank you. Then I will stay. But just for tonight." He pulled a chair over by Dani and sat.

"I'll get you some hot chocolate," Kitree said.

Tuck retreated to the small office off the living room and Sage followed Kitree into the kitchen.

Hawke leaned forward and gave Dani a chaste kiss on the lips. "Are you really okay?"

She nodded. "I didn't start shaking until Tuck was driving me here." She put a hand on Dog's head that rested on Hawke's knee. "He heard them before I did. I realized it was motorcycles and got my gun." She went on to tell him what happened. "Mr. and Mrs. Woodly are going to ask me to leave and it's going to be months before the apartment is livable."

Hawke studied her face. He saw worry and something else. A grin spread across his face. "Is this your way of saying we need to sign papers on that place we looked at yesterday?"

Her face flushed. "We haven't had time to talk about it, but it is sitting there empty and I'm in need of a place to stay."

He laughed and hugged her as Kitree and Sage walked into the room with hot chocolate for everyone and a plate of blondies.

"Wow, you two look joyous. Did you figure out who did this?" Sage asked.

"No," Hawke said. "We decided to purchase the land we looked at yesterday. Dani needs a place to stay, and I'm ready to move out of my one-room apartment and give my geldings more space to exercise."

"That's wonderful. Where is the place?" Sage asked.

Dani told Sage and Kitree all about it as Hawke wandered into the office.

Tuck looked up from the computer he was typing on. He spun the screen and Hawke had a view of the gate coming up to the house. "My brothers installed the cameras a couple of years ago when there were some high schoolers stealing gas. They come in handy now and then."

Tuck, Sage, and Kitree stayed in a house on Tuck's family's ranch when they weren't up at the lodge working for Dani. One of the brothers was a bronc rider who was gone a lot on the weekends and the other brother managed the ranch with the help of the nieces and nephews. Tuck helped out during the winter feeding the cattle and helping with calving before they went back up to the lodge to work.

The two men walked back into the living room.

Kitree handed them each a mug of hot chocolate. "Did Hawke tell you he and Dani are moving closer?"

Tuck glanced at Dani and then Hawke. "What's this?"

Kitree began telling him all about the house, while Dani and Sage smiled.

Hawke returned to his seat next to Dani and listened.

In the morning, Hawke and Dog in one vehicle, and Tuck and Sage in their truck drove to Dani's apartment. The men assessed the damage and took photos, which Hawke sent to Dani so she could send them on to her landlords. While the men were checking things out, Sage went up to the apartment and started filling the boxes they'd brought with Dani's belongings. There was no sense for her to come back here. The stairs were hard for her to climb, and the apartment wouldn't be livable until the insurance company paid for the repairs.

Hawke left the husband and wife boxing up Dani's things and headed toward Alder and the Sheriff's Office. He wanted to find out what he could about the man who had tried to break in. On the way, he called Sergeant Spruel to let him know he would be ready for work in two more days and then he called Special Agent Pierce.

"Pierce," the agent answered in a distracted tone.

"It's Hawke. Some of the Brother Speed tried to break into Dani's place last night. When they couldn't get in, they set it on fire."

That got the man's attention. "Is she okay?"

"Yes. She and Dog heard them, and she called a friend for help."

"Where the hell were you?" Pierce asked, his tone accusatory.

"I was coming from Moss Spring, I found the plane that crashed, or more like, did an emergency landing. There wasn't a dent, crack, or scratch on any part of the plane that we uncovered. I went with a trooper and deputy up to the crash site yesterday. We grabbed all the evidence that might be in the plane. It should be in Pendleton at the OSP lab this morning."

"How do you know it was Brother Speed who tried to break in?" Pierce asked.

"I'm guessing. They were on motorcycles with Idaho plates. I'm headed to see if the one they caught is saying anything."

"Where is he being held?" Pierce asked.

"At the county jail."

"I'll be there in two hours. If no one has questioned him yet, ask them to wait until I get there. I might have information that will help make him talk."

Hawke wondered if it would shed light on who drugged Barclay and why Gilmore killed him. "I'll see what Sheriff Lindsey says."

"I hope you do better than that." Pierce ended the call.

Hawke stared at the road ahead of him. There were

times when the FBI agent was too full of himself.

At the Sheriff's Office, Hawke parked behind the building and walked in the back door past the jail. He walked up the hall and listened at the doors of the interview rooms. No one was inside. He stopped at Sheriff Lindsey's office and knocked on the door.

"Come in," the sheriff called.

He opened the door and walked in. Lindsey was on the phone. A frown said the sheriff didn't care for whatever was being said on the other side of the call.

"I'll see what I can do," he said and hung up the phone. "That was your FBI friend. It seems he found out about the man we caught last night and wants to interview him. Hell, he knows nothing about what happened last night."

Hawke cleared his throat. "Actually, I told him about it. Since he was the one who told me about the connection between Gilmore and the Outlaw Motorcycle Gang, I thought he should know they had come after me."

"Oh. Well then, I guess we'll wait to interview the man until Pierce gets here."

"Have you learned anything about the suspect you picked up last night?" Hawke asked.

Lindsey handed him a file. "Alden said the man didn't say a word through the ride here, booking, and putting him in a cell."

Hawke opened the file and began reading.

# Chapter Thirty-two

FBI Special Agent Pierce sat beside Hawke in the interview room waiting for a deputy to bring in Howie Powell, AKA Hammer. From the file Lindsey had handed Hawke, the man had been a part of Brother Speed since he graduated from high school. He was thirty-three and worked as a mechanic when he wasn't going around breaking bones for the motorcycle gang.

Deputy Corcoran opened the door and shoved a man whose head just missed touching the top of the threshold and whose shoulders scraped the door jambs. Hawke could see how the man got his name Hammer. His fists were as large as cantaloupes. His head was shaved, and he had a wild brown beard that rested on his chest.

He was in handcuffs. Hawke was glad to see that and equally grateful that Tuck had responded so quickly to Dani's call the night before. Bile rose in his throat thinking of that man's hands hitting Dani to get information she didn't have.

Pierce introduced himself and poised his pen over his notepad. "Please state your name."

The man glared at him.

"Howie, we know you are part of Brother Speed, and you were sent here to silence this man," Pierce pointed to Hawke. "You'll be helping yourself if you cooperate."

Howie stared at Hawke. The biker's gaze slid over Hawke's face and across his body, shoulder to shoulder. Then Howie grinned.

Fear should have been Hawke's reaction, but he was too angry to fear the man. "I wasn't in that apartment you tried to burn down." He barely raised the corners of his lips. "You and your buddy messed up." Hawke set his gaze on Pierce. "I wonder what happens to members of the gang who screw up?"

"I think they are the ones we find shot in the back of the head out in the desolate areas around Boise," Pierce countered.

"Just shot? I'd think they'd torture them for not taking care of the business they were sent to deal with." Hawke noticed Hammer flinch in his peripheral vision.

"Yeah, we have found a couple that had their fingers chopped off. Not with a knife. ME figured it was an axe, because the bones were splintered."

Hawke winced. "That sounds painful."

Pierce looked at Hammer.

Hawke studied the man as well.

"You heard me state I'm with the FBI. I can make this," he waved his hand between Hammer and Hawke, "go away. But in return, I'd like to know what you know about Kieran Gilmore and Patrick Barclay. The reason you were after my friend, here."

Hammer's gaze moved from one man to the next and back to Pierce.

"If you're afraid the others in the gang will think you ratted on another member, we can say you got loose when we were transporting you. That you never made it to the jail." Pierce circled a hand, showing off the interior of the room. "Do you see a camera or recording device? The only people in this room are you, me, Hawke, and a deputy who I'm sure would like to go up the ranks and that can be done with my help." Pierce glanced at Corcoran.

Hawke knew Pierce would never undermine any police officer or help them illegally. He was playing to the gang member's mentality of you help your own kind. Though Corcoran had raised his brows at Pierce's comment.

"I'm not asking you to rat on anyone that's important. After all, Gilmore is only a weekend Brother Speed, isn't he? He's only a member because he started laundering money for the Outlaws." Pierce closed the notebook he'd been poised to write in. "We only want to know about Gilmore. Was the money he hid money he'd stolen from the gang?"

Hammer's eyes narrowed. "If Irish stole money, Bear would have told me to kill him not kidnap him." Hammer's chin came up pointing at Hawke.

"Your leader wanted me kidnapped? Why?" Hawke found this interesting.

Hammer just stared at him.

"Back to 'Irish,'" Pierce said. "Did he approach Bear about the laundering or did Bear approach him?"

Hammer just sat there his lips pressed together,

staring at the wall between them.

"Take him back to his cell. Guess I'll call my operative in the gang and let them know Hammer spilled his guts." Pierce picked up his notebook and the file and stood.

Corcoran grabbed Hammer's arm and the large man stood. He stared at Pierce, spit a blob of saliva on the agent's jacket, and walked out of the room.

When the door closed, Hawke said, "I don't think you intimidated him."

"Why did they want to kidnap you?" Pierce asked.

"They obviously believe I know something." Hawke stood. "Where's Gilmore?"

"He arrived in Seattle yesterday and went straight to the Barclay residence." Pierce walked to the door. "Do you have any idea why Barclay was drugged?"

"I think to make him land before they got to Seattle. The whole thing happened too soon after they left Boise. I'm thinking Gilmore had planned to stage a plane wreck, only he would survive, and Barclay wouldn't. Barclay felt the drug taking effect and landed sooner than Gilmore had anticipated. Being a skilled pilot, the victim landed them without physical danger and proceeded to get them to help at the lodge. When Gilmore realized they were alone, he tried to kill Barclay who still managed to get a bullet in his attacker." Hawke opened the door. "I think Dani and I arriving at the lodge scared Gilmore. I would bet he had planned on taking Barclay's body to the plane and leaving it there, so people would think he died in the crash."

"And Gilmore would be found on the mountain stunned from the accident," Pierce said.

"It makes more sense than anything else I've been

able to piece together." Hawke leaned against the wall.

"Why would he fake Barclay's death?" Pierce asked.

"I think that answer is in Seattle, where he is staying." Hawke studied the FBI Agent. "He would want to console the grieving sister and eventually marry her and have access to laundering money for the Outlaws at all Riches Pawn shops. That would make him indispensable to the motorcycle gang."

Pierce's sharp eyes sparked. "It could make him the leader of the motorcycle gang."

"After Hammer said he was to kidnap me, I think Bear wanted to know exactly what all happened on the mountain. He's afraid he's going to lose his status to Gilmore."

"I can set up a meeting with you and Bear. Maybe we can get him to have anyone in his organization who might have some information we can use against Gilmore talk to us."

Hawke grinned. "I like the way you think." He started down the hall and stopped. "Call me when you get that set up. I'm off to sign papers on a house and property."

<><><><><>

Hawke stood in the middle of the house he and Dani had signed for the day before. Because it was empty, Dani needed a place to stay, and they had more than half to put down on the property, Gail had handed them the keys this morning when they'd taken their respective cashier's checks into the realty office.

"I can't believe we can move in this quickly," Dani said for the third time since being handed the keys.

"Me either." Hawke studied her. "While you needed

a place to stay, neither one of us has any furniture." He stared at the empty rooms he could see from this vantage point. The kitchen, living room, and dining room.

Dog barked and Hawke glanced out the window. Two pickups with furniture in the back were driving up to the house. He and Dani walked to the door. The tires crunched on the frozen snow as Herb's pickup backed up to the yard.

Herb and Darlene got out and walked to the back. Herb opened the tailgate and Darlene continued up the walkway to the porch.

"What is this?" Hawke asked.

"I knew some people who had furniture in storage. You can use it until Dani is able to get around and purchase what she likes." Darlene waved Dani into the house, and said to Hawke, "Go help Herb."

Two hours later, the two pickup loads of furniture were in the house. Herb, Darlene, Tuck, and Sage, sat around the table in the dining room with Hawke and Dani. Darlene had brought a cooler with food, and they were all enjoying a friendly lunch.

"This furniture is thoughtful," Dani said, running her hand over the dining room table. She glanced at Darlene. "Please thank the person responsible for letting us use their furniture."

"I will. It saves them paying for storage while you are using it. Which makes it a win-win situation." Darlene smiled at Dani and Hawke.

Hawke's phone buzzed. He glanced at the name. Pierce. "I need to take this."

He heard Dani say, "He goes back to work tomorrow," as he walked outside.

"Hawke," he answered.

"I have a meeting set up for six this evening with Bear. You need to meet him at their Boise Clubhouse."

Hawke held the phone away and peered at it. Then he brought it back and said, "You set up a meet with the head of a biker gang at his clubhouse? Are you sending me in there with the National Guard as backup?"

Pierce scoffed and said, "No. Just you, me, and Rose, an FBI informant in the group. You need to meet us at five-thirty at the Steel Horse Saloon. I'll send you the address and meet you there." The call ended.

Hawke glanced at his watch. He needed three hours to get there and had three and a half until 5:30. Walking back into the house, he wondered what one wore for a meeting with a leader of a motorcycle gang?

# Chapter Thirty-three

There were close to twenty motorcycles parked in the lot in front of the Silver Horse Saloon. Hawke spotted Pierce's SUV parked a block away from the business. Not sure if he should pull up behind the FBI Agent's vehicle or park in front of the bar, Hawke decided to park in the lot nearest the exit.

Before stepping out, he texted Pierce: *I'm here. Where are you?*

A reply came at nearly the same time he sent his message: *We'll be right out.*

Hawke stepped out of his pickup, locked the doors, and headed toward the front of the bar.

Pierce dressed in boots, jeans, and a denim jacket walked out with a young blonde woman dressed in black leather. They sauntered up to Hawke.

"Rose, this is Hawke. Hawke, Rose. She's our ride to the clubhouse." Pierce looked and acted differently. It

276

appeared he'd been on more than one undercover assignment.

"Do they know you are a Fed?" Hawke asked.

The woman shook her head. "They don't know I am, but they know I've been dating a Fed for intel." She smiled. "They just don't know that I'm only sharing what I'm told to share."

Hawke heard the roar of motorcycles coming down the street. "Am I supposed to know you are a Fed?" he asked Pierce. "It's evident they know I'm a cop."

"Yes. I set this up through Rose, so they would know I called you to come talk to Bear."

The motorcycles rolled right up next to them, revved their engines, and idled.

"Get on!" the guy next to Hawke said.

The man rode a low-slung, long-framed black Harley. He had on black goggles over a scarf patterned with skulls and crossbones.

Hawke didn't want to make the man think he was scared to ride with him by asking for a helmet, so he grabbed his Stetson in one hand, swung a leg over the bike behind the man, and held his hat between him and the man as the bike started rolling. He cast a glance behind him and spotted Pierce on behind a woman and Rose rode sitting behind a smaller man. It appeared they were being taken to the clubhouse.

Twenty minutes later Hawke had a bad feeling. They had left the city limits and were headed south into open barren country. And there were now fifteen bikes in the group that guided them down what appeared to be a paved county road.

He was beginning to believe they weren't going to a clubhouse but rather out in the middle of nowhere to be killed. Glancing back at the other bikes, he tried to get a glimpse of Rose. She would be the one to know if they were going the wrong way. She sat behind her driver, staring out at the landscape. He found the woman Pierce was riding with. Pierce had a smile and his arms comfortably wrapped around the woman's middle. Hawke decided if they weren't worried, he shouldn't be either. They must know the club was out this way.

The biker throttled down, and Hawke spotted a low building hidden by a grove of birch and a couple of tall cottonwoods. His chauffeur swung down onto the dirt road leading to the structure in the trees.

A dozen motorcycles were propped up on kickstands in the grassy area in front of the double doors. Hawke thought the building with curled gray paint had once been a grange hall from the rectangular shape, size, and wide entrance.

"Get off." The man ordered as the bike rolled to a stop.

Hawke swung his leg over, placed his hat on his head, and scanned the area for Pierce and Rose. They were stepping off the bikes that had transported them here.

A man nearly as large as Hammer, and with twice as much dark hair, threw the double doors open. "Rose, I see you have brought friends." His voice boomed and everyone stopped moving forward.

"Bear, this is my boyfriend." She wrapped an arm around Pierce's arm. "And this is the man you wanted to talk to." She pointed at Hawke.

Hawke walked forward with his hand extended. "Bear, I think we both have something in common."

The gang leader crossed his arms over his chest.

"What is that?"

"Neither one of us trusts Kieran Gilmore."

Bear stared at Hawke for a few seconds and slowly extended his hand. "True."

They shook and Bear said, "I asked you here to speak with you about him."

Hawke had released the man's hand. Now it was his turn to cross his arms. "Asked? You sent two men to my friend's home and when they couldn't get in, they tried to burn her house down. I'm not here as a friend. I want to get evidence that will put Gilmore in jail for killing Patrick Barclay and I want to make sure that no one," Hawke glanced around at the bikers, "ever bothers my friend again."

Returning his gaze to Bear, Hawke saw annoyance and respect flicker in the man's eyes.

"Come inside." Bear pivoted, walking into the building.

Hawke followed. The large open room had two pool tables set up with mismatched couches and chairs set along the sides of the room and one corner had plastic coolers stacked up. The one on top was open showing ice and cans of beer.

Bear walked over to a corner. He sat down in the largest chair and motioned to the one beside him.

Hawke sank onto the overstuffed cushion and inspected the people in the room. Half of them looked like they were laborers who had stopped by on their way home from work. The other half were dressed in leathers, vests, and scarfs tied around their heads. They were predominately male. He found Pierce and Rose had been led to the pool table farthest from where Bear had sat.

"Beer?" the gang leader asked.

"Not right now. What can you tell me about Kieran Gilmore? When did he become a member of your gang?" Hawke wanted to get down to business and get home to Dani for their first night in their new place.

Bear raised a hand and shook his head. A young woman in tight leather pants and a top that barely covered her breasts arrived with a can of beer. Bear took the can, pulled the tab, and drank, swallowing what had to have been half the contents. He set the hand down holding the beer and said, "Irish was never a member. He rode with us a few times, but he refused to do the initiation."

"Then why are you so interested in him?" Hawke asked.

"Because he is luring CeeCee away from me. He only bought a motorcycle because she likes the feel of a big machine between her legs." He winked. "And I can provide that on and off a bike. That prick Irish could only give her a ride on a motorcycle. She knows he could never thrill her on his own."

Hawke studied the man. "I heard that after she hooked you and Kieran up to launder money, you dumped her."

Bear finished off the can and crushed it. "We only pretended I dumped her to get her brother off her back. He had a vindictive streak. Especially when it came to the family business."

"Then you had a reason to want Patrick Barclay dead. Did you help Kieran kill him? Did you think the heiress to the Riches Pawn shops franchise would marry you?"

"No. She doesn't want to marry. She just wants to have a good time. CeeCee liked that her brother enjoyed running the family business. But she got in over her head when Irish asked her to help him meet people like me. People who were looking for places to launder money."

"Why did she get in over her head?" Hawke asked, finding it interesting that Bear talked as if the woman was in trouble. She was set to take over the family business.

"Because she didn't realize what Irish was up to until it was too late. Then her brother found out and threatened to turn her and Irish in to the police. She called me upset and asked if I could come see her. Help her figure out how to get out of the mess."

Hawke peered at the man. He did seem to have a soft spot for the woman. His eyes no longer held sparks of animosity. "Did you go help her?"

Bear shook his head and his shaggy hair whipped about his face. He shoved it back with a large hand. "I had business to take care of here first. I heard about her brother's death before I could get up there to see her."

This took Hawke to an idea he'd had earlier. "Do you think Miss Barclay would have tried to stop her brother?"

The gang leader narrowed his eyes. "You aren't going to put her in jail for her brother's death. I've talked to her. She's devastated. She never wanted to run the business and doesn't want to deal with any of the family's obligations. CeeCee just wants to have fun and enjoy life."

"Would Kieran give her that if she married him?"

Bear came up out of his chair and the whole room went silent. "I'll wring that ferret's neck if he does!"

"Then help me build a case against him. I'm certain he drugged Patrick. But I'm not sure how. Do you know if he was asking around for Vicodin before he left town?" Hawke asked.

Bear waved a hand. "Mickey, over here!"

A young man set down the pool cue and crossed the room. "Yeah?"

"You did work for Irish. Did he ask you where he could get some Vicodin?" Bear studied the young man.

Hawke also watched Mickey.

"He did ask me where he could get some drugs that would knock someone out. I told him to ask Wally." Mickey glanced at Hawke. "Wally steals jewelry and drugs."

"Where can we find this Wally?" Hawke asked.

Bear snapped his fingers. Two gang members appeared. "Go get Wally and bring him here."

The men jogged out of the building.

"How long will this take?" Hawke asked.

"Long enough for you to tell me about the money I heard Irish had stolen."

Hawke glanced across the room at Pierce who was talking to a woman bent over the pool table, aiming her stick at a ball. He wasn't sure how much of what they knew was to be told to the gang leader, but he was bringing someone who might help them connect Kieran to Barclay's death.

Hawke cleared his throat, asked for a beer, and started telling Bear about finding the body and what Kieran had said about having a bullet wound in his arm.

The beer arrived along with Pierce who raised an eyebrow. Hawke took a swallow of the beer to ease his dry throat and told Bear about learning of the suitcases with money and finding them, only to be hunted by two men who Barclay had hired to extract himself and the suitcases from the mountain.

"You mean Barclay had planned to leave Irish on the mountain, but ended up dead?" Bear asked.

"That is my guess. Why else would he have hired the men to get him and the money?" Hawke studied the gang leader. He could see the man was thinking hard about what Hawke had said.

"Where were they going in the airplane?" Bear asked.

"From the flight plan Barclay gave the Boise airport, they were headed to Seattle," Pierce said.

Hawke and Bear both faced him.

Bear spoke first. "Did I ask for your input?"

"No, but Hawke didn't know about the flight plan." Pierce stared back at Bear.

The gang leader dismissed Pierce. "Hawke? That's your name?"

"Yes."

"Then we have more in common. Names that are from nature." Bear almost smiled. "Back to the money and Barclay. Do you think Barclay offered the money to Irish to get him to leave his sister alone?"

"That was one of my theories. We know that Barclay had been up to the lodge that they landed near during the summer. The people who work there said he seemed to be looking around more to see the area than asking questions about having a group come up. Which was his cover for being there." Hawke thought about that. "How would Kieran have learned that Barclay planned to kill him rather than just pay him off?"

"How do you know that?" Bear asked, crossing his arms.

Hawke took another sip of the beer that was growing

warm. "Because why wouldn't Kieran have taken the money and started up his own pawnshop business?"

Bear's brows met above his nose as he frowned. "Because he wanted the Barclay business, not to start from scratch."

"The only way to accomplish that is to marry CeeCee," Pierce said.

Bear growled and Hawke nodded.

The two gang members returned with Wally. The man was in his thirties, unshaven, and wearing clothes three sizes too big. When Pierce grabbed the man's jacket, he revealed pockets sewn onto the lining, containing bottles of prescriptions that didn't have Wally's name on them.

"Did you sell or give Kieran Gilmore a bottle of Vicodin three weeks ago?" Hawke asked.

Wally didn't look at Hawke. His gaze was on Bear.

"Answer him!" Bear said.

The man nodded his head. "Yes. He said he needed some to help him relax so he could sleep."

"Did you give him a bottle or just a few?" Hawke asked.

"A bottle." Wally scratched his head.

"Was there a name on the bottle?" Pierce asked.

Wally swallowed. "No." He pulled out a bottle. "I use a marker to black out the names. All people care about is what kind of pill they are getting."

"Have you searched Kieran's place?" Hawke asked Pierce. There was no sense in them trying to pretend that he wasn't there in his capacity as an FBI Agent.

"They did. No pill bottles were found."

Hawke stared at Bear, wondering just how much the man cared for CeeCee Barclay. "Do you know someone in Seattle who you trust?"

The man returned the stare. "Why?"

"We need to get CeeCee away from Kieran before he talks her into marrying him. I have a feeling if she goes against his wishes, she'll be the next homicide we're solving."

Bear pulled out a cell phone and stalked out of the building.

"What was that all about?" Pierce asked.

"He's in love with CeeCee. He'll get her away from Kieran, but we are going to have to find a way to force Kieran's hand."

# Chapter Thirty-four

Hawke and Pierce were delivered back to the Steel Horse Saloon after Bear came in and said he'd called CeeCee and told her to meet his friend. The man would get her to Boise.

At the parking lot, Hawke leaned against his pickup. "Can you contact whoever is watching Gilmore? I'd like to know what he does when CeeCee disappears."

"Go home. I'll talk to them and let you know what is happening." Pierce walked toward his vehicle.

Hawke slid in behind the wheel of his Dodge and pointed it toward home. He pondered the relationship between the heiress to the Barclay fortune and the motorcycle gang leader. Who would forsake their reign for the other?

The drive home was uneventful. As he turned into the driveway to their new place, he saw a light glowing on the porch. He smiled. It was nice coming home to a real house and a light shining for him. Tomorrow, he had to go back to work. But he'd work a short day so he could haul the horses over and set them up in the stalls in the barn and let them kick up their heels in the pasture that would be their new home.

Dog met him at the door, whining and wiggling.

"Hey, boy. Did you have fun peeing on everything outside, marking your territory?" He scratched the animal's ears, head, and neck before straightening and walking down the hall to the master bedroom. The room was as big as his apartment over the arena but with a larger bathroom.

The lamp on the bedside table had a low glow to help him navigate the path to the bathroom. He showered and slipped into bed. As he reached to turn the light off, Dani rolled toward him.

"Is it over?" she asked.

He wanted to tell her, yes, but it wasn't. Not until Kieran Gilmore was behind bars. "No. But we should be able to get him in the next day or two. The victim's sister was being manipulated by Kieran. She should be away from him tonight and hopefully, Pierce can talk to her tomorrow."

He pulled Dani into his arms. "Go to sleep. It's not our problem anymore."

"What about the men who burned my apartment?" she asked, her face snuggled against his neck.

"We don't have to worry about them. Their boss and I came to an understanding."

"Good."

Hawke held Dani as her breathing slowed and she fell asleep. He remained staring at the ceiling and running everything he knew over and over in his head.

They were missing something. But what?

Hawke sat in his work vehicle waiting for a group of hunters to arrive back at their camp at Sled Springs. Only youth hunts lasted this long into December. He wanted to make sure that the hunters in this group were only the youth. There was one carcass hanging from a tree. It was properly tagged which led him to believe this was a law-abiding hunting camp, but it was his job to check on them.

His engine was running to keep the vehicle warm. Hawke had a cup of coffee and cookies Darlene had left at the house yesterday after lunch. It had been nice of her to talk her friend into letting them use their furniture until he and Dani could have time to purchase their own.

His phone buzzed.

Pierce.

"What did you find out?" Hawke answered.

"Miss Barclay is in Boise. Bear's friend drove her to the airport and she took the first plane out of Seattle, arriving in Boise early this morning. We met her and have been questioning her all morning."

"Did you learn anything interesting?" Hawke asked.

"She didn't know anything about her brother going to Boise to buy off Gilmore. He told her, he needed to talk to Gilmore about the losses from his store."

Hawke jumped on that. "Do you think the money in the suitcases was money Gilmore was siphoning off the business?"

"If so, that was another good reason for Barclay to want the man out of his life." Pierce cleared his voice. "Miss Barclay swears up and down, that her brother didn't own a gun and he would have never tried to kill

Gilmore. He would have paid him off, not killed him."

"Did you ever check to see who the gun was registered to?" Hawke asked.

"Yes. It came back as registered by Patrick Barclay."

"Where was it purchased?"

Pierce was quiet for several seconds. "A gun shop in Caldwell, Idaho."

"Barclay's death was premeditated."

"Shit! I'll get someone over there with a photo of Gilmore and see if they recognize him. You can bet he paid in cash." Pierce ended the call.

"But if Gilmore bought the gun, how had Barclay come to have it in his possession?" Before he could think about that a pickup pulled up to the camp trailer.

Hawke exited his vehicle and walked over, introduced himself, and asked to see the tags and licenses.

As he'd figured, they were following all the rules. He thanked them and settled back in his vehicle. He drove away, headed for Alder, and home.

His phone rang. Herb.

"Hello?"

"There was a man here looking for you. I told him you don't live here anymore. He was adamant that he needed to talk to you or Dani."

Hawke sucked in his breath and then asked Herb to describe the man.

It was Kieran.

"You didn't tell him where Dani is, did you?" His heart started pounding and he pressed down on the accelerator.

"No. Do you want me to go over and stay with her?"

Herb asked. "Or bring her to our place?"

"If you can't get her to go home with you, call Tuck." Hawke recited Tuck's number. "I'm going to try and meet up with this guy and see if I can't get things settled once and for all." He ended the call and stabbed his finger on Pierce in contacts.

"What is Gilmore's cell phone number?" He asked as soon as the agent answered.

"Why?"

"He's looking for me or Dani. I'd rather he talked to me and thought I'd set up a meeting."

"You will make sure there is backup when you talk to him?" Pierce asked.

"If you give me his number, I'll set up a meet and make sure I have backup." Hawke had been through enough the last few weeks, he didn't want to mess with a crazy person on his own.

Pierce rattled the number off. "And call me back with the place you're meeting."

Hawke agreed and pulled into the Shake Shack parking lot. He dialed Kieran's phone number.

"Who's this?" Kieran answered in an agitated state.

"I heard you were looking for me," Hawke said.

"Hawke? Yes, we need to meet. I need your help." The man sounded as feeble and ineffectual as he'd portrayed himself to be when they escorted him off the mountain.

"Why do you need my help?" Hawke asked.

"Just meet me and we can talk about it."

"Okay. Do you know where the High Mountain Brewery is in Alder? I can be there in an hour." Hawke hoped the man wouldn't pull out a gun in the middle of a populated business.

"No. That's no good. I don't want to talk to you in front of a lot of people. How about Dani's apartment?"

Hawke didn't like that idea. Even if Dani wasn't there, he didn't like the fact the man knew where it was. "Can't. It was burned by your friends."

"My friends?" Kieran questioned.

"The Brother Speed gang. Two of their members came looking for me and burned the building trying to get me to come out. Only I wasn't in there. Dani and Dog were in there." He said the last with all the anger he felt toward everyone involved in trying to hurt his dog and woman.

"Are they okay?"

He wasn't going to tell this killer anything about Dani or Dog. "How about the parking lot of the Rusty Nail Café in Winslow." Hawke knew it would be closed by now. There wouldn't be anyone around to get hurt and it was close to the OSP office.

"In an hour." Kieran ended the call.

Hawke immediately called Sheriff Lindsey, Sergeant Spruel, and Pierce. The first two said they'd send backup, and Pierce said, he'd be there as soon as he could.

Wanting to get the whole thing over with, Hawke drove through the Shake Shack, ordered fries and a shake, and headed to Winslow.

# Chapter Thirty-five

Hawke circled the block before pulling into the parking area behind the Rusty Nail. There weren't any vehicles, and the lights were all out. He backed into a spot so he could see the street and both entrances to the parking lot.

The back door of the building opened, and Justine stepped out. His stomach twisted. He and Justine had been friends since he began working in Wallowa County. And now she and Dani were friends.

She walked up to his vehicle, smiling.

He rolled down the window. "What are you doing here so late?"

"I dropped my car off at Doug's. He's putting the snow tires on. He just called and said it's done." She smiled. "Want to give me a lift?"

"Any other time, I would. Right now, I'm waiting for someone, and it would be best if you hurried away from here."

She studied him. "What are you caught up in now?" Her eyes widened. "People at the restaurant today said an apartment over a garage caught on fire. Was it Dani's place? Oh my God! Is she okay?"

"Why don't you walk out through the trees behind my vehicle and then head on over to Doug's. You can call Dani and talk to her while you're walking but don't tell her you saw me." He gave her a steady stare. "Go. Now." And he rolled up the window.

She frowned but did as he said, walking between the trees.

His body started to uncoil until a car pulled into the lot.

It was a rental car with a Washington plate. Kieran must have rented it when he'd discovered CeeCee wasn't coming back.

Hawke flipped on the dash camera and his body cam.

Kieran parked the car in front of Hawke's vehicle. He stepped out, standing behind the door.

Hawke had his Kevlar vest under his shirt. It would be stupid of the man to shoot him here, but dealing with as many crazy people as he had over the years, Hawke knew to always be ready for the unexpected. He opened his door and stood on the running board, keeping his body mostly hidden. "What did you want to see me about?"

He didn't see a gun in the man's hands as he stepped out from behind the door. "I want you to go for a ride with me. We need to talk. You are telling people lies about me. I want to tell you the truth." Kieran stood with his body in full view.

However, his bulky coat could conceal several types of firearms.

"We can talk right here." Hawke remained where he was. He knew the cameras would record Kieran's actions and words.

The man shook his head and pulled a handgun out of his pocket. "No, we can't talk here. It's cold and I want to have a long private discussion with you. Put that camera and radio inside your vehicle along with your belt."

Hawke held up his hands. "Why would I do that? You're going to shoot me anyway, might as well do it here."

Kieran's lips tipped into a nasty grin as his eyes flashed to Hawke's left. "That may be so, but if you don't do as I say now, that woman standing behind a tree will get a bullet."

Before he even glanced over, Hawke knew he'd see Justine. The woman stood behind one of the trees. She must have circled back after he'd watched her walk away.

Shit! She had nothing to do with any of this. He pulled off the body camera, his radio, and the duty belt. He didn't want anyone to get hurt. Kieran was obviously not thinking clearly. It would be best to get him away from town and the possibility of his shooting an innocent bystander.

Piling everything he'd been directed to lose on the driver's seat, Hawke felt secure knowing he still had his knife in one boot and a backup gun in the other. He stepped out from behind the door, keeping his body between Kieran and Justine. He hoped like hell she took off running when he blocked her from the dangerous killer.

"Get in the car," Kieran said.

"You first." Hawke didn't want him shooting at Justine if she hadn't had the sense to take off.

The man smirked. "No, you're driving."

Hawke wondered what had happened to his backup. They'd all had plenty of time to get here. He walked over to the open driver's door and dropped down into the seat.

Kieran glanced around and settled into the passenger seat. "Back out and head up that road." He pointed the weapon at Lostine River Road.

Hawke thought he caught a glimpse in the rearview mirror of a county car headed around the corner to the Rusty Nail.

The Lostine River Road was paved the first ten miles. After that, the road was rutted from local people traveling into the snowy mountains for Christmas trees in four-wheel-drive vehicles. The rental car bogged down in the snow halfway up the incline after the Pole Bridge.

Hawke used this to his advantage, revving and spinning the tires to help the vehicle become more embedded in the snow. "That's as far as we're going to get on this road," Hawke said, turning the vehicle off.

"Get out!" Kieran shouted.

Hawke did as he was told. The sides of the road had either an upward climb or a downhill drop into the icy Lostine River.

"Walk!" Kieran said, pointing up the road.

Stepping into the track of a four-wheel-drive truck, Hawke stared at the incline, his mind whirling with how to get the jump on Kieran without either of them getting hurt. "You do know that once you shoot me, you'll be lost out here in the forest. Who are you going to have save you this time?" He knew he was taunting the man, but he found it ironic that the man who was lost up at the lodge was putting himself into the same situation.

"Shut up. I'm thinking."

The road leveled out a bit.

"Go to the right." Kieran was directing him toward the drop off to the river.

If he didn't start asking questions, he wasn't going to have answers before one of them ended up in the river. "Did you skim money from the business just to get Patrick to come to Boise with plans of exposing who you were to his sister?"

"Who told you that?" Surprise caused his voice to rise an octave.

"No one. I figured it out with what the Feds found out about you and your pawnshop. I have a feeling it wasn't just the business you were skimming from. You took one suitcase of money from the Outlaw Motorcycle Gang, didn't you? Did you hope they would think Patrick stole it and go after him? Then when that didn't happen you bought a gun and registered it in Patrick's name. After all, you either asked his sister for all his information or you found it when you were visiting pretending to be dating CeeCee."

"You aren't as smart as you think. Laundering the Outlaw's money was CeeCee's idea. Patrick didn't know anything about it." Kieran's breathing had quickened.

The snow was up to their knees. Hawke was in his work boots with feet warmers, long johns, and his heavy-duty pants. It was cold enough the snow wasn't melting. His feet were warm, and he was toasty in his work coat. Kieran was wearing the same type of clothing he'd had on when Hawke found him lost on the mountain. His toes would be going numb soon.

"It was CeeCee's idea? Because she is in love with Bear, the head of the Brother Speed gang." Hawke glanced over his shoulder.

Kieran stopped; his gaze focused on Hawke's back. "She and Bear? No way!"

"That's where she is now. He called her last night, and she caught the first plane out of Seattle." Hawke faced the man. "You might as well give up. The woman you did all this for doesn't want you. Doesn't want anything to do with the business you killed her brother for."

"Yes, she does!" He pointed the gun at Hawke.

A blur of tan, brown, and white came from the side and hit Kieran's outstretched arm. The gun went flying and the man fell to the ground covering his head.

Hawke watched, as on silent wings, a large horned owl flew off through the trees. Shaking his head, Hawke ran over and grabbed Kieran by the back of his coat and hauled him to his feet. A quick pat didn't produce any other weapons.

Without his duty belt, he didn't have handcuffs. He pulled the drawstring out of the hood of Kieran's coat and tied the man's hands behind him. Then shoved Kieran all the way up the side of the incline to the road.

Walking back down the road, Hawke spotted a county car, state vehicle, and Pierce's SUV parked behind the rental car.

Deputy Alden ran up to them.

"Put cuffs on him." Hawke left Kieran to Alden and walked over to Pierce. "Take me back to my vehicle. I'll check on Dani and then be at the county office to write up my statement."

Pierce didn't say a word until they were almost to Winslow. "Did he confess to killing Barclay?"

"No. But if the right buttons are pushed, he'll tell you everything. He has nothing to gain by keeping his mouth shut at this point. He kidnapped a police officer at gunpoint. It's all on camera and the woman he was doing it all for is with a gang member. She's not going to stick up for him. Especially since one of those suitcases of money was skimmed from the gang."

Pierce smiled. "Good job." He parked next to Hawke's vehicle.

Hawke opened the door. "I'll give my statement and let you and the county do the rest of the work. I want my life to get back to normal." He was through with the Barclay homicide. As for life getting back to normal— What he'd witnessed while being buried in snow and more recently when the owl flew into Kieran's arm, he knew it was a sign from his ancestors.

# Chapter Thirty-six

Hawke stood at the gate watching his three geldings run, kicking up snow. Next winter they would also have the horses from the lodge here. Dani didn't want to take away the money the family who kept them through the winter would get this year.

Dog ran up to the gate, barked, and ran back toward the house. Hawke turned and spotted the Kimbals' truck, Herb and Darlene's pickup, and Justine's car. Dani had invited them all to dinner.

"Looks like our company arrived at the same time." Hawke patted Dog on the head and walked back to the house.

Dani wore a walking cast now. With the snow, she had to stay inside but she had been making the most of having two hands to carry things. She had hung pictures on the walls and set out all of her travel collectibles. The house became more inviting each time he came home.

He greeted everyone, helping them hang their coats in the closet by the door and settling them in the living room.

"Does Dani need some help in the kitchen?" Darlene asked, peering into the kitchen area.

"I'll go see." Hawke walked over to where Dani stood mixing something in a bowl. "Darlene wants to know if you need help."

The retired Air Force pilot glanced at him. "I have everything under control." Her cheeks were red and her eyes glowed. "I never thought I'd be happy puttering around in a house all day. But the last week has been fun. I'm looking forward to working on the yard when spring comes."

Hawke laughed and said, "I didn't take you for the domestic type when I met you."

"I didn't take myself for that either." Dani laughed and hugged him around the waist with one arm. "I'm so glad everything has been cleared up about the body you found in the lodge barn. And to think I spent all that time alone with Kieran and he was a murderer."

"He only really had one person he wanted dead. The man that stood between him, and the money and woman he loved. You were never in any danger. And I only was when he became desperate. Greed and passion, two of the reasons most murders happen."

Hawke spun to head back into the living room with their guests when he spotted a framed photograph of a great horned owl hanging on a wall. "Where did you get that?"

"I found it in one of the crates Uncle Charlie left me. I hadn't opened it until Tuck and Sage brought me all the boxes that were in the apartment." She walked over to him and whispered in his ear. "Do you think that was Uncle Charlie who warned us?"

He and Dani had forsaken the spiritual side of their heritage, which they now needed to embrace as they filled their new home with new traditions.

"Maybe…" Hawke drew her close to him, smiled and stared at the photo. "But we may never know."

*Murder of Ravens*
Book 1
Print ISBN 978-1-947983-82-3

*Mouse Trail Ends*
Book 2
Print ISBN 978-1-947983-96-0

*Rattlesnake Brother*
Book 3
Print ISBN 978-1-950387-06-9

*Chattering Blue Jay*
Book 4
Print ISBN 978-1-950387-64-9

*Fox Goes Hunting*
Book 5
Print ISBN 978-1-952447-07-5

*Turkey's Fiery Demise*
Book 6
Print ISBN 978-1-952447-48-8

*Stolen Butterfly*
Book 7
Print ISBN 978-1-952447-77-8

*Churlish Badger*
Book 8
Print ISBN 978-1-952447-96-9

While you're waiting for the next Hawke book, check out my Shandra Higheagle or Spotted Pony Casino Mystery series.

**About the Author**

Paty Jager grew up in Wallowa County and has always been amazed by its beauty, history, and ruralness. After doing a ride-along with a Fish and Wildlife State Trooper in Wallowa County, she knew this was where she had to set the Gabriel Hawke series.

Paty is an award-winning author of 52 novels of murder mystery and western romance. All her work has Western or Native American elements in them along with hints of humor and engaging characters. She and her husband raise alfalfa hay in rural eastern Oregon. Riding horses and battling rattlesnakes, she not only writes the western lifestyle, she lives it.

By following Paty at one of these places you will always know when the next book is releasing and if she's having any giveaways:

Website: http://www.patyjager.net

Blog: https://writingintothesunset.net/

FB Page: https://www.facebook.com/PatyJagerAuthor/

Pinterest: https://www.pinterest.com/patyjag/

Twitter: https://twitter.com/patyjag

Goodreads: http://www.goodreads.com/author/show/1005334.Paty_Jager

Newsletter: Mystery: https://bit.ly/2IhmWcm

Bookbub: https://www.bookbub.com/authors/paty-jager

Thank you for purchasing this Windtree Press publication. For other books of the heart, please visit our website at www.windtreepress.com.

For questions or more information contact us at info@windtreepress.com.

Windtree Press
www.windtreepress.com

Hillsboro, OR